Priori...

"What's the threat magnitude?"

"We have total default potential." Mason's flat statement confirmed the worst. The changes being caused by the anomaly could wipe out almost everything in future history.

"Wave speed estimate?" Vitterand asked. His mouth was suddenly dry, his heart racing. Everything in the future was going to depend on him—did depend on him!

"Three subjective days, tops," Mason said. "That's our best estimate. Could be less. It's already passed over you, of course."

"My God," Vitterand muttered. Mason's statement meant two things. First, the change in history that had started with the explosion at the Louvre was traveling into the future like a wave moving along a rope. In three days of time, as Vitterand measured that time subjectively, the wave would have reached the absolute limit of the future, that point beyond which time travel into the future was impossible . . .

Don't miss
the thrilling debut of the Time Station series in
<u>TIME STATION: LONDON</u>

and

the electrifying return of the Temporal Corps in . . .
<u>TIME STATION: BERLIN</u>
coming in September 1997

Ace Books by David Evans

TIME STATION PARIS

DAVID EVANS

ACE BOOKS, NEW YORK

This book is an Ace original edition,
and has never been previously published.

TIME STATION PARIS

An Ace Book / published by arrangement with
Bill Fawcett & Associates

PRINTING HISTORY
Ace edition / May 1997

The Putnam Berkley World Wide Web site address is
http://www.berkley.com

Make sure to check out *PB Plug*,
the science fiction/fantasy newsletter, at
http://www.pbplug.com

ISBN: 0-441-00441-5

ACE®
Ace Books are published by The Berkley Publishing Group,
200 Madison Avenue, New York, NY 10016.
ACE and the "A" design are trademarks
belonging to Charter Communications, Inc.

PRINTED IN THE UNITED STATES OF AMERICA

10 9 8 7 6 5 4 3 2 1

TIME STATION

PARIS

Prologue

Place: Karinhall, Bavaria, Germany
Time: Estimated 3 a.m., Munich time, May 5, 1943

Fat Hermann Göring, *Reichsmarschall*, Commander in Chief of the *Luftwaffe*, and the named successor to Adolf Hitler in the unlikely event of the Führer's death, roused from his stupor. His big, flabby body, lying on a soft feather mattress on silk sheets in the middle of his large, hand-carved, oak four-poster bed, jiggled like pudding. Slowly, Göring realized he was jiggling because someone had a hand on his leg and was trying to awaken him.

"Please, *Herr Reichsmarschall!*" an urgent voice intoned. "You have an important communiqué from Berlin!"

Reluctantly, Göring opened one of his small blue eyes, sunk deep in a swollen pouch of reddish flesh. The room was dark.

"Stop shaking me!" Göring ordered.

The insistent hand was removed from his leg.

"Turn on the light," the Reichsmarschall commanded. "Who are you anyway? Where is my valet?"

"I was afraid the light would disturb you, *Herr Reichsmarschall,*" the voice replied. Göring didn't like the cold, satiric tone with which the anonymous voice had dripped out his title. Something was wrong.

The fat man sat bolt upright, both eyes open now. He squinted, then opened his eyes wide, trying to gather in enough light to see the figure at the foot of his bed. It was a man, wearing some kind of military uniform. In the darkness Göring couldn't make out the service. But this man was in his bedroom at . . . What time was it?

"Turn on the light, damn you," Göring barked. He swung his heavy legs out from under the sheets. His swollen feet plopped onto the cool hardwood floor. He squinted again, this time in the direction of the antique, Swiss grandfather clock that ticked away in the nearest corner of his bedroom.

Three in the morning! Something was definitely wrong. No one disturbed the second most powerful man in Europe at three a.m., not without going through his staff of servants. Göring turned his head back to the uniformed figure. It was a full uniform, complete with hat and side arm. Even in the darkness the old veteran could see the bulge of the Luger in its holster.

"If you're here to assassinate me, get on with it. You might have shot me without interrupting my sleep," Göring said wearily.

"I'm sorry to disturb you, *Herr Reichsmarschall*," the man replied, his voice still haughty. "I assure you I am no assassin. I have merely brought you an urgent communiqué from Berlin. My instructions were to deliver it to you personally."

"Then show the decency to send in my valet while you wait in the sitting room," Göring ordered, relieved to know that if his enemies had sent this man, they had already failed. The fat man reached up and yanked on the thick bell cord that hung by the side of his bed. The ringing would roust his valet. In less than a minute the hall outside his room would be filled with sycophantic servants and his Luftwaffe bodyguards. Any shot from this bedroom now would be the death warrant of the man who fired it.

"And," Göring added, "give me this communiqué so urgent that I have to be awakened." Göring held out his hand expectantly. "What is it? Has Tunisia fallen?" he asked.

"Not to my knowledge at this time," the soldier replied vaguely. He stepped forward, snapping to attention and delivering the one-arm salute. "Heil Hitler!"

"Yes, of course, Heil Hitler," Göring answered, listlessly lifting his own arm to return the salute while his feet searched vainly on the floor for his warm slippers. He could see the man more clearly now. He wore the uniform of a Luftwaffe colonel, though it did not fit him well. The jacket was too short and tight for this man's build. And there was something about the face that didn't look quite right . . .

The raised arm dropped. The communiqué passed into Göring's hands.

"Lights," he ordered once again, examining the single sheet of white paper with its neatly typed message.

The colonel produced a small flashlight and shined it on the paper.

"You've read it, I assume," Göring snapped, his eyes wincing from the sudden beam of yellow light. "Now answer me. What is it?"

"I do not make it a habit to read the Reichsmarschall's communiqués," the colonel replied smoothly. "I only deliver them."

"Liar!" Göring snapped. The old man made his eyes focus on the white paper illuminated by the flashlight. The letterhead was from the Ministry of Cultural Affairs. And the signature looked genuine. It was a memo from Otto

Albrecht, a Göring crony in the ministry most responsible for looting artworks from the occupied territories.

> New shipment of objets d'art from Louvre, Paris, by order of Himmler.
> Suggest you visit Paris immediately to safeguard shipment.

"Damn him!" Göring sputtered. Himmler had found more loot at the Louvre—maybe some of the best items, which the French, those swine, had hidden for years. Now he was planning to pilfer it all back to Germany. No doubt some priceless pieces would be gifts from Himmler to the Führer, a fine bit of toadying. Well, not if Göring had anything to say about it. Himmler might have the power of the SS, but Göring could pull strings at the Ministry of Cultural Affairs—it was loaded with his spies and friends. And any shipments would have to go through that ministry.

Göring stood. "Turn off that damned flashlight," the Reichsmarschall barked as his still bare feet plodded across the room. He reached for the main light switch.

The colonel cocked his head. He heard footsteps coming from the hallway beyond the heavy, ornate oak door. Those, he knew, would be the valet, and possibly the bodyguards.

Göring flipped the switch. Light flooded the room from the electric chandelier overhead. "And now," he said to the colonel, "as for you . . ."

Göring heard a loud *snap* in the air, like the firing of a small caliber rifle. The colonel vanished before his eyes.

A fist pounded on the door. "*Herr Reichsmarschall,*" cried a concerned voice. "Are you alright? You rang for me?" The fist pounded harder.

Göring flung the door wide open. He reached by reflex to

pull his robe tightly closed, and realized with annoyance that he wasn't wearing his robe, only his red silk pajamas.

"Turn out the guards. Have the entire hall searched, and the grounds as well. There was an intruder here!" Göring barked.

"At once, *Herr Reichsmarschall*," his loyal valet exclaimed.

"I will want a full report from my security forces," Göring continued. "No one, no one is to enter my bedroom in the middle of the night unannounced! How did he get in here? How did he even get inside the house?" Göring demanded.

"I will make inquiries, sir," the shaking valet responded.

"I will make my own inquiries," Göring snorted. "And there will be blood running in the courtyard when I learn who is responsible for this!"

Running footsteps sounded in the hallway as bodyguards began to fan out through the luxurious expanses of Karinhall, Göring's Bavarian dream lodge.

"And keep this quiet!" Göring suddenly shouted. He stuck his head out the door, calling after the guards, but they were already gone.

"I will tell them," the trembling valet volunteered. "Here, sir, are you alright? Won't you lie down? May I get you something?"

"Nothing. Perhaps some warm milk, to help me back to sleep."

Göring staggered back to the bed, the memo still in his hand. He sat, shaking his head in confusion. Then he carefully folded the memo and placed it in a drawer in a small stand beside the bed.

"Begin packing," he ordered the valet. "I will leave first thing in the morning for Berlin. From there we will take my special train to Paris. And this particular trip will be kept secret, especially from the prying eyes of the SS and the Gestapo," Göring grumbled. "Ring up Munich, get my aide. I want my personal security forces doubled, and a guard put on my family as well."

He leaned back into the softness of his bed, his eyes already closed, sleep already clouding his brain. He wondered how a Luftwaffe colonel, one he didn't know, at that, had managed to get into his quarters. He would have to replace his chief of security, perhaps. Who was this colonel, and why did Albrecht use him as a message boy? More puzzling was how the man had simply vanished, as if he had completely disintegrated in an instant. What could have caused such a thing?

Maybe, he thought dreamily, it had something to do with those wonder weapon experiments—he had heard of a bomb that could disintegrate things, that bomb with atoms, or molecules, or whatever. He would ask Speer about that. Speer stayed out of the intrigues; he could be trusted to give a straight answer.

1

Alert!

Place: Paris, France. Temporal Warden's Station
Time: 0200 hours, Paris time, May 10, 1943

"Temporal Warden Jean Vitterand, please awaken," the computer's low, feminine voice called. "You have a priority alert communication from uptime."

Vitterand awoke instantly and was fully alert in two seconds. In one smooth motion he raised himself from the plain cot to his feet. His hands grabbed his simple off-white linen pants, which he pulled on while answering the computer's urgent summons.

"Vitterand here," he said. "Proceed with uptime link."

He snatched the green cotton blouse from the foot of his cot and slipped into it quickly, even as the uptime voice was piped into his sleeping quarters.

"Vitterand, is the communication secure?" the deep male bass asked.

Vitterand reached over to the small keyboard on the desk near his cot and punched in a command. A monitor screen lit up, showing the location of every person in the Paris 1943 Time Station.

"Test sound transmission," Vitterand ordered.

Random voice recordings sounded in his quarters. On the monitor, Vitterand could literally "see" the sound waves produced, as they bounced around in his tiny room and then were absorbed by the sound-deadening walls. Only minor perturbations reached anywhere else in the station; no one could hear him. He also saw the flashing red indicator in the corner of the monitor—an anomaly alert. Whatever temporal distortion the uptime computers had picked up had been noticed by the station's system as well.

"Vitterand to uptime. Communications secure within station."

Vitterand quickly buttoned the blouse as he spoke, then pulled tight the rope belt around his pants and tied it with a quick double knot. He grabbed a black beret and stuck it on his head, while his eyes cast about for his sandals.

"This is a Priority Two alert," the uptime voice declared. "All hell's broken loose."

"Clear, Priority Two alert," Vitterand responded. He forced himself to sit down at the small terminal, even though he was experiencing an adrenaline rush and the whole of his lean, hard, five-foot, eleven inch body ached for action. There'll be action soon enough, he thought. Priority Two alerts were very rare—so he'd been told in training. A Priority Two alert could only mean a definitive threat to the integrity of the entire Timeline. Failure to correct a Priority Two anomaly could mean the end of everything uptime, and with it the end of the Temporal Wardens as well.

"Temporal origin point?" Vitterand asked, cutting to the heart of the matter quickly. Whenever this anomaly had begun, it had to be stopped in its place and time of origin. Knowing that something was "wrong" with history at a certain, specific time was just as important as knowing what was wrong. Often it was easy enough to tell what was wrong as the wave of change raced into the future, changing event after event. But it was not always easy to determine when the wave of change had started.

"Undetermined," the uptime voice answered.

"First anomalous manifestation recorded?" Vitterand queried. If uptime didn't know exactly when the problem had started, they would at least know when the first noticeable result had appeared; the first point on the Timeline where history was noticeably diverting from its original, set pattern.

"Explosion at the Louvre Museum, Paris, at 11:07 p.m. Paris time, May 9, 1943," the voice answered. "Multiple works of art presumed destroyed. German Reichsmarschall Hermann Göring killed in the blast," the voice replied.

"Couldn't have happened to a nicer guy," Vitterand quipped—and then instantly regretted the joke.

"Jean, this is serious," a new voice answered from uptime. "There's no time right now for humor or your twentieth-century American morality."

"Yes, sir," Vitterand answered. The new voice he recognized instantly. It was not one of the Temporal Warden HQ functionaries; it was Bill Mason, the Chief of Operations for a five century period. Mason had trained Vitterand personally. He wouldn't be on the pipeline himself unless there was a threat to the very existence of uptime and the Temporal Warden Corps.

"What's the threat magnitude?"

"We have a total default potential." Mason's flat statement confirmed the worst. The changes being caused by the anomaly could wipe out almost everything in future history.

"Wave speed estimate?" Vitterand asked. His mouth was suddenly dry, his heart racing. Everything in the future was going to depend on him—did depend on him!

"Three subjective days, tops," Mason said. "That's our

best estimate. Could be less. It's already passed over you, of course."

"My God," Vitterand muttered. Mason's statements meant two things. First, the change in history that had started with the explosion at the Louvre was traveling into the future like a wave moving along a rope. In three days of time, as Vitterand measured that time subjectively, the wave would have reached the absolute limit of the future, that point beyond which time travel into the future was impossible. That was the point in time occupied by the Temporal Wardens' main HQ. Second, the wave had already passed through May 1943. No one native to the time would know that anything was amiss. Everything would seem to be exactly as it should be, as it had "happened." Local memories of the real events that had taken place in the last three hours were already changed; people would only remember the changed, anomalous events.

"Why are you calling me now?" Vitterand demanded. By "now" he meant his own present time, about two in the morning on May 10, 1943 in Paris, France. If the anomaly were as threatening as Mason made it sound, why hadn't he been alerted days ago, so he could have taken steps to prevent it? Once the uptime HQ detected an anomaly, it could communicate that knowledge back to any point in time.

"Downtime com links are blocked by a damper field," Mason answered. "Computer links are still up, but those carrier waves are inviolable without shutting down the entire detection system—no way to superimpose more data on them without risking missing additional anomalies."

"Roger that." Vitterand knew now that they were up against someone with a lot of time travel resources at their disposal, someone with access to enormous amounts of energy. To create a damper field around an entire area of the

Timeline required an amount of energy that only linked fusion reactors or higher tech could possibly produce. "How about an earlier period?" Temporal Warden Stations, often called "Time Stations," existed in several decades of the turbulent twentieth century, and in several locations around the globe. If communications were blocked to the Paris Station, or even to all stations in the 1940's, no field could be powerful enough to lock out all communications to earlier times and places in the twentieth century.

"Wrong personnel," Mason said flatly. "You're our best bet. No one else knows the period and culture as well. Downtimers could hardly be expected to adjust."

Vitterand reflexively nodded his agreement. The nearest station in time was near the end of World War I. Life in France then was very different from the life now; anyone coming into 1943 Paris without special training would be stepping on cultural land mines the moment they arrived. They'd probably be arrested within hours, then chucked into a concentration camp.

"Request Priority One resource release," Vitterand said. A Priority One resource release would put virtually unlimited use of time travel technology at his disposal. The Wardens had never granted a Priority One resource release since the priority system had been established. There was too much danger involved in entrusting that much power to any one individual, no matter how well intentioned. The use of the ability to time travel was strictly rationed and monitored. But in this case, Vitterand knew he might well need the kind of power, resources, and flexibility in action only a Priority One release could provide. He waited tensely for the reply. There was a long silence on Bill Mason's end.

"Denied," the answer finally came. "You know that no Priority One release has ever been granted, and you know why."

"Damn it, Bill, I may need—"

"May need," Mason snapped back. "Not do need, just may need. If it changes to a definite need, let me know."

"I will, if I can get back to this time," Vitterand said bitterly. "I can't call you from downtime, remember? The damper field."

"Quite. Happy hopping," Mason said. "We're all counting on you. Out."

Swell, Vitterand thought. Somebody with enough power to damp out months, maybe years, along a Timeline blew up the Louvre and fat Hermann with it three hours ago. Now I have to go sort it out in under three days with limited resources.

"Implant chronometer, activate," Vitterand said aloud. A small electronic implant near the base of his brain was activated by that thought sequence. "Set subjective chronometer to seventy hours," Vitterand said. Quite literally inside his head, a tiny clock began ticking. Now, by simply thinking about it, Vitterand could know how much time had passed, and how much time he had left before the entire future was eradicated by the wave of change riding down the timeline. Mason had said three days—that was seventy-two hours. Vitterand knew that all estimates of wave speed up a timeline were just that—estimates. He wanted the extra couple of hours as a margin of safety.

Vitterand punched another key on his terminal and an alarm sounded through the Time Station putting the station on its top alert status. Personnel began scrambling to be ready for costuming, equipping, emergency RNA data storage implanting, all the things that might be needed when the Time Warden stepped into the Beamer portal to hop backward or forward in time.

"Equipment, TCAF good for seventy-two hours," Vitterand called over the intercom system. "And I'll need a scooter with a full six loads for hopping."

"Roger that," answered Pat Mulhoon, the Equipment Chief for the station. "How would you like that scooter to look?"

"German, military issue," Vitterand replied. "Beams, set for 10 p.m., May 9, 1943. Put me down anywhere near the Louvre. Not inside this station—I don't want to confuse myself."

"Your request creates no problem," answered the voice of C'hung C'hing, one of the best Beam operators in the business. "I suggest the Place de la Concorde, near the Egyptian obelisk. It will be nearly deserted by 10 p.m., and is only a short walk from your destination."

"Good choice," Vitterand concurred. Only tourists were in the Place de la Concorde after dark, and in occupied Paris, there weren't many tourists. Now, he thought, if only Costumes can come through with something appropriate. . . .

Place: The Thomason residence, north side, Chicago, Illinois
Time: 7 p.m., local time, August 6, 1940
John William Thomason, Ph.D., former Associate Professor of History at Cornell University, leaned against the marble mantle above the fireplace in the drawing room of his parents' Chicago residence. He sipped lightly from the extra dry martini held in his right hand; not even the best spirits had any taste or appeal for him tonight. Besides, he told himself, he wanted to be clearheaded for the confrontation that was coming. His parents would have a very difficult time understanding his recent decision, and he feared his father's reaction, in particular, could create an unpleasant scene.

Thomason set the glass on the mantle. He cast his cool, brown eyes about the familiar room, a space that managed to convey formality and coziness at the same time. It was the room the Thomason family always preferred for intimate conferences about the most private family matters. The fireplace was not lit on this warm August evening, but the curtains were pulled back from the west windows, so the setting sun could still illuminate the familiar nooks and crannies where Thomason had made almost every important decision of his life. It was in front of this mantle that his father had told him he would be enrolled in Eaton, and young John had acquiesced. It was in the two short, fat, overstuffed chairs with their floral print coverings that the two of them had sat and read together his acceptance letters from both Harvard and Yale. His father had paced the handwoven, imported Persian rug that covered the center of the drawing room floor, weighing aloud the pros and cons of the two institutions while young John had listened intently. His father and mother had shared tea and biscuits on the awkward love seat that faced the fireplace the night John had returned home, his Ph.D. degree in history in hand, and his letter of appointment to the faculty at Cornell proudly displayed on the small, carved mahogany table.

Now Thomason paced the Persian rug, slowly, pensively, straightening the expensive tie that accented the slight touch of color in his otherwise gray, double-breasted suit. He had rehearsed his speech dozens of times in his head, but there seemed to be no good way to explain himself. He had acted on his own inner convictions, convictions which defied the logic of the times and with which most of his peers disagreed, vehemently. He had come home tonight, unannounced and unexpected, to announce what he had done. He did not expect his parents to react joyfully.

The elegant, narrow wooden door to the drawing room

opened without a sound. Thomason heard the voice of Stuart, the family's butler for longer than he could remember. "Master Thomason," Stuart said (he always called John "Master Thomason," even though he was long since a grown man with his own distinguished if controversial academic career), "your father."

William Thomason barreled in, his robust, barrel-chested form as uncomfortable cramped into its evening tux as it seemed in this confined, dusk lit room. "John, boy, why, you're back early!" the senior Thomason exclaimed. He clapped his son heartily on both shoulders, his clean shaven but weathered face beaming with a smile. "Why did you cut short your trip to New York? Stuart said you wanted to see me."

The older man cocked his head and gazed inquisitively into his son's eyes. Handsome young devil, the father thought. Tall, lean, hard, smart as whip. Damned shame to waste all that in some dusty university library.

"That's right, Father," John replied, extending his hand and giving his father's a firm shake, even as he backed away from the potential embrace implied by his father's greeting gesture. "I have something to tell you. And I should tell Mother, too."

"She'll be along," the older man said, his eyes squinting. The boy wasn't going to blurt it out, whatever it was. That meant it couldn't be good. "Nothing is amiss, I hope," he said, forcing his frame into the further constraints of one of the overstuffed chairs.

"Not at all, Father. At least, nothing is amiss with me." Thomason paced slowly back to the mantle and took another sip from his martini. "I'd say there's plenty amiss on a larger scale."

"Hmmm," the older man grunted his agreement. "Damned Nazis have overrun half of Europe, and now they're getting ready to bomb England into submission," he said. "I'd say that's plenty amiss on a larger scale. Although if you ask me," he added, not noticing that he had not been asked, "I'd say the Brits are getting what they deserve; yes, and the French, too. If they'd stood up to that goose-stepping house painter in 1938, they wouldn't be in this mess today."

"I'm glad you see it that way," John said, eagerly seizing the opening this provided. "It was Britain and France's unwillingness to prepare seriously for war that led to this war in the first place."

"Oh, war, war, war—is that all you men can talk about?" A feminine voice chided the two men from the doorway. John's father stood, and John turned to greet his mother, hurrying toward her with a kiss for her cheek. She accepted his peck with smile, before continuing her remonstrance. "I suppose I should be glad that at least you're discussing the origins of the war, rather than its effects on business. Goodness knows I hear enough about that every evening from your father."

"Ah, Mother, I would suppose that the effect on business is quite positive," John teased. "I can't imagine Father complaining about it." John extended his arm and led his mother to the second of the chairs.

"It hasn't hurt," the senior Thomason conceded, reclaiming his own seat. He cast a quick smile at the woman who was still the joy of his life. In her late fifties, Helen Thomason retained the slightest hint of girlish prettiness in a face that was distinguished by its warmth and framed by undisguised graying hair. Tonight, she looked especially beautiful and distinguished, for she was dressed in her new gown, purchased especially for the symphony performance due to begin at eight. That she was already going to be late seemed not to disturb her in the slightest.

"Now, darling," Mrs. Thomason said, "why don't you tell

us what your sudden return is all about, so we can discuss it and not miss the Mahler in the second half of the program tonight."

"I would think Debussy might be more appropriate," John quipped.

"I'm afraid, Son, that your beloved French are drowning in Wagner now," his father retorted. One thing that the older man regretted about his son's upbringing was the extensive amount of time the very young boy had spent in France, where the family had had diverse business interests in the 1920's and 1930's. It had always bothered the older man that his offspring seemed to be as much a Frenchman as an American, with decidedly Gallic tastes in foods, and an even worse Gallic tendency to embrace a sentimental idealism ill suited to the realities of life in the business world. Even as a nine- or ten-year-old playing with his fellows, young John would dream of glory on the baseball field, but express it in downright Napoleonic terms.

"There you go," Mrs. Thomason chided, "right back to that dreadful war again. Thank God that it's none of our affair, and won't be unless . . . *that man* drags us into it." Mrs. Thomason always used the term "that man" in reference to President Franklin D. Roosevelt.

"Not likely, my dear," her husband reassured her. "Not even the Democrats are stupid enough to get us involved in another European war."

"Well, Father," John interjected, "that's really what I wanted to talk to you and Mother about tonight."

"What's that?" the older man said. "You came all the way from a vacation in New York to talk to us about the Neutrality Acts?"

"Not exactly," John said, shaking his head and pacing, his back to his parents as he tried to explain himself. "I've studied this Hitler, and the forces that brought him to power in Germany," he began. "He's not going to stop, ever, unless someone stops him by brute force. And there is only one power on this earth strong enough to stop him."

"John!" Mrs. Thomason's exclamation betrayed the sincerity of the shock she felt. "You're not suggesting that we should become involved in this European affair, are you?"

"I'm saying that we certainly will be involved, whether we want to or not. That we already are involved; only we just don't know it."

"Now, see here, John," his father protested. "I despise these Nazis as much as anyone, but I don't see how we're involved in this war with them."

"The great theme of world history in the past century was the emergence of the common man, the rise of meritocracy over aristocracy in all the advanced nations. This produced enormous convulsions, changes in the class system from an hereditary to a monetary—which in a free economy is to say, a merit—basis, the necessity for abolishing the last vestiges of hereditary privilege or lack of privilege—witness our own Civil War," John began.

"There you go with that intellectual stuff," his father cut in. "Speak in plain English."

"The last hundred years did away with aristocrats and replaced them with businessmen, like yourself," John said flatly. "That was the underlying theme of the whole country."

"I can see that," the senior Thomason agreed warily. "What's that got to do with Roosevelt dragging us into some European adventure?"

"The theme of our century is the struggle to determine whether these meritocracies will also be democracies—or whether they will be tyrannies," John explained. "The world is divided between the democracies on the one hand and military tyrannies on the other—look at Germany, Italy, Japan, and the Soviet Union."

"You came from New York, dear," his mother asked, "to tell us this?"

"No. I came from New York to tell you that I will not sit idly by while the issue of the century is being decided in blood," John declared. "That is why I have resigned my post at Cornell and joined the United States Army. It is inevitable that we shall be involved in this struggle, and I intend to be well prepared when that time comes. I leave tomorrow to begin basic training. After that I should qualify for Officer's School."

"Oh, dear," his mother whispered. She slowly and instinctively reached out her left hand and laid it gently atop her husband's hand.

William Thomason stared at his son in numb silence. Bad enough he had turned into an intellectual. But now he was going to throw away even that career, wasting himself in the ragtag rabble generally known as the U.S. Army?

"Have you signed the necessary documents?" the older man asked at last. He spoke slowly, his voice deep and grave. "Have you already given your commitment?"

"Yes," John replied.

"Well, then," his father said, standing and extending his hand. "I'll shake your hand, because you have the courage to act on your convictions. Personally, I don't agree with them and I think you're a damned fool. But you're a damned fool of good character, and I could hardly ask for more in a son; the same was once said of me."

John shook his father's hand with a firm grip. "I imagine we won't see much of you before you go, Son, though you are welcome to join us at breakfast tomorrow if you have time," the older man said. He then turned and held out his arm to his wife. "Come, dear, we don't want to miss the entire program."

Place: Time Warden Corps Headquarters
Time: Classified

"So, William, you are going to check out this recruit for yourself?"

"Yes, I suppose I'll have to," William Mason replied. The broad, round-faced man with still a trace of British accent pursed his lips thoughtfully. "Dreadful business, having to travel back in time one's self. Been quite a while since I've seen fieldwork." Mason sat his drink thoughtfully on the plain, square white table. He stood and paced once about the small, completely white conference room. His companion, Arkady Grigoravich Gallybin, was his closest subordinate, and the one who would take Mason's place should anything go awry on this recruitment mission.

"Perhaps I should go," Arkady volunteered.

"No," Mason shot back, his hands folded behind his back, his brows furrowed. Arkady was good, very good. But his background and training, no matter how good, hardly fitted him for the time period which would be Mason's target zone. "Very decent of you to offer, though," he added quickly, so as not to hurt Arkady's sensitive Russian feelings. "But, no, I should do this myself. I'm the one who'll be in charge of his training, if he works out, and the post he'll be assigned will undoubtedly be very sensitive. You know I have him in mind for the Paris Station, in the early 1940's. German conquest, French resistance, that sort of thing. Have to judge him for myself. Make sure he cuts the grade."

"Of course," Arkady demurred. "When are you going to? And what cover will you use?"

"Bloody awful place," Mason answered with an attempt at a smile. He sat down again, retrieved his drink, and took a sip. "Philippines, early during the Japanese conquest at the start of 1942. American forces are reeling back from the Japanese onslaught. Our lad gets himself killed by a sniper. Body was never recovered."

"So you will be a soldier?"

"Yes, I will be a soldier," Mason said, wrinkles of disgust growing on his cheeks. "An American soldier, no less. Ah'm Billy Mason, just a private from down in Georgia," Mason attempted to drawl in his best impersonation of a Southern American accent.

"Georgia?" Arkady asked. "Isn't that where Stalin was from?"

"Wrong Georgia," Mason answered dryly. "Your area is supposed to include the twentieth century—good heavens, it was once called the American century. I'd supposed you'd be up on your American geography."

Arkady nodded his graying head, and a tint of bright red crept up his face at the rebuke. That Georgia, he thought.

"You'll be briefed on the operational plan before I Beam Back tomorrow morning. The idea is, I'll tag with him as a wounded comrade, check him out, and then more or less die—well, I will die as far as he's concerned—and then observe his death. If he passes muster, I'll signal a retrieval team. If not, I'll just come back alone."

"Dangerous, Beaming into a war zone," Arkady observed. Both he and Mason knew full well that a person who had never traveled in time could be brought back from even the most horrible of deaths, in many cases, by the marvels of medical science. But once a human being had traveled in time, death was irrevocable, final, nonreversible, no matter what steps were taken to either prevent it or to resuscitate the victim.

"Damned dangerous," Mason concurred. "But all for the good of the Time Warden Corps, eh? Duty, you know." Mason finished his drink, stood, and walked out of the room. "Do be on time for the briefing in the morning, Arkady," he said as he strode out.

Place: Philippine jungle
Time: 6 a.m., local time, March 16, 1942

John William Thomason tripped on a root in the fetid stream and fell headlong into the water. The weight of the wounded man slung across his shoulders threatened to keep his head under, drowning him. He could see nothing in the brackish water, but the stream was shallow; he was resting on the bottom. He flattened his palms in the muck and heaved upward with all his strength, blowing bubbles as he exhaled.

Thomason felt his back break the surface. He rolled over, slinging the horribly wounded man off him. He fell back into the water on his back, sat up quickly, and spat foul-tasting mud from his mouth. He turned to his side, slid an arm down under the wounded soldier, and lifted the man's head back above the water.

The soldier coughed and sputtered. Thomason noticed the blood that gushed out with the water. He would not be carrying this particular burden much longer.

"C'mon, pal, let's get you somewhere on solid land," Thomason muttered as he stood, hoisting the crippled man. Still staggering from exhaustion, Thomason half carried and half dragged the man across the narrow stream. Holding his charge around the chest with his left arm, Thomason drew his machete with his right and hacked away at the underbrush and tangled, dangling vines that cluttered the bank. In a few minutes he had a barely usable path hacked out that led to a tiny clearing ringed by the jungle trees. Here he deposited the man, sitting him up with his back against a tree. Then Thomason allowed himself to sink to the ground, exhausted.

They'd been running for two days, and always the Japanese were just behind them. Thomason could hardly remember just how he'd become separated from his unit; there was so much confusion when the Japanese attack came in force. The jungle had come alive with mortar explosions, and machine gun fire had cut swaths through the underbrush. Men were screaming, falling and dying all around him. Thomason had fought back as best he could. It was hard, fighting an enemy you couldn't see. He'd fired blindly into the jungle, tossed his full load of grenades in the direction of the enemy, and then, noticing that no one else was left around him, he'd started to run.

He'd picked up the wounded man that night. He'd found the fellow lying on the jungle floor, blood gushing from the stump of his right leg, severed above the knee. Mortar, probably, Thomason had thought. A crude tourniquet torn from his shirt had checked the worst of the bleeding, and Thomason had been dragging and carrying the wounded man ever since, hoping to find some way back to the American lines, hoping that one of them or maybe both of them might live.

All that night and all of this day he had run, and always he had heard the Japanese not far behind him. He needed rest, food, clean water. He needed some solace. So far through their ordeal, the wounded man had never spoken; incoherent moans were all he could manage.

"Thanks, buddy."

Thomason heard the words, barely whispered.

He raised his head and looked at the wrecked human being leaned against the tree.

"I said, thanks, buddy," the man repeated.

"It's okay," Thomason replied, feeling new strength flow through his own body at this sign of revival from his heretofore silent comrade.

The man slapped at a huge mosquito that had landed on his cheek and begun sucking with impunity. The bug left a greasy black and red smear down his face.

Thomason laughed. "You showed him!" he joked.

"Yeah," the man answered. "Where are we?"

"Somewhere in the jungle—damned if I know where," Thomason answered truthfully.

"Japs?"

"They're around," Thomason acknowledged.

The man gazed at his tourniqueted stump. White bone gleamed in the sunlight that trickled down from the canopy above, standing out sharply from the red meat. "I ain't gonna make it," he said simply.

"Sure you will," Thomason said matter-of-factly. "Our own lines can't be far from here."

"What I remember, we ain't got no lines," the soldier said. "No use pretendin'. You best be goin' on, save yourself. If you got a rifle, I'll take a few of them with me if they come this way."

Thomason shook his head. He'd dropped the rifle when he ran out of ammo. No use carrying deadweight.

"What's your name, soldier?" Thomason asked, trying to change this unpleasant subject.

"Billy Mason. From Georgia. Who're you?"

"John Thomason."

"Captain Thomason, if them bars is real," Billy said, a grin on his face. He slapped at another mosquito, then brushed his hand over his stump in a futile effort to run off the flies that clustered on the open wound.

"They're real, but I don't feel much like an officer and a gentleman right now," Thomason said. He sat up, glanced around the clearing, and cocked his head, listening for the tread of the pursuing Japanese. He heard nothing. Then he slapped at two mosquitoes of his own.

"Gotta smoke, Captain?" Billy asked.

Thomason shook his head.

"I don't feel much like talking," Billy said. Blood began to trickle again from his mouth. He spat it out. "You talk."

"What about?" Thomason raised himself to a crouch. Had he heard something in the distance, back toward the stream?

"'Bout yourse'f," Billy said. "I'm dyin'. I'd like to know about the man that tried to save me."

"Not much to know," Thomason said. "Born in Chicago, signed up a while back, like a lot of fellows."

"That ain't what I heard," Billy whispered. "You ain't like a lot of the fellas at all. Been to college. Made officer right out. You was somebody before this war began," Billy said, his eyes suddenly gleaming. "You was somebody, and you risked it all for me. Sorry to let you down by dyin', Cap'n."

Billy's head fell back against the tree trunk as the last breath left his lungs.

Thomason reached over and closed the man's eyes. "Yeah, Billy, I was something. Rich parents, raised all over the world. I've probably spent more time in Paris than you have on your folks' farm. Ivy League. Ph.D. in history. Enlisted in 1940, back before the Americans got in the war, because I knew we'd have to be in it sooner or later. But I couldn't save you, could I, Billy? Sorry to let you down."

Thomason staggered to his feet. He looked around for something to dig with, and somewhere to dig. He was so tired he was puzzled when he could find neither a tool nor a suitable place to bury Billy. Confused, he just stood in the clearing, staring, until a single shot rang out. The bullet caught him square in the forehead and passed through, exiting the back of the skull, blowing bits of brain and bone and blood all over the jungle floor. Captain John William Thomason, United States Army, fell dead, shot by a Japanese sniper in the Philippines, March 16, 1942.

Billy Mason waited, seemingly dead, until the Japanese sniper had appeared and satisfied himself that his victim was in fact dead. As the man disappeared back into the jungle, Mason stirred. First, he ripped open his pants leg, undid several straps, and removed the meticulously crafted "stump" of his wounded leg.

"Ah, that's better." He extended his healthy leg, felt the needle-sharp tingling of the nerves as he willed the muscles to move again. Then he grasped his dog tags, raised them to his lips, and whispered, "Retrieval team. Now. Fifteen minutes maximum metatime available, maybe less."

Mason had no sooner uttered these words than four Time Warden Medical Corps officers materialized in the midst of the jungle, bearing a full complement of field equipment.

"Hook him and get him back fast. He has a single bullet through the brain."

The chief medic nodded. Neuronal tissues deteriorated rapidly. The team, well drilled, swung at once into action on the body of Captain Thomason.

Mason struggled to his feet, watched the medics at work, then shook his leg vigorously. "Oh, damn!" he muttered. "Activate recall."

Instantly, Billy Mason disappeared from the jungle. A few seconds later, the medical team as well vanished into thin air, taking with it Thomason's body.

Place: Classified
Time: Classified

Thomason awoke with the worst headache he had ever suffered. He grunted with pain, and would have cried out, but the mere sound of the grunt increased the pain so much that he stifled the urge to scream. He saw lights, very bright lights, and smiling faces. He tried to speak, but the words wouldn't come. Thomason blacked out.

Thomason awoke again. The headache was terrible. Was it as bad as it had been? Thomason couldn't remember. Had he only dreamed about waking up once before?

"Where am I?" he heard his voice say.

"All in good time," a pleasant female voice replied.

He saw her face—a beautiful face—framed by the brilliant white lights.

"Is this . . . heaven?" Thomason asked.

The beautiful face frowned just a tiny bit. "No, not quite," she replied. "But you might think of it as your afterlife."

"Let me see if I understand," Thomason said. He sat back in the extremely comfortable chair that automatically molded itself to provide the best support for his new body position. "I can either join up, or I can go back where I came from?"

Bill Mason leaned forward in his own chair, which flowed automatically forward beneath him, supporting his weight perfectly.

Thomason pointed at the movement of the chair. "I like that," he interjected.

"Yes, quite nice," Mason said. "Let me correct you on one point. You can either join up, as you put it, or you can go back to *when* you came from."

"Yes, yes, when I came from," Thomason responded. "Which means I'd be dead in a clearing in the jungle in the Philippines, if I understand all this correctly."

"That is correct," Mason conceded, leaning back.

"Whereas, if I elect to join up, I'll have a chance to learn about the entire history of mankind, from the earliest civilizations up to . . . when? No one has ever told me exactly when this moment is. What year is it? I mean, using my calendar. Is this 2015 A.D.? Is it 2505? When is this future you've pulled me to?"

"I'm afraid that's not for you to know," Mason said. "As a matter of fact, I don't know myself. But it is significantly later than either of the dates you've suggested. I know of Wardens recruited from as late as 2993 A.D., using your calendar."

Thomason stood, stunned by the thought of that much elapsed historical time. He paced thoughtfully around the small white room. It seemed to him that everything in the future was white—almost sterile. White rooms, white carpets, white ceilings. Buildings all of white, with huge, open airy spaces towering into the pale blue sky. In a way it *was* like an afterlife—if he was being allowed to see it all.

"Is everything in the future like . . . this?" he asked. "I mean, all beautiful buildings, everything white, furniture that moves, people without physical blemishes—is this all that there is? What is mankind doing? What are the challenges? Have we evolved? What is the meat of the history of this future?" Thomason demanded. "I'm an historian by training—I have to have some answers," he added, almost pleading.

"Sorry," Mason said, his voice, as usual, dead flat. "I haven't the foggiest notion of how to answer any of those questions. I was recruited myself, just like you. Don't have the slightest idea where or when this place is. But I can tell you that one of the challenges this civilization faces, whenever it may be, is time travel."

"Yes, disruption of the historical process," Thomason responded. "So you've all been telling me. Disruptions brought about by unauthorized, uncontrolled use of time travel technology for—how many years?"

"Sorry, couldn't say," Mason answered. "The fact is, that doesn't matter. What does matter is keeping history sorted out more or less the way it's supposed to be."

Thomason paced around the room again, pausing to look out the one large window onto the cityscape outside. Gleaming white buildings towered upward for miles; the caps of white skyscrapers bit into the horizon. Beams of light flashed from point to point among the buildings— transportation beams, Thomason had been told, carrying people and goods from place to place at the speed of light.

"For whose benefit?" Thomason asked. "Why should I care about keeping the past straight, so the present can be what it is, when I can't know what the present is? For all I know, I'd be preserving some monstrous culture with inhumane values."

"That's a damned fool thing to say," Mason retorted. "Whatever it is we're preserving, it's what humanity has become, what we were meant to become, if you believe in that sort of thing. And that's quite better than any version of the future where people don't care about what they've become, don't care about preserving the past or the present. But it's even simpler than that. You've been told about the outcome of your own time, that war business you were involved with. Do you want someone mucking about with history so that Hitler wins that bloody war?"

Thomason stared thoughtfully at Mason. Mason was a big bull of a man, thickset, with a squared-off face, heavy jaw, big bulbous nose, and sandy brown hair that fell in a loose tangle down over his forehead. His eyes were crystal blue, his mouth large, with full lips. It was an honest face that deserved an honest answer.

"No," Thomason said quietly.

"Well, then, there it is," Mason said. "In any event, I

should think it beats ending up as food for maggots in the jungle."

"Which," Thomason said, suddenly awestruck, "I've already been. I mean, I did die in the jungle, and rotted there, until there was not a single trace left of me, I'd imagine, until . . ."

"Until our chaps came along and pulled you out just at the point of death. Damned near thing, too, I have to tell you, even with what our medicine can do."

"So you've changed history!" Thomason concluded. "Oh, not a lot, probably, but you've changed it, none the less. Whereas I was a rotted corpse in the jungle . . ."

"You aren't now," Mason concluded for him. "Yes, that is a change in history, if you will. Fortunately, it doesn't seem to be a very large change. We've detected no anomalies caused by the removal of your body, at least none yet. And by the way, you're wrong to assume that the change caused by removing your body from its resting place would be minor. As it turns out, it is minor, but it's wrong to assume that. Even the tiniest change can have enormous repercussions over a long enough period of time. That's why, as a Time Warden, you'll undergo extensive training prior to your first assignment."

Thomason bounded down the white corridor with the throng of graduates, all of them shouting, laughing, clapping one another on the back. White cadet uniforms were crisp and clean, but the new graduates came in all colors, a variety of ages, and from a wide variety of times. Among them were a Zulu warrior from the nineteenth century, a Crusader knight from Normandy, a Chinese Confucian monk, an Egyptian priest from the time of Rameses, a Roman foot soldier who had fought with Caesar at Alesia, a space fighter pilot from the twenty-first century. Temporal Wardens all now.

It had taken extensive training, as Mason had predicted. By Thomason's own reckoning, it was three years. In that time he'd become even more expert in certain areas of human history, especially the twentieth century, which he came to love, not only because it was his own time, but because it was the American Time, a time when the ideals on which he had been nourished were spread across the globe. Beyond that, he'd learned more than he had ever thought it was possible to know about the basic sciences, including the physics of time travel. He'd become an expert in several forms of martial arts, personal combat with weapons from several time periods, demolitions, acrobatics, escape techniques, interrogation techniques, hypnotism, and a dozen other skills that might be vital to his calling.

Above all, he had learned a sense of mission, a sense of the absolute necessity to preserve the past as it had naturally evolved, without interference from time travelers. And he'd learned how delicate that web of past events really was. A dead mosquito could change a century; yet the assassination of a key political leader might have minimal effect in the long run.

Thomason raced to his own quarters, filed away his certification, and touched the transport button.

"Destination please," the computer asked.

"Locate Bill Mason and transport to him," Thomason ordered.

Thomason vanished in a flash of light, and a nanosecond later materialized in Bill Mason's presence. He noticed it was the same small white room where the two of them had had that critical conversation three years ago, the conversation that resulted in Thomason's decision to live, and to become a Temporal Warden.

"Ah, Thomason. All trained, I understand."

"Yes, largely thanks to you, and ordered to report to your division for assignment."

"Very good, very good indeed. Do sit down." Mason indicated one of the two chairs in the room. "I have just the assignment for you," he said, taking the other chair himself. "One I think you will find very interesting, if not pleasurable."

"Well?" Thomason asked.

"You had extensive experience in Paris during your life, didn't you? More or less grew up traveling from Paris to Chicago and back all the time. Something to do with the family business?"

"That's right, that's right. Is it Paris, then?"

"Yes. We've a Time Station in Paris that's ready for its first full-fledged Temporal Warden—and not a moment too soon. The events in this time period are critically important to the stability of the entire line."

"When?" Thomason asked, becoming impatient with Mason's phlegmatic approach to handing out news.

"When? Oh, yes, I suppose that would be of paramount importance, wouldn't it? We're going to place you on station starting May 1, 1943. You'll remain at the station for the duration of the Second World War. After that, you may be reassigned. In Paris you'll be known as Jean Vitterand to the locals, if that's quite all right with you. Our computer picked the name as the one least likely to lead to any anomalies."

"Occupied Paris . . ." Thomason muttered.

"Quite," Mason said. "I suppose you should know that there was some opposition on the Council to my appointing you to this particular post. There are some who believe you won't be able to overcome your own strong cultural biases in a time period so close to your own."

"But I know the time, the place, the culture. I know it to my bones," Thomason said, smiling.

"Yes, that was my argument, and it prevailed. Nevertheless, you will do me the great favor of not 'going native,' as they say."

Thomason recognized the importance of Mason's statement. One of the dangers to the Temporal Warden Corps was that small percentage who, away from the strict training environment, could not resist the charms of the cultures to which they were sent. Inevitably, a few Wardens turned bad. They tried to "go native," to live normal lives in the time period to which they were assigned. Of course, because the Wardens could never allow such a thing to happen, those who made such attempts went to great lengths to hide their own past from the Wardens—to literally bury themselves in time. Much time and effort was spent tracking down these renegades, who of necessity stole time travel equipment and more importantly, the knowledge of how to make such equipment.

"I'm no renegade," Thomason said.

"Good, then." Mason stood and extended his hand.

"A twentieth-century gesture to see me off?" Thomason asked, shaking the hand heartily.

"Quite. You'll find your station new, fully equipped. Computers are on line, constantly in contact with computers here at HQ, comparing local events with our records of them, searching for anomalies. You'll have a good Beams operator, one of the best. Equipment man is first rate. Costuming may be a bit weak—but she'll make up in creativity what she lacks in available equipment. You'll need to do something about increasing our stores in that area."

"Very good, sir."

"Then, off with you. You arrive at six a.m., May 1, 1943, at Paris Station. Good luck, Thomason."

Place: Paris, France, Time Station
Time: 0243 hours, Paris time, May 10, 1943

"Communications, I need an update!" Vitterand snapped. He tugged at the black jersey, slightly too tight, of his Gestapo colonel's uniform. His feet ached already from the gleaming black boots that were a full size too small.

"Damn it, Sandy, this uniform doesn't fit!" Vitterand had to shout to be heard above the din of the control room. The energy processors were working at full output, storing the charge that would punch a hole in the space-time continuum and hurtle him backward in time. C'hing's technicians called back and forth to one another, double checking the complex calculations needed to transmit an object or a person through time with anything approaching accuracy. Lights of a dozen different colors glared off of terminal screens. And the personnel at the Communications consoles were all babbling at once, apparently over the latest communiqué from uptime on the progress of the wave of temporal change toward the future.

Sandy Deweese turned from her computer terminal and stuck out her lips in a mock pout. "It's the best I could do on such short notice. In case you weren't aware, Gestapo colonels don't conveniently drop dead, in uniform, in your size, on the spur of the moment. And I'm afraid beating one up and stealing his clothes might cause a tiny bit of an anomaly. If you'd have given me some warning I could have had one fabricated for you uptime."

C'hung C'hing stifled a snort of laughter. Vitterand shot him a cold glance, and the Chinese, still grinning, turned his full attention back to the keyboard controls of the energy modulation system.

"Hmph," Vitterand grunted. "Where did you get this, then?" he muttered under his breath. "I didn't know the SS recruited dwarves."

"They don't," Sandy snapped. Vitterand was prone to forget that, among other things, as a genetically engineered human from the year 2341 A.D., she had a powerfully developed sense of hearing. "He was a normal sized man who happened to die of a heart attack in a house of ill repute. You should be grateful I have such black market and underworld connections that I could find it in time."

Vitterand knew she was right. If he'd been thinking more clearly, he'd have had a complete set of uniforms, all services, prepared immediately upon his arrival. Instead, he'd concentrated on the clothing of the common Frenchman, focusing on blending in inconspicuously among the Parisian working class. But tonight he would need authority.

"Sorry, Sandy," Vitterand muttered.

"Stow it. And take this—may you never know what I had to do to get it." Sandy extended her right arm. In her hand she held a shining black riding crop.

"Oh, my God!" Vitterand exclaimed. "Is that really necessary?"

"Clothes make the brute," Sandy wagged.

"Here's the Com update!" Vu Nguyen, a nineteenth-century-born Vietnamese, handed Vitterand a printout summary of the progress of the anomaly just sent from uptime. The pages spilled onto the floor as Vitterand began quickly devouring the data:

May 9, 1943: Hermann Göring killed in explosion at the Louvre Museum in Paris.

May 12, 1943: Gestapo crackdown in Paris results in

mass arrests and executions. In Berlin, power struggle begins between Himmler, Heydrich, Bormann, and Goebbels for succession to the Number Two spot.

May 14, 1943: Goebbels assassinated; Gestapo seizes Ministry of Propaganda.

May 15, 1943: Himmler assassinated. Heydrich and Bormann arrested by order of Hitler for complicity in Himmler's death.

May 16, 1943: Conference of Nazi Gauleiters summoned in Berlin. Hitler addresses Gauleiters, breaks into hysterical frenzy. Rommel arrives in Berlin, as do several other "nonpolitical" generals.

May 17, 1943: Gauleiters ratify Hitler's choice of Albert Speer as Deputy Führer of the Third Reich. Speer is little known, nonaligned within the party. Hitler chooses him because he has no enemies. SS military formations ordered by Hitler and Speer to "consolidate the situation" in key cities of Germany—outside of Berlin. Hitler reported ill from exhaustion.

May 20, 1943: Speer announces "tragic" death of Adolf Hitler, summons *Reichstag* to meet in three days. *Wehrmacht* reserve formations seize all key points in Berlin.

May 24, 1943: Reichstag witnesses Speer taking oath as Führer of the German Reich. Speer announces von Rundstedt as new Chief of Staff of the Wehrmacht. Erwin Rommel named to command all German forces on the Eastern Front. SS military formations are subjected to Wehrmacht authority.

May 25, 1943: Speer secretly inaugurates new secret weapons research.

June–July 1943: Rommel cancels planned Kursk offensive before it starts, assumes strong defensive posture on Eastern Front. Russian offensives are mounted in force at key points along the front, but timely retreats, consolidation of reserves, and savage German counterattacks keep Russians off balance.

October 1943: As campaign season nears its end, Eastern Front is stabilized with German control of Ukraine, Belo-Russia, and Leningrad intact. Soviets have suffered massive casualties for minimal gains. Allied campaign in Italy stalemated. Germans launch major "anticommunist" propaganda campaign. Speer suggests Germany will recognize and even restore the British Empire and promises recognition of "legitimate American economic and military interests in China, the Philippines, and the Far East" should the "unfortunate quarrel" between the "Aryan nations" be negotiated. Speer proclaims the now "independent" Ukraine a "model liberated republic," typical of "new nations" to be formed in Eastern Europe as part of the "New World Order."

February 10, 1944: World's first atomic explosion destroys staging area for three Soviet tank armies deep behind Soviet lines.

February 22, 1944: Moscow destroyed by world's second atomic explosion. Bomb delivered by V-3 remote-guided rocket. Soviet government is effectively "decapitated."

March–April 1944: Soviet Front collapses from loss of morale, mass desertion, and recall of units by separatist republican movements. Latvia, Lithuania, and Estonia declared free republics; Georgia and Armenia recognized by Speer government as independent neutral states with favored trading status with Germany. German armored columns drive deep into Russia, bypassing the Moscow "death zone" and seizing critical rail and communications lines.

May 3, 1944: Speer passes secret ultimatum to Western

Allies through neutral diplomatic channels. Britain can be restored to the leadership of her empire while embracing a treaty of friendship with Germany, or London will be destroyed. U.S. troops begin evacuation from southern England invasion staging areas.

May 4, 1944: Winston Churchill's government in England collapses. Parliament declares an unprecedented state of emergency.

May 5, 1944: U.S. releases Britain from its pledge of "no separate peace."

May 6, 1944: Great Britain signals acceptance of Speer ultimatum.

May 10, 1944: British and German representatives sign the Peace of Paris. Speer proclaims the triumph of the New World Order in Europe, while pledging British independence. U.S. Congress pressures Roosevelt for a "Japan first" policy. . . .

June–August 1949: Utilizing basing facilities in Greater European Siberia and American-occupied Japan, forces of the European *Reichsbund* savagely suppress the Communist revolutionary forces in China. While guerilla warfare will continue in China for years, a pro-German, pro-American, military totalitarian government under Chiang Kai-shek takes recognized power with capitals in Peking and Nanking. . . .

November 1952: Incumbent President Harry Truman is defeated in his bid for a second term. Truman campaigns hard for "maintaining the American tradition of liberty." His opponent, Thomas Dewey, in his second run against Truman, stresses the "need for global security against Nazi plutocracy" and the "clear destiny of the American nation to defend and liberate its hemisphere from the European totalitarian menace."

June 1954: U.S. invades Mexico in response to Mexican demands for reform in economic relationships and threats to import German "military and economic advisors." Lightning campaign overwhelms the Mexican army, but armed guerilla uprising begins in the countryside. By the end of 1954, U.S military is clearly embroiled in a large-scale guerilla war throughout Mexico that threatens to spill over into all of Central America. . . .

Summer 1963: Race riots erupt in American cities of Little Rock, Jackson, and Birmingham. The U.S. military responds with unprecedented ferocity, providing further provocation to the growing antiwar sentiment among middle-class American youth. Draft riots break out in Chicago, Los Angeles, and New York, followed by further racial eruptions in Atlanta, Jacksonville, Memphis, Gary, and Baltimore. Collapse of constitutional authority follows the assassination of President Joseph McCarthy. Richard M. Nixon succeeds to office, declares a state of national emergency, proclaims national martial law. Congressional protests result in official "temporary suspension of the Constitution" and dissolution of Congress. . . .

Vitterand shuddered in revulsion. He wasn't going to let this happen, even if it did mean he had to dress up like some SS bastard and save the life of Hermann Göring.

"You all know already that this anomaly is a particularly nasty one," Vitterand shouted, claiming the attention of the entire staff. The din in the room lowered to the dull hum of the energy processors.

"*Jawohl, Herr* Colonel," Sandy shouted back, clicking

the heels of her pumps and snapping a one-armed salute. A wave of laughter broke the tension in the room.

Vitterand forced a grin. He was in no mood for laughter, not now, not when some idiot with a time machine was destroying the natural history of . . .

Vitterand broke that chain of thought. What had Mason said about the dangers of "going native"?

"Now, people, this will be a short investigative hop," Vitterand continued to his staff. "I just want to see what's happened firsthand. If I can take preventive action that will downgrade the impact of this anomaly, of course I will. But the main purpose of this particular hop is information gathering. Any questions?"

"You will be wanting this," C'hing called. He tossed a small black rectangle to Vitterand, who caught it, smiled, and clipped it onto his uniform belt. He pushed the tiny "On" button, and made sure the indicator light was glowing red.

"I was about to ask for this," he said.

"Sir? What about the scooter?" Pat Mulhoon asked. He indicated the beat up looking German military motorcycle parked near the Beamer platform. Vitterand examined it closely. The bulging front body panels hid a multitude of sins, including a small but effective temporal drive and six short fuel pods. Immediately in front of the seat a small flip-up panel contained a digital readout screen and three controls for setting the space-time coordinates. The drive could be activated by merely pushing a small button on the end of either handlebar. But first, the operator would have to program in the correct identity code; this was to prevent any "local" citizens from accidentally transporting themselves backward or forward in time while joyriding on a stolen cycle.

"Excellent job, Mulhoon," Vitterand said with approval.

"No one would ever suspect that this isn't exactly what it appears to be. But this time, I think I'll be going on foot. I'll be setting down very close to where the anomaly occurs, and I shouldn't need any fast transportation."

Vitterand strode toward the gleaming steel arch that framed the Beamer platform. "Beams," he called, "now." As Vitterand passed under the arch, the archway filled with a brilliant flood of intensely white light, and the time traveller disappeared. The entire process lasted less than a fraction of a second from the perspective of those observing in the control room. C'hung C'hing looked up from his control panel and smiled. For all the times he'd Beamed men and women into the past or future, the process still amazed and delighted him.

"You see?" he asked the silent crew of technicians and staff. "We have done it again. It is as though we make God blink."

2

A Plan

Place: Kingdom of Ukluk, an historically unknown city of ancient Sumer Time: Exact day and hour unknown. Year 4903 B.C.

Golden sunlight streamed onto the flat rooftop of the one-story, rambling, dried mud brick palace of the greatest of the merchant princes of Ukluk. George Faracon grunted with pleasure as the short, naked, dark-skinned slave girl poured scented oil over his feet and began his afternoon foot massage. He squirmed slightly on his S-shaped reclining couch, burrowing his head back further into the soft, satin-covered pillows. He chuckled with delight as a second girl, black hair framing her almond-shaped green eyes, her firm, round breasts only inches from his face, plopped a fresh date between his thick lips. The ancients, Faracon thought, had known how to enjoy luxury.

From the tangle of narrow streets below came the stench and clamor of hundreds of people and thousands of animals. Goats, sheep, and cattle bleated their death songs; pheasants and squab beat feathers against metal bars in vain efforts to escape. Humans babbled, bartered, and argued. Slave sellers, clothiers, and tradesmen sang out the virtues of their wares. The smells of dung, urine, sweat, and oily smoke clogged the air.

Faracon turned up his nose slightly—he was still not accustomed to the intensity of the smells. He made a vague gesture to the nude male slave boy who hovered attentively behind him. Instantly the boy appeared, swinging a censer filled with an oil that gave off a minty scent as it burned. The youth took great care not to look into Faracon's eyes, and to keep his gaze averted from the nubile slave girls who also attended the great master. To look at the master would show disrespect, punishable by beating. To look at the girls would betray lust for the master's property, punishable by death.

Faracon's gaze, on the other hand, wandered where it would. The plump but sturdy man raised himself on one elbow, the better to see out over the jumble of flat roofs that stretched to the horizon formed by the city's high wall. In only one place was the constant tangle of rooftops broken. About half a mile to the east of Faracon's palace the buildings disappeared, revealing the emptiness of a huge open plaza. In the center of this plaza a ziggurat tower soared toward the blazing sun, towering higher, even, than the city's protective walls and their occasional fortified towers. From the plaza, a single, broad avenue sliced through the city toward the main gate.

Soon, Faracon expected, he should hear a great clamor from that avenue, one that would rise above the daily din of life in the ancient city. Soon, he thought, the king would come to see him.

"Ahhh," Faracon moaned, lying back down. The slave girl's thumbs slid up his arches and massaged the ripple of spaces in the metacarpus. Too much of this kind of living could make one soft, Faracon mused. But for the moment he was content to indulge himself.

Beneath the roof, in the stretches of the palace below, a good thirty slaves and a handful of free overseers went about the daily tasks that sustained Faracon in luxury in the ancient city. The cooking rooms, pantries, and garners buzzed with activity. Other slaves labored, somewhat fruitlessly, to remove the endless clouds of grit and dust that constantly intruded into the sleeping chambers, hallways, reception rooms, and eating hall. In a set of closely guarded, connected rooms in a separate wing of the palace, still more slaves sorted, cleaned, counted, and carefully stockpiled a vast inventory of bolts of cloth, gold and silver chains, pendants, necklaces, earrings, gemstones, carvings of both stone and wood. Short, fat scribes oversaw this work, the bright colors of their calf-length tunics lost in the gloom of these airless, lightless storerooms. The scribes squinted in the semidarkness, striving to make sure each count was accurate, and then engraving the tally with cuneiform markings on the moist clay tablets they carried.

Today's bustle in the palace was even greater than normal. For today, the servants had been told, the King of Ukluk would come to see the master. So even more smoke from the cooking rooms roiled in black greasy clouds through the hallways. The servants lighted all the wall torches, and these smoked and sputtered as they illuminated those areas of the palace untouched by the sunlight, which could only peep in through the few tiny square windows in the outer walls.

Faracon enjoyed his luxury on the roof until the sun moved distinctly to the west in the afternoon sky. Eventually, he heard above the clamor of the streets the sound of braying horns from the area near the ziggurat. The King of Ukluk, living incarnation or personification or whatever of Enlil, God of the Sky, was rousing himself from his palace. Time to get ready. Faracon toyed with the idea of allowing his slave girls to bathe him—a practice he usually enjoyed—but decided against it. He needed to be sharp of mind while negotiating with old King Utnapishtim. Reluctantly, he kicked away the ministrations of the slave girl at his feet and hoisted his bulk off of the reclining couch. With a stroke of his large, pawlike hands he brushed an assortment of bread crumbs, date pits, and grape seeds from his white tunic and flowing blue robe with gold embroidery. "Senlak," he barked at the slave boy. The youth ran toward him, eyes downcast, and knelt at his feet.

"Tell the chief overseer that the master will retire at once to the Place of the Gods."

The youth nodded without looking up, turned while still in his crouch, and scuttled toward the stairway that led down to the main floor of the palace. The slave girls dropped their oils and plates of food and ran to Faracon, each wrapping herself around one of his arms.

"Oooh, master," one pouted. "Will you not stay and allow us to pleasure you?"

Faracon hesitated, smiling for a moment at the images her suggestion brought to mind. Then he yanked his arms free, stepped forward, and turned, striking the girl in the face with a backhand blow that sent her sprawling across the sunbaked bricks, blood streaming from an open gash on her cheek cut by one of his many gem-studded rings.

"Stupid wench! You will pleasure me when I choose! Remember that, if you want to live," he growled. He stomped off down the stairs, bellowing to announce his impending presence to the household staff. Work came to a halt as he entered and lumbered through the largest of the house's reception halls; slaves fell forward on their faces to register their humility before their generous and merciful owner.

Faracon made his way through the palace, past the

clumps of terrified silent slaves whose presence he did not even acknowledge with a glance. At the entrance to the warehouse wing he paused. On either side of the double doors stood an armed guard. These men were also short by comparison to Faracon, who at six feet, one inch towered over them. They were lean, hard men with sun-darkened skins. Their nearly hairless heads were covered by tarnished bronze helmets. At his side each wore a sword of bronze, and each carried a spear about six feet in length with a bronze tip. Their armor consisted of simple padded leather breastplates worn over their mid-thigh length tunics, and leather bracelets to protect their wrists.

"Master," one of men said, nodding in acknowledgment of Faracon.

Faracon scowled. Try as he might, he could not teach these ancient clods military discipline. In any reasonable century, these guards would have snapped to attention at his approach.

"Open the door," he barked.

"At once, master," the soldier responded. Using the butt end of his spear shaft, the guard pounded three times, slowly, on the solid, heavy doors. Then he shouted, "The master comes."

"What is the password?" a voice asked from the opposite side.

"Falcon," the first sentry shouted back.

Faracon fidgeted while he heard the heavy beam that blocked the door from the inside being lifted from its place. At length, the doors swung open, and the master of the house strode into the warehouse rooms. Just inside, the chief overseer awaited him.

"Master!" he called. "The slave Senlak informed me you wished to visit the Place of the Gods." The chief overseer was dressed more like Faracon, only his richly embroidered robe was of red silk, and he carried on his person a sharp sword with a keen steel edge, a fine black whip, and, unbeknownst to any save Faracon, an automatic, self-charging, short-range laser pistol. He was a swarthy, thin man with a thick, black beard and moustache, and his eyes were tiny, dark brown, and cold. He smiled sardonically at Faracon.

"The slave informed you correctly," Faracon replied, rolling his eyes upward in response to his chief overseer's smile. "You will escort me there."

"Yes, master," the overseer replied. "Clear the way for the master. All leave the wing at once!" the overseer barked. Throughout the warehouse wing, slaves were herded by scribes and overseers toward the guarded double doors. Faracon and his chief overseer waited until they were alone in that wing of the palace, save for the two guards on the inside of the door.

"Close and bolt the doors," Faracon ordered. "No one is to enter this wing until I personally return and give my permission."

The soldiers nodded dumbly.

Faracon made his way through the tiny dark rooms crowded with the treasures of his merchant profession. Neither he nor the chief overseer spoke until they were alone in the innermost of the tiny chambers, a seemingly empty room, a room never seen by any other occupants of the palace, and known to them only as "the Place of the Gods." Faracon closed and barred the door.

"Going back to the ship?" the chief overseer inquired.

"Yeah. We have some plans to make. I want to be sure everyone understands what they need to be doing. Then I'll come back here, meet with old Utnapishtim, and get the ball rolling."

The chief overseer nodded.

"Activate recall," Faracon muttered. The chief overseer said the same words at almost the same instant, and the two of them vanished into thin air from the Place of the Gods.

Place: *La Liberté*, interstellar-capable time travel ship in synchronous orbit above the Tigris-Euphrates Valley
Time: Exact day and hour unknown. Year 4903 B.C.

"Captain on board!" the Beam operator reported to the bridge of *La Liberté*. "Decontam program running now."

Faracon and his chief overseer, better known to his comrades as Antonio Vitelli, materialized on the Beamer platform on *La Liberté* and stepped immediately into the decontamination chamber. There, the two men stripped as biosensors scanned them and a variety of high-intensity energy waves played over every inch of their skin.

"Attention. Please attach respiratory masks," a computerized voice sounded in the white, sterile chamber.

"Crap," muttered Vitelli. "These damned temporal backwaters are nothing but disease pits."

"A small price to pay for the benefits to be gained," Faracon replied. The bulky time traveler reached out and plucked a small breathing mask from its holder on the wall. The mask extended from the wall on the end of a clear tube. He placed the respirator firmly over his mouth and nose and began breathing as forced air rushed into the tube at a constant pressure. Vitelli did the same. Faracon noted the slight but distinct, almost metallic odor of a vaporized antibiotic agent in the air.

"Treatment completed. Danger of pulmonary infection averted. Contagion probability less than 0.5%. Acceptable risk level," the computer droned.

The two men replaced the masks on their holders on the wall, waited for the air lock door to open, and stepped into the adjoining, sparsely furnished dressing chamber. There, each quickly donned a set of routine issue white space coveralls and slippers. When they were dressed, Faracon gave a voice command, the next air lock door opened, and the pair stepped into the temporal control room of *La Liberté*.

Faracon nodded to the small, thin, weasel-faced man known as Jonesy, his Beam operator. "Secure from recovery," Faracon ordered. "Join us on the bridge."

"Aye, Captain. Very good to have you on board again, sir," Jonesy squeaked.

"Stow it, you bootlicking wimp," Vitelli snapped.

"That's enough from both of you," Faracon snarled. "We have work to do." Faracon strode to the hermetically sealed air lock across the control room. "Captain entering bridge," he told the computer monitor. The door to the bridge slid open soundlessly.

"Report!" Faracon ordered, striding swiftly onto the bridge of the antique, yet awesomely powerful interstellar-capable time travel ship. His executive officer and second in command, Liu C'hien, snapped to attention and saluted.

"Situation unchanged, sir," C'hien reported. C'hien, a short, wiry man of mixed descent from southeast Asia, was nothing if not efficient. He rigidly demanded the strictest military discipline from all crew, which was the main reason Faracon had made him his executive officer. Faracon was also aware that, like many execs, C'hien commanded the personal affection of the crew. When the day came that their affection for C'hien outweighed their fear and awe of their captain, he would rebel, an event Faracon intended to prevent. "Maintaining synchronous orbit over ordered coordinates," C'hien continued. "Temporal drift zero. Spatial drift within standard tolerances. Sensors indicate no temporal intrusions simultaneous with our presence. All weapons and

spatial drive systems fully operational. Temporal drive—"
Liu C'hien broke off his report. Everyone on the bridge
knew the situation with respect to their temporal drive.

"Ship's temporal drive is still not operational," Faracon
said, smiling benignly. "Status of damper fields, temporal
shuttles, and onboard, individual temporal transport systems?"

"All operational," C'hien reported. "We have sufficient
power left for several individual time transports and recalls.
Our shuttles remain deployed on station at various points
throughout the timeline. The damper field you ordered
installed to block communications downtime in the area of
spring 1943 remains operational, although the power drain
is significant and contributes to our inability to activate
ship's main temporal drive system."

Faracon grunted an acknowledgment as he flopped into
the bridge command station.

"Kill visual," he ordered.

The ship's eight by ten main viewscreen at the front of the
bridge went blank.

"Okay," Faracon said. "Gather round and listen up."

C'hien, Jonesy, Vitelli, and ten other criminal dregs from
the backwaters of history gathered around their commander,
ready to hang on every word he uttered. With the exception
of Vitelli, and perhaps C'hien, they all held him in awe. He
was George Faracon, a.k.a. the Wolf, a.k.a. TimeEater, a.k.a.
the Time Boss. What his real name might be, and where and
when he had come from, no one knew except the Wolf
himself, a state of affairs he maintained with constant
vigilance. Over an unknown period of time, he had managed
to acquire more time travel technology, and hence more raw
power, than any of the hundreds of renegade time travelers
spawned by the Temporal Wars of the thirtieth century. With
the ending of the wars, he had not only survived, he had

thrived, making himself eventually the most powerful and most feared of the crime lords who ran the temporal black markets and the illicit trade through time in everything from valued ancient artifacts to time-displaced technology to programmed human slaves. He had murdered many of his competitors, and others had disappeared from history altogether. It wasn't as if they had never existed; thanks to Faracon's manipulations of time, it was a simple fact that they had never existed. Faracon was a constant target of probes, raids, and attempts at execution by the Temporal Wardens, but so far he had always eluded them, and continued to elude them, at every point in the Timeline where he appeared.

No proof of his power was greater than the *La Liberté* herself. Built by the South American Union at the height of the Temporal Wars, the ship was a time traveling vehicle also capable of deep space flight, and armed sufficiently to attack an entire planet. She had been designed as a super weapon, a temporal dreadnought. The very fact of her existence had helped to end the Temporal Wars. The threat of such monstrous ships wreaking havoc throughout history was so great that peace had become the only viable option. That was the reason Faracon had decided to steal her; the Temporal Warden Corps did not dare travel back in time to interfere with her construction and initial deployment. The peace which had come about because of those facts would be jeopardized, and with the peace, the future existence of the Corps itself.

But all power has limits, as even Faracon had learned. Maintaining his possession of the ship against the Temporal Warden Corps required his every trick of time war cunning. Equally problematic was operating the behemoth. She required enormous amounts of energy. Faracon was obsessed with this energy problem.

"As you know," he began telling the bridge crew, "we're a little short of temporal drive energy."

No face dared smile at humor of his understatement. Every member of the bridge knew that the orbiting dreadnought was now stranded in time. Faracon's earlier excessive use of their time travel capability had drained all the stored power, power that had taken years to accumulate.

"We're trying to store up some more, but I understand from our friend Mr. C'hien that the collector fields are not operating properly. Is that correct, Mr. C'hien?"

Liu C'hien nodded agreement.

"Why don't you go over it for us once more, to be sure we all understand," Faracon demanded.

C'hien squeezed through the assembled crew and stood beside Faracon's command seat on the cramped bridge. With the main visual screen off, the bridge presented an odd visual contrast. The room seemed dark, even though there were thousands of small lights coming from the numerous readouts, monitors, and displays. But the LCD light was cold; it did not illuminate. C'hien hated the bridge in this twilight state of darkness pierced by a thousand lights. He liked open spaces and bright lights. Faracon knew this—that's why he had killed the main viewscreen before putting C'hien on the hot seat.

"We collect energy from the sun in a variety of forms, with a variety of collectors, to provide the power necessary to propel the ship through time," C'hien began. The young Oriental squinted, trying in vain to see, in the cold dark, the expressions on the faces of his comrades.

"In our last minor encounter with the Temporal Wardens, in an environment where both sides had deep space capability, our collector systems were damaged," C'hien continued. He discreetly did not mention the all out space battle between *La Liberté* and a force of ten cruisers from the old human-Vegan federation that had ambushed *La Liberté* and nearly crippled her there. The ship had had only enough main temporal drive power available for one last hop—the hop that had placed her in orbit above earth in the year 4903 B.C. "Not all of the collectors were damaged," C'hien continued. "We have photon collectors operable, of course, as well as other radiation collectors, and tachyon collectors. What isn't working are the antimatter collectors. Every star radiates low levels of antimatter. But without the capability to collect that antimatter, we cannot operate the ship's main temporal drive."

"And what is needed to repair the antimatter collectors?" Faracon prompted.

"Tin, Captain," C'hien replied. "As everyone here knows, we need a very, very large amount of . . . tin."

"And so, Mr. C'hien—just to make sure I have this right—there we were, fighting off the human-Vegan federation, taking damage on an unprecedented scale. As I recall, I gave you the order to get us out of that situation—to hop the ship to another time. Correct?"

"Correct, sir."

"And you did. Correct?"

"Correct, sir," C'hien replied again, his face a blank mask.

Faracon stood and snarled into C'hien's face. "And you happened to hop us into a Bronze Age period, with mining operations based on illiterate, unskilled slave labor, when our antimatter collectors were no longer operable and we needed massive quantities of tin for repairs! Is that correct, Mr. C'hien?"

"Correct, sir." C'hien did not add that the temporal coordinates for the ship's next hop had already been set by

Faracon himself, nor did he defend himself by asserting, correctly, that the extensive damage to the antimatter collectors had not been assessed until after the hop. He further restrained himself from mentioning that had the ship not made an excessive number of prior hops, at Faracon's command, there would still be sufficient stored power for the massive temporal drive.

Faracon knew everything that C'hien knew. He was also aware that the bridge crew, sympathetic to C'hien, was well aware of all the things C'hien had left unspoken.

The captain walked slowly around C'hien, eyeing him up and down from front and back. "Your actions were incompetent, Mr. C'hien."

C'hien did not respond.

"Do you agree that incompetence should be punished?" Faracon asked, still circling C'hien like a vulture, glancing from the corners of his eyes at the reactions of the bridge crew. They stood rigid, their faces expressionless. Good, Faracon thought. Fear is a very good thing.

"Yes, Captain," C'hien replied.

"And you are incompetent?"

C'hien remained silent. That proved to be a fatal mistake.

Faracon swung back with his right leg and kicked C'hien squarely in the stomach. The Oriental doubled over. Faracon grabbed the medium-length black hair at the back of the man's head and shoved his face forward, hard, into the sharp edge of an arm on the metal command chair. He felt teeth crunch and saw dribbles of blood spill over the chair arm. He yanked C'hien's head back up, twisting the man around so that the entire bridge crew could see his bloodied face. The gasping C'hien spit two bits of tooth out between his bloodied lips.

"Do you know what happens when a time traveler dies, Mr. C'hien?" Faracon bellowed.

"Yes, sir," C'hien stammered.

"What?" Faracon demanded.

"He is dead forever. No attempt to change the historical fact of a time traveler's death can prevent that death from occurring."

"That is correct, Mr. C'hien," Faracon said, smiling, tightening his grip on C'hien's hair. "And do you know the punishment for displeasing me?"

"Captain," C'hien begged, his face contorted from the pain of his hair being pulled. Too late, C'hien understood his situation. Faracon had made a big mistake, and the crew knew it. C'hien was a good exec, one the crew respected. In this instance, he had inadvertently made Faracon look fallible. Faracon's grip on the crew was based on fear, and fear alone. Fear of his cunning, and fear of his ruthlessness. Faracon's own mistakes had brought his cunning into question. C'hien should have taken all the blame for those mistakes in a credible way. He should have admitted to incompetence, let Faracon off the hook in the eyes of the crew. He had not. Now his death would serve the purpose, enhancing the crew's fear of Faracon's ruthlessness. "Captain, I swear I am loyal to you!"

"That touching affirmation will be your last oath, Mr. C'hien," Faracon said dryly. Faracon spun C'hien around and slammed his forehead into the heavy metal chair arm with all his strength. Immediately, he yanked the Oriental's head back and slammed the head forward again. C'hien's body went limp. Still, Faracon slammed the man's head into the chair arm again, and again, and again. Flecks of blood, bits of bone, and finally pieces of brain flew out over the bridge. Faracon did not stop until C'hien's head was an unrecognizable mush.

Faracon finally tossed C'hien's head to the floor with

disgust. He casually placed one foot on the dead man's torso. "Antonio Vitelli is now executive officer of *La Liberté*," he announced to the silent, immobile bridge crew. "He will explain to you how we are going to get the tin we require."

Faracon strutted off the bridge without so much as a glance back.

Vitelli strutted forward from the semicircle of stone-faced crewmen.

"We are stuck, thanks to this piece of garbage," Vitelli began, kicking the dead form of C'hien in the ribs, "in a primitive time. The metal we need is buried in the earth in ore form. It has to be mined, smelted, and processed before it's of any use to us. The captain is striking a deal with one of the local kings to get the entire year's output of the largest tin mine currently existing on the whole stinkin' planet," Vitelli explained.

"In order to do this, he and I will be traveling back and forth to the surface quite a bit. We're also going to be doing some time traveling into the Second World War period, to get what this king wants in exchange for his tin. We need to do a little caper at the Louvre. There, we're going to take some statues this king is gonna want. Once we have them in hand, we wait a year, then we take the tin and blow this time period. Questions?"

"I'll need to get ready for any time transports," Jonesy chimed in. "I'll need exact information. And the captain will need RNA implants for the French and German of that period. I'll need to get medical onto that right away. Also, I was wondering, what about costuming? The captain has that Luftwaffe uniform he used last week when he went to 1943 Bavaria, but won't any strike team be larger? We can't just synthesize the clothing we need; it would take too long to make the microcomputers we'd need. And then there's—"

"Shut up, Jonesy," Vitelli barked. "The captain is a master at covering his tracks. He already went to Germany to make sure Hermann Göring shows up in Paris at the same time we're pulling our heist. The statues we take will show up as missing, alright, but everyone will presume they were stolen by the Nazis, especially if Göring is in town when it happens."

"What's the backup plan?" the communications officer asked.

Vitelli nodded his understanding. Faracon always had a backup plan. Whenever his activities were interfered with by Temporal Wardens, he'd hop somewhere else, near the same time period, and create a change wave so devastating Temporal Wardens would have to divert all available resources to dealing with the second anomaly. By the time they got that solved, there'd be so many other things of priority that what Faracon had done would take a permanent backseat and never be acted against aggressively.

"Don't worry," Vitelli said. "There is a backup plan. But we won't be needing it unless the skipper and I get chewed up pretty good during the heist. As always, you and Jonesy will have everything you need to know before it all goes down. As for now, me and the skipper gotta go back to the surface and cut the deal with this king.

"Now, before we go, you oughta know that what happened to C'hien here," Vitelli added, again nudging the limp body with the toe of his standard issue space boot, "was absolutely his own fault. He got what was comin' to him. Anybody disagrees, come talk to me personal and I'll help you get straightened out on this."

Vitelli strode off the bridge, looking for something decent to eat before preparing to transport back to the primitive culture below. Jeez, he thought. Working for Faracon was just like working for the Big Fella in Chicago. Only there were a lot more gadgets and a lot more angles, and Faracon sure did like to scare the crap out of his *soldati*.

Place: Kingdom of Ukluk, Sumer
Time: Late afternoon, exact day and hour unknown.
4903 B.C.

Utnapishtim, King of Ukluk, swatted at the flies that buzzed constantly through the dusty air. He knew the exercise was pointless; flies were a ubiquitous annoyance in Ukluk, and even a king, or in his case, as he liked to claim, a god, could not do anything about them.

The king turned his mind to more pleasant matters. Tonight he would be entertained at the palatial home of his good and loyal subject, Enkidu-galal. There would be a great feast, and the pleasure of dancing slaves, fine wines, royal revelries. And then there would be business.

Utnapishtim normally did not visit a subject's home. This litter borne trip through the streets of Ukluk was almost unprecedented. His priests, jealous of Enkidu-galal's wealth, power, and influence with the king, had insisted that if Enkidu-galal wanted to speak with the king, he should come to court, like any other subject, and make his suit in public — where their jealous priest ears could hear every word.

Utnapishtim had overruled them. Enkidu-galal's chief overseer and steward had made it clear, in his secret communication to the king, that Enkidu-galal would make the king an offer that would indeed be worthy of a divinity on earth. Utnapishtim was intrigued. Besides, it would be great fun returning to his court with Enkidu-galal's trade offer in hand, watching the priests and scribes and sycophants scurrying and plotting in their efforts to find out just what this offer entailed, how it would affect their standing in court, and what they could say against it to undermine Enkidu-galal. Such entertainment, Utnapishtim thought, was not to be missed, even if it did mean the king would pay Enkidu-galal the unheard-of honor of a personal visit.

It was such disdain for the court that had made Utnapishtim king in the first place. Once he had been a mere soldier, one who had risen on the merits of his strength and personal courage to the command of a hundred men. Then, when chaos had threatened Ukluk, when the war gods had turned against the old king Enlagamesh, when the priests had despaired and the general fled, Utnapishtim had seized command. He had given orders, and the people had obeyed, because no one else knew what to do. It was Utnapishtim who had unleased the stored-up waters of the flood upon the enemy hosts at the gates of Ukluk. It was Utnapishtim who had led the common soldiers forward into the chaos of the enemy camp after the floodwaters receded. It was Utnapishtim who had fought with the sword and spear, slaying scores himself, directing the slaughter of an entire generation of soldiers from the Kingdom of Uruk. And when he had returned to the city, and the priests and scribes and sycophants had insisted on crowning the scrawny, puling babe son of Enlagamesh by one of his royal whores, it was Utnapishtim who had dashed the babe's brains out on the steps of the great ziggurat, proclaimed himself king, and led the victorious army in the ruthless slaughter of the priests who cried out against him. Finally, it was Utnapishtim who had directed the building of the new system of ditches and dikes and pools to protect the city from the waters of chaos that bounded annually out of the great river Tigris, fecundating the soils but threatening to wash away the city in the process.

For this achievement, he had taken the royal name of Utnapishtim, the name of the one man who had saved mankind from the greatest of ancient floods, and who even now dwelt on the mountain of the gods.

But those accomplishments were in the old days, Utnapishtim reminded himself. He stroked his long, oiled, scented beard thoughtfully. Now he must have some regard for the priests, and even more the gods, of whom he was one. Now he must have order, stability, regularity in the affairs of the kingdom. There must never be an opportunity for an ambitious youth to climb to royal, or even divine heights, as he himself had done.

Still, a little bit of spirit must occasionally be indulged. If this Enkidu-galal's offer did not please him, he could always have the man put to death. And his palatial estate would make a nice addition to the royal properties inventory.

The slaves bearing the royal litter halted. The king looked up as a cacophony of horns blared, announcing his presence at the front of the home of Enkidu-galal. Already the gates were flung open by naked slaves, and a bevy of nude young girls were running toward the royal litter, giggling and strewing flower petals everywhere. Then Enkidu-galal himself appeared in the doorway to the palatial residence. The old merchant looked resplendent in his gown of blue, shimmering material with gold embossed throughout in delicate designs. He wore his beard long, curled and carefully shaped, like the king's. He bowed deeply to the royal presence, arms extended fully out from his sides in a gesture of welcome.

Utnapishtim stepped from his litter. The slaves at once knelt, facedown, in the dirt of the street. Enkidu-galal, Utnapishtim noted with pleasure, also fell on his face in the presence of the living god. These negotiations would go well, the king thought.

Place: Kingdom of Ukluk
Time: Late evening of the day of the king's visit to
Enkidu-galal; exact time unknown. 4903 B.C.

Utnapishtim belched. Enkidu-galal belched. Both reclined
on soft pillows, breathing air scented with incense and
burning oils, their bellies bloated with food, their senses
sated with pleasure.

"You mentioned, in your invitation, some type of trade
arrangement," Utnapishtim began. "Your hospitality has
been worthy of our person. We trust your commercial
proposition will be of equal delight."

Enkidu-galal leaned forward, his eyes intent, boring into
those of the king. Utnapishtim frowned. He was not
accustomed to being looked in the face except by the slave
girls and wives in his harem, and then only in the most
intimate of moments.

"I have much to offer the living god," Enkidu-galal
replied slowly. "But I have much to ask."

Utnapishtim forced himself to meet the gaze of this
subject. He was king and god, and would not avert his eyes
from any face. "What is it that you ask?"

"All the tin of the mines of Ukluk for a period of one year.
Every scrap of ore, smelted and pounded out into sheets or
poured out into blocks—I care not which. But I must have
it all."

Utnapishtim roared with laughter. "Bring me my litter
slaves!" he called aloud. "I have enjoyed the evening's
entertainment, but my host has been made mad, no doubt
from staring rudely into the face of a god. For it is said no
man can actually see the gods face-to-face and live, save
Utnapishtim himself."

Faracon, a.k.a. Enkidu-galal, caught the warning in the king's humor. He at once lowered his face.

"I assure the Great King that I am neither mad, nor full of unwarranted pride. I humbly seek the Great King's forgiveness for my rudeness. Only an intense desire to see the joy in the Great King's face when he learns of what I offer in return for the tin drove me to look into his eyes."

"And what, for the sake of more laughter, is it that you offer?" Utnapishtim replied, his tone of voice indicating that his amusement was growing less by the moment with this display of hubris and lèse majesté.

"The gods of Uruk," Faracon rumbled back, his voice intentionally low and the words drawn out slowly, so there could be no mistaking their meaning.

Utnapishtim plucked a grape from the plate nearest him and plopped it into his mouth. He sucked out the seeds and spit them onto the rich carpet. "Leave us," he suddenly bellowed with a wave of the royal arm. The dozens of slaves and courtiers at once scurried from the banquet hall. The plucking of lyres and droning of lutes ceased as the musicians followed the slaves into the royal-ordered exile from the banquet.

"Am I to perceive that the Great King has interest?" Faracon asked with an oily sneer in his voice.

"You presume much in your attitude toward us," Utnapishtim roared, leaping to his feet. Wine cups topped as the royal robes caught on them and swirled around them. Utnapishtim's dark eyes glowed with the dark, angry fire of an offended king. "Live long enough to explain how you could possibly make such an offer!"

Faracon rose slowly, again locking his gaze with Utnapishtim's. "Believe me when I say that before I came to Ukluk—and after—I was both a warrior and prince among my own people. You and your priests do not know the . . . magic of my people. I can reach out and pluck the gods of Uruk from the very altar of its king with greater ease than you can pluck another grape or grab a slave girl's breasts. I offer these gods to you, with all that means. In return, I want a year's worth of tin. And when we are before other eyes, I will bow and scrape as any subject, but when we are alone, I am your equal. Do not speak down to me again," Faracon hissed.

"You are mad," Utnapishtim said quietly, a look of sincere disappointment on his face.

"I can prove what I say," Faracon said, smirking. "I can go now, to the Great Temple of Uruk, and remove the King of Uruk's Enlil and Ishtar, and bring them here, to you, now."

"It is five days' march to Uruk," Utnapishtim protested. "Now I know you are mad."

"If I do what I say, you will give me the tin?" Faracon persisted.

Utnapishtim paused to think. His eyes burrowed into Faracon's, and his fingers played in the curls of his oiled beard. He turned away from Faracon and paced the dining hall, his sandaled feet stepping over the bowls of oiled dates, figs, chopped meats, and roasted fowl. In the sputtering torchlight, all these familiar things took on a certain strangeness to Utnapishtim, as though the whole world were suddenly jarred from its foundations and tilted. He had seen strange things in his time—things as strange as a poor freeman, indentured into the army, rising to become a king. But such strange things were dangerous. Was this Enkidugalal dangerous? Was he mad? Or did he have the magical power to do what he claimed he could do? This Enkidugalal was a strange man, after all. He had come to Ukluk only a year and a half before, and in that time he had erected this great palace, greater than any building in Ukluk save the king's residency and the great ziggurat. His trade had prospered as no other merchant of Ukluk had ever prospered, and yet he himself was never seen to actually work. He had proven a good ally of the king, had paid his taxes without whimpering, and shamed the merchants and artisans who grumbled at the king's share of their wealth.

Certainly, Utnapishtim thought, there could be little harm in finding out what Enkidu-galal's magic could perform. True, the price was high. A year's worth of tin from the mines of Ukluk—that would mean no bronze for a year for spear points, helmets, shields, greaves, and all the accoutrements of the warrior. And yet—to possess the very gods of Uruk! While both Ukluk and Uruk worshiped Enlil, each had their own sacred images of the god, which were the presence of the god in their midst. In war, Enlil was often fickle, favoring now one side, now another. But how could Enlil fight for Uruk, when Uruk's Enlil himself marched with Ukluk's army? With the gods of Uruk in his possession, Utnapishtim could achieve the dream of three generations of kings of Ukluk: the conquest of Uruk!

Utnapishtim turned slowly in the dimming light and faced Enkidu-galal. "Let it be as you say. Bring me the gods of Uruk, here, tonight, and place them in my hands, and the tin you desire shall be yours. I, Utnapishtim, King of Ukluk, Chosen of Enlil, Renewer of the Earth, Savior from the Flood, have spoken it."

"Great King," Faracon replied, smiling and bowing slightly, "let yourself witness that I will now vanish, and before you can count twelve twelves, I shall return and place within your hands the gods of Uruk."

Utnapishtim nodded his assent.

His head still bowed, Faracon quietly said in the common language of the twenty-ninth century, "Activate recall."

Utnapishtim's eyes grew wide with fright as Enkidu-galal muttered a short incantation in a strange tongue and vanished into thin air. Shivering with fear, the Great King slowly began counting to 144.

3

A Meeting in Time

Place: *La Liberté*, in synchronous orbit above the Tigris-Euphrates Valley
Time: Exact day and hour unknown. Year 4903 B.C.

"Jonesy, recall Vitelli," Faracon ordered. The big man was already shedding the rich robes of the merchant Enkidugalal as he stepped into the decontamination chamber. "And be sure my next costume is ready!" Faracon shouted.

The captain of *La Liberté* hurried through the decontamination process and stepped into the dressing room, where his 1943 German Gestapo colonel's uniform, coat, hat, and boots were carefully displayed, ready for him to don. Next to his uniform was one in Vitelli's size, but with the rank of a mere captain and in the *feldgrau* of the *Waffen-SS*.

Faracon was half dressed when Vitelli entered from the decontamination field. "I was listenin'," Vitelli announced. "Things seemed to go pretty well with the old king down there. You shoulda seen his face when you Beamed out! Say, them's pretty nice uniforms."

"I somehow thought you would find them aesthetically appealing," Faracon muttered sardonically.

"Whatever," Vitelli agreed.

Faracon stepped to the mirror as he pulled the black uniform jacket over the regulation shirt and tie. He carefully adjusted the shining lightning bolts on the jacket collars, straightened the tie, and carefully placed the black uniform hat squarely on his large head.

"*Sprechen Sie Deutsch?*" he casually asked Vitelli.

"Huh?" Vitelli replied, struggling to stuff his gray pant legs neatly into the tops of his mid-calf leather jackboots.

"Computer, RNA prep," Faracon ordered. The ship's computer immediately alerted the duty crewman in the time travel preparation section that the captain wanted him in the beamer dressing room.

"Kang here, Captain," the man called over the computer operated intercom system. "What will you be needing?"

"Short term RNA implants for German language, 1943," Faracon said. "Historical and cultural package for the same period. Two doses of each. One for me, one for Vitelli. Ready for injection in five minutes."

"As you order, Captain," Kang's voice answered.

"I already gave Jonesy the coordinates for this hop," Vitelli commented. "Looks like he did a good job gettin' ready. These clothes look real authentic. He was sayin' we couldn't replicate—"

"Spare me the details of Jonesy's problems," Faracon replied. "Just remember: You're a captain in the Waffen-SS, a kind of elite fighting force. You've been assigned to me as my aide. I'm a colonel in the Gestapo, the secret police of the period, and a rank high enough to keep anyone much from bothering us. We'll break out the statues we want, and loot a few other items for good measure, so it won't be obvious to any Temporal Warden what we were after."

"Got it," Vitelli said, glancing in the mirror to straighten his own uniform cap. "Don't look bad. What about fire-power?"

"We'll take the photon rifle as well as period side arms—gunpowder slug throwers called Lugers. Keep the rifle slung under your overcoat," Faracon commented.

Vitelli went to the rack of standard armaments in the dressing room, opened the case, and pulled out a lightweight photon rifle. The piece was two and a half feet long with the stock folded in, and weighed only one and half pounds. He loaded it with one power capsule, an energy storage device of oval shape three and one half inches long. He stuck two other capsules in the pocket of his German military overcoat. Then he slung the light, folded rifle over his shoulder and donned the coat over it. A few practice swings convinced him he could produce the rifle quickly and easily, even from beneath the bulky outer garment.

Vitelli next looked questioningly at the pistol in the holster on his pants belt.

"That's the Luger," Faracon explained. "Just point and pull the trigger. It fires one lead round each time you pull the trigger, until the clip is empty. Clip is in the handle."

Vitelli drew the weapon, withdrew and checked the clip, reloaded, and chambered a round, nodding understanding. He'd spent a lot of time in the twentieth. This "new" model of automatic pistol felt just like old times to him—only better.

Lastly, each man placed in the pockets of his period overcoat a mid-twentieth-century flashlight.

Kang entered the dressing room. Without a word, Faracon and Vitelli hung their heads forward, exposing the backs of the necks. Kang went to Faracon first and pressed a hydro-injection gun to the back of his neck, just below the base of the skull. With a soft *pop*, the gun shot a rapidly self-replicating, short lived RNA implant into Faracon's brain. Within ten minutes, the RNA would spread throughout Faracon's neural net, interfacing with his language and data storage centers, giving Faracon an outstanding ability to speak and understand German as spoken by any class or social group in 1943. Also implanted was a general working knowledge of the cultural rules of the period, and key reactions—such as recognizing and saluting superiors, knowledge of the names of key cities, politicians, monetary denominations, vehicles, and foods. This RNA was programmed to self destruct in twenty-four hours: at the end of that period, all of the information it stored would be cleared from Faracon's brain. Kang gave a similar injection to Vitelli.

Ten minutes later a trembling Jonesy punched in the final coordinates ordered by Faracon, and Faracon and Vitelli stepped through the Beamer portal.

**Place: Place de la Concorde, Paris, France
Time: 10 p.m., Paris time, May 9, 1943**
Jean Vitterand, riding crop tucked neatly under his left armpit, the black leather of his Gestapo getup oiled and polished, silently materialized just to the left of the Egyptian obelisk in the Place de la Concorde, the large square at the end of the Champs-Elysees opposite the Arc de Triomphe. The square was brilliantly illuminated by the banks of lights along the interior walls of the Louvre and the Jardin des Tuileries, and the illumination of the magnificent fountain that stood between the obelisk and those gardens. But with a curfew in place, there were few pedestrians strolling the famous square. Only a few sleek, black Mercedes unloaded their wealthy occupants at the front of the nearby Hotel Crillon, and the still elegant Maxim's, now catering especially to the higher caste of German officers and a lower than normal class of French females.

Vitterand immediately adjusted the leather belt of his

overcoat, checking, as he did, to make sure that the activated light was glowing on his Temporal Collision Avoidance Field (TCAF) device. Without that small device, and the quantum effect it created, Vitterand knew he would be almost instantly dead. For he had taken the enormous risk of hopping back just a few hours in time, to a time when he was already in existence. Right now, he could walk back to the secret entrance to the Paris Time Station, go inside, and talk to himself, should he so desire. But he could do so only with the TCAF activated. The device subtly changed the quantum vibration frequency of the matter of his body, putting it out of phase with the matter "native" to this particular time. Without this "out of phase" effect, one of nature's basic rules would take over: No one thing can be in two places at the same time. If he had Beamed Back without an activated TCAF, Vitterand's body would have instantly sought out its duplicate self in this time period and collided with it, producing an explosion of great severity and killing Vitterand in the process.

Certain that the field was operating properly, Vitterand reached into his uniform's interior jacket pocket and produced his identity papers. For this evening's foray he was Col. Hans Jurgen of the SS Gestapo, on special assignment from Berlin with authenticated plenipotentiary orders to investigate French underground and resistance activities. His authorizations were signed by Himmler himself—or at least a computer's duplicate of Himmler's signature. With these papers, he could go anywhere, question anyone, and generally raise all the hell he wanted to without anyone in Paris having the authority to stop him.

"Mit diese papieren, Ich kann . . ." Vitterand-Jurgen noticed that he was thinking in German; his RNA implants were functioning well, augmenting his already fluent knowledge of that language.

But pleased as Vitterand/Jurgen might be, John Thomason felt his heart sink in his breast and a lump rise in his throat as he gazed across the fountain and beautiful gardens at the great stone facade of the Louvre. Even as a child he had had a special fondness for this seemingly endless building. Originally constructed in the early 1500's, the Louvre had been a fortress, royal palace, and finally museum that had been touched by every great royal and republican hand that had ruled France for over 450 years. Francois I, Henry IV, Louis XIV, and Napoleon had all played a special role in creating both the building and priceless treasures which it now displayed. The huge structure, shaped like a giant letter *U*, was, in many ways, part of the heart of Paris, and to the young American John Thomason, it had been an almost living testimony in architectural and artistic form to the very best in the spiritual and political history of the western world. Now, above the frieze covered cornices atop the ends of the great building flew neither the tricolor of the Revolution nor even the eagles of the Empire, but rather the hated red banner with the black swastika obscenely emblazoned in a circle of white.

In the far distance, he could see German soldiers standing guard at the entrance of what was once the Palais Royal, the residence of the kings of France.

Thomason shuddered, then caught himself. "*Ich bin nicht Amerikaner, nur Pariser . . .*" he forced himself to think. He cast a harsh, suspicious, and hopefully sufficiently arrogant glance around the Place de la Concorde and strode off, stomping, toward the Quai des Tuileries, which ran above the banks of the Seine and eventually became the Quai du Louvre, from which one could enter the museum.

There was little traffic in the streets, other than German soldiers and a few women who chose or were forced to be

their escorts for an evening of sight-seeing in the famous
city. The former gave the Gestapo officer a wide berth; the
latter turned their faces. No native of Paris wanted her face
recognized by a member of the Gestapo, no matter how
innocent the activity in which that person might be engaged.

Jurgen walked on along the river, the Louvre looming up
into the night to his left. He passed entrance after entrance,
each properly closed and guarded by soldiers who cast
wistful gazes at the couples strolling by. Perhaps tomorrow
night someone else would pull guard duty, and they could
romance a local girl along the banks of the fabled river.
Jurgen walked on, noticing every guard position and entrance, looking carefully for anything that seemed amiss,
any anomaly, any tiny sign of something that didn't belong
in 1943. He found nothing. Disgruntled, the Gestapo colonel turned to make his way back the way he had come.

Jurgen passed the end of the Louvre when he heard the
sirens. He quickened his pace and marched quickly back to
a vantage point with a view of the square and the gardens.
Two motorcycles led a military procession, followed by an
armored car. Behind that came an extra long Mercedes limo,
its huge hood followed by the characteristic high cab. From
the front fenders flew the banners of Commander in Chief
of the Luftwaffe. Göring's car was followed by another
armored car, then a large truck, loaded with Luftwaffe
troops. Two more motorcycles brought up the rear of the
column. Reichsmarschall Hermann Göring was coming to
visit the Louvre. Sirens blaring, the lead cycles swung
through the Place de la Concorde and took the narrow lane
in the gardens. The Reichsmarschall would enter through
the Palais Royal, Jurgen noted.

Quickly turning, Jurgen returned as rapidly as he could
without attracting attention to the farthest entrance to the
building along the Quai du Louvre. A quick check of his

watch, carefully preset before his Beam Back, showed the time to be 10:48 p.m. Whatever was going to happen would happen soon, Jurgen thought.

Place: The Louvre, Paris, France
Time: 11 p.m., Paris time, May 9, 1943

"Jonesy did well," Faracon said flatly.

Vitelli spun around quickly, shining his flashlight along the walls, taking in his surroundings. The duo stood in a large hall of stone, the walls of which were lined with glass cases with nasty looking locks and alarms. Little placards in French and German identified the countless bits of statuary, jewelry, pottery, and baked clay tablets displayed in the seemingly endless hall of cases.

"First time at the Louvre?" Faracon asked mockingly.

"Yeah," Vitelli answered. "I ain't never seen so much rubbish in one place in my life. And this place looks like a tomb."

"Fitting," Faracon agreed. "It was originally built as a fortress. Can't remember right now who it was supposed to defend the French against—probably the English or the Spanish. Or maybe one of their own archdukes."

"If this is what high culture is all about, I ain't interested," Vitelli commented.

"Your lack of interest will dismay centuries of aesthetes, I'm sure," Faracon replied. "Let's find what we're looking for."

"Good idea. I think we've got company," Vitelli replied. No guards were in sight, but they could hear voices shouting and footsteps in the distance, echoing though the chambers of the huge building.

The burly SS colonel strode down the corridor, shining his own light on case after case, his gaze drinking in every piece and placard as his eye sought what his own research had told him could be found here. After a few minutes' search, he stopped in front of one large case crammed with a variety of statues ranging in size from a few inches to two larger pieces, each about three feet in height.

"It's these two," Faracon said. The placard identified the pieces by catalogue number, and noted that they were believed to be statues of the Mesopotamian god Enlil and his consort Ishtar, excavated from the ruins of Uruk, time period uncertain but probably prior to 4000 B.C.

"Hey, boss," Vitelli asked, sliding back into the vernacular of his home culture, "how come it matters which crummy statues we take that old king? How's he gonna know a fake from the real thing?"

"You forget that to the people of Ukluk these statues are, in fact, gods. Utnapishtim has visited Uruk and seen these very statues. He will have noticed every detail about them, including, if I am not mistaken, the mounting holes on the bottom, the peculiar way in which that left eye of Enlil's is slightly off line with his right eye, and the somewhat odd position of the left foot, which is just ever so slightly forward from the right. Any mistake in replicating any of these details would tell Utnapishtim in a second that we were frauds."

"He knows the real stuff when he gets it, huh?" Vitelli summarized.

"Aptly put."

Place: The Louvre, Paris, France
Time: 11:03 p.m., Paris time, May 9, 1943
"I swear, *Herr Reichsmarschall*, there have been no unauthorized removals of artworks from this facility!" The fat, bald sergeant of the guard was sweating profusely,

despite the cool May weather. Bad enough that tonight, on his duty watch, the Reichsmarschall himself had to visit the museum. Worse still that his commanding officer had ditched his duty post, leaving the sergeant in charge while he romanced some more than willing French girl, who, truth be told, was probably in the resistance—weren't they all? But unbelievably bad that the Reichsmarschall, in a terribly foul temper, was accusing other German officers of looting the Louvre—and demanding a full inspection tour! There would be hell to pay for all this, and Sergeant Willy Gunther wanted none of it.

"You will admit my troops at once!" Göring screamed at the trembling man. "Do you know who I am?"

"*Jawohl, Herr Reichsmarschall.* Open the doors! Admit the troops at once, you fools!" he shouted to the stunned guards. Luftwaffe troops in pale blue uniforms stormed manfully through the doors of the Palais Royal, then looked stupidly about for orders.

"Search this place!" Göring shouted. "Search the whole damned museum! Find anyplace where it looks like something is missing—and any damned Gestapo or SS troops who might be around!"

"There are no SS troops or Gestapo here," Sergeant Gunther tried vainly to assure the Reichsmarschall. "I would know if there were."

"Well, then," Göring stormed, "you won't mind if we just have a look for ourselves, will you! And while we're at it, I will personally take into custody for safekeeping certain of the pieces here which these corrupt looters no doubt intended to steal for their personal gain."

"*Jawohl, Herr Reichsmarschall,*" Gunther said weakly, a sick feeling growing in the pit of his stomach. Now there would really be hell to pay. . . .

"*Heil* Hitler," he essayed, hoping to assuage Göring's wrath.

But the Reichsmarschall paid Gunther no more heed. He was already pacing down the great hallway, musing aloud to a sycophantic aide who seemed glued to his side.

"I must have something that will please the Führer, something of more interest to him than whatever it is that that damned Himmler is after," Göring said.

"The Führer himself was a painter . . ." the aide offered.

"The Führer has no real interest in painting," Göring countered, a look of scorn on his face. "His tastes run in more . . . bizarre directions. Now, what would really please him would be something very old, something ancient, something from the time of the Old Testament—you know how superstitious he is about anything Semitic," Göring stated, a smile breaking on his face.

"Sergeant!" Göring bellowed. "Which way to the Semitic antiquities?"

Gunther quickly checked one of the visitor's maps available near the Palais entrance and gave directions to Göring. "You!" he shouted to one of his own men. "Go with the Reichsmarschall. See that he finds his way. And . . . turn on the lights as you go," Gunther ordered.

"But, Sergeant, I don't know where the lights—"

"Go!" Gunther bellowed.

The soldier ran off behind Göring and his aide, looking frantically for a light switch.

Gunther leaned back against a column, exhaling deeply. He snatched a handkerchief from his hip pocket and patted the sweat off his bald forehead and pate. "*Mein Gott*," he thought. "Himmler and Göring fighting over treasure that I'm supposed to guard. What can happen next?"

"You there, Sergeant of the Guard," a cold voice called.

Gunther looked up, startled. He saw a black gloved hand

slam into his throat, pinning him against the cold stone column. Then he saw the eyes of the meanest looking SS Gestapo colonel he had ever seen boring through him.

"The Reichsmarschall was just here," the colonel said. He released his pressure on Gunther's throat slightly.

Gunther nodded in the affirmative and gasped.

"Which way did he go?" the officer demanded.

"He was looking for SS troops. He thought they were looting the Louvre. I assured him, *Herr* Colonel, that nothing of the sort was happening. I—"

The hand choked off Gunther's air supply. His arms began to flap and his legs began to kick aimlessly, but the terrified sergeant never even considered taking physical action to defend himself against an officer of the Gestapo.

"Did I ask you what he wanted or what he said?" the colonel demanded. Again, the air supply was partially restored.

Hacking and choking, Gunther shook his head, indicating a negative answer.

"Very good," Colonel Jurgen said, smiling at Gunther. "What I asked you was one simple question, and you will give me one simple answer. Which way did the Reichsmarschall go?"

His throat burning and his lungs on fire, Gunther pointed in the direction Göring had disappeared.

"Did he mention a specific area as his destination?" the colonel wanted to know.

Gunther nodded, coughed up phlegm, and spat. "He wanted to find the Semitic antiquities," he managed to gasp. The colonel released the hapless man, who staggered forward and grabbed another of the visitor's maps from the nearby stand. He pointed on the map to the general area for Mideastern Antiquities.

"Thank you, Sergeant. You have done a greater service

for the German people and whole world than you can possibly imagine," Colonel Jurgen said. Then he began running full tilt down the great hallway of the Louvre.

Place: The Louvre, Paris, France
Time: 11:07 p.m., Paris time, May 9, 1943

"That's it, smash up a few more of these cases," Faracon suggested.

Vitelli enjoyed himself. With the butt of the Luger and the front end of his heavy flashlight he smashed glass cases right and left, raking their contents onto the floor. The clanging of the alarms that sounded as each case broke didn't bother him in the slightest. The more the alarms clamored, the more he went about his work with enthusiasm.

At each end of the hallway, heavy, steel, portcullis type grills dropped automatically from the ceiling, crashing to the floor and sealing off all means of egress from this particular exhibit area.

"That's good," Faracon called, noticing that the area was sealed. "Now pick up some of this rubbish and stuff it in your pockets. Be sure to take things from several different cases."

Vitelli grunted and nodded. His holstered his Luger and shined his flashlight over the cold stone floor, looking for the more interesting bits of ancient jewelry strewn about. He was examining a copper hair ornament studded with tiny emeralds and rubies when he heard the first shouts from beyond the portcullis. Beams of light slashed into the hall, streaking across Vitelli, then coming back to rest on him.

"*Achtung! Halten Sie!*" a voice cried in German from the darkness.

"Boss, we got company," Vitelli reported calmly.

"Yes, I see. We'd best get what came for." Faracon strode to the glass case containing the desired statues, and with a stroke of his flashlight shattered the panel. He reached into his overcoat pockets and produced two leather straps, each with a small black box attached. He carefully placed one strap around the neck of each statue, and then pushed a small button on each black box. A tiny red light glowed from each, indicating the activation of a TCAF. Then Faracon calmly tucked one statue under each arm.

Place: The Louvre, Paris, France
Time: 11:07:45 p.m., Paris time, May 9, 1943

Jurgen ran full tilt down the dark hallway of the Louvre, his flashlight cutting swatches across masterpieces that, as John Thomason, he had once spent hours adoring. Just ahead he saw a portcullis grillwork falling in front of the body of Luftwaffe troops who were rushing toward the sound of clanging alarms. Behind the troops ran the enraged form of Hermann Göring.

"*Der sind SS!*" one trooper screamed.

"*Ja!*" Göring shouted. "I knew it! It's that damned Himmler! Raise that gate at once!"

Jurgen was closing on Göring, looking at his watch as he did so. If the anomaly report was correct, there were only seconds until the explosion. He could at least save Göring's life and stop the worst effects of the wave of change that was rushing toward the future, if he could only catch up to him! For a fat, morphine-addicted derelict, Göring could display amazing energy when his temper aroused.

"*Ich kann nicht!*" a soldier cried. He was unable to find the release to raise the grillwork.

Jurgen peered past Göring's body into the now demolished display room full of Mesopotamian antiquities. He saw glass and rubble everywhere, and a short, wiry, dark-haired man in a Waffen-SS uniform grabbing pieces at random and stuffing them in his pocket. The man watched the alarmed with amusement.

"*Halten Sie selbst!*" he shouted back at them. "*Wir sind das SS! Wir sind Gestapo!*"

"*Feuer!*" Göring shouted. "Kill those SS bastards!"

"Let's get out of here," Faracon shouted to Vitelli. "Activate recall!" Faracon disappeared.

"*Nein!*" Jurgen shouted, "*Nicht feueren!*" He threw his body forward, his arms outstretched toward the back of Göring.

A shot rang out as Jurgen's arms closed around Göring's body. The momentum of his tackling leap propelled both men forward.

"Activate recall," Vitelli said.

The bullet, fired with great accuracy by one of the Luftwaffe soldiers, struck the pocket of Vitelli's coat, and slammed through the casing of one of the proton rifle power capsules. The full load of energy released in an enormous, searing flash at the same instant Vitelli disappeared from May 9, 1943. The blast ripped through the grillwork of the gate, shearing the metal and sending twisted spears flying back down the corridor.

The concussion of the blast blew Göring backward even as Jurgen's tackle pushed him forward. The fat Reichsmarschall bent nearly in half, the back of his head crashing into the small of Jurgen's back as both men fell to the floor. Then a foot and a half of steel bar, blown out from the explosion, flew just over Göring's face. The deadly missile ripped into the chest of the Luftwaffe colonel who, as always, had been just behind the Reichsmarschall. The man gasped in shock, clutched the bloody portion of the metal that had exploded his heart, and fell over, dead.

"Mein Gott!" a Luftwaffe trooper screamed. *"Das Reichsmarschall!* The Gestapo has tried to assassinate the Reichsmarschall!"

Uh-oh, Jurgen thought. He arched his back, rolled the heavy, unconscious Göring off himself, and staggered to his feet. Through the smoke and dust he could see that Göring was badly burned, and several of the troops killed. Those who weren't were leveling their weapons at him, looking from the sprawled, burned body of their comatose hero to the Gestapo colonel who was somehow involved in his injury.

This was definitely not part of the plan. He had wanted to observe what happened—and he had failed. He'd seen only one culprit—but heard the voice of a second. And now he was about to be butchered by these emotional young Luftwaffe fanatics who'd just seen their hero half blown to bits and believed that somehow he was in on it.

Jurgen shook his head. If it's not one damned thing, it's another, he thought, the old Americanism running through his mind. It was then that Jurgen noticed his face felt flushed.

"Activate recall," he said softly.

4
When Things Go Wrong

Place: *La Liberté*, in synchronous orbit above the Tigris-Euphrates Valley
Time: Exact day and hour unknown. Year 4903 B.C.

Pale-faced with fright and shock, Vitelli materialized on the Beamer platform aboard *La Liberté*.

"What the hell happened?" Faracon demanded.

Even Jonesy could tell that something was amiss with Vitelli. Usually arrogant, cool, and nonchalant, Vitelli was pale and trembling. He didn't even seem to know where he was. From Jonesy's perspective, of course, not much at all had happened. One moment, he had activated the Beamer and watched Faracon and Vitelli disappear in a flash of light. The next instant, the recall switch had automatically activated, and the two had reappeared. To Jonesy's eyes, they had been gone less than a second—he had barely seen them flicker out and then back in.

But Vitelli was definitely changed in that instant. That meant something had gone wrong—and it meant Faracon would be in an even more foul mood than usual. Without a word Jonesy thumbed the alert button that roused the crew from their normal routine and put them on standby alert, ready for any emergency action Faracon might order.

Vitelli shook his head vigorously, trying to clear his mind. What had happened?

"There was big flash, boss," he said. Eyes wide with wonder, Vitelli began patting his torso with the palms of his hands. He was still solid, still in one piece, still alive. Why shouldn't he be? Because there had been that flash of light . . .

"An explosion!" Vitelli exclaimed. "Something blew up just when I bugged out!"

"An explosion? What exploded, you dolt?" Faracon demanded. "Here, take these damned statues!" he roared at Jonesy.

"Decon," Jonesy reminded him.

"Damn! Vitelli, get your wits about you and meet me on the bridge. I need to know what happened, and I need to know now!"

In the decontamination chamber, Vitelli discovered the answer to his quandary.

"Look, boss," he said. "Look at this hole in my coat pocket." Eagerly, he thrust a hand in the pocket, feeling for the power capsules for the photon rifle. There was one. . . . Where was the other? The hole had a strange, burnt look to it. . . .

"How many power capsules did you have?" Faracon demanded, his burly body bathed in the decontaminating beams. From the floor of the decontamination chamber, the statues of Enlil and Ishtar looked up at him with their frozen, stone disdain. "How many?"

"I thought I stuck two in this pocket, but there's only one here now, see?"

"I heard an order to shoot," Faracon said thoughtfully.

"That's it!" Vitelli shrieked.

The decontamination chamber door slid open automatically as the process concluded. The two men stepped into the dressing room, Vitelli nearly dancing with joy as he understood the nature of his narrow escape from certain and permanent death.

"There was a shot fired—you remember?" he asked the boss.

"I heard someone order the troops to fire," Faracon said. "That's when I got out—and that's when you should have gotten out."

"I did," Vitelli protested. "I was just an instant behind you. There was a shot, then a big flash of light, and I was out. I think the bullet hit one of the power capsules, and I transported just as it blew."

"Then you can rot in ten thousand hells!" Faracon exclaimed. "Do you know how devastating an explosion of a power capsule can be? Especially in 1943, a blast like that will stand out like a sore thumb. When the police or the Germans investigate—and they will—they'll find a residue unlike anything they've seen before. They were still learning about plastic explosives then. An explosion like this will be a sure tip-off to the Temporal Wardens!"

"Hey, this was supposed to be easy, you said. And I don't remember you mentioning anything about those capsules bein' explosive if they get hit. You're the expert in these future weapons. I coulda been killed," Vitelli bitterly challenged.

"Hmmph," Faracon snorted. "It's a miracle you weren't. The chance shape of the capsule and the angle at which the bullet entered must have directed the energy of the explosion outward, away from your body. By the time the explosion reached any size, and we're talking about thousandths of a second, you were gone." He threw on his white space coveralls and strode off to the bridge. The crew snapped to attention as he entered, and he noted with a grin that the arm of the bridge command chair, and the floor around it, had been meticulously cleaned since he had last been there. He slumped into the chair, leaving the crew to stand like silent statues while he pondered.

It was no use blaming Vitelli. He was, after all, merely a thug—a not very smart thug—from the twentieth century. He was right; Faracon should have warned him about the power capsules—or better yet, not taken any high-tech weapons at all. The question was, had the Temporal Warden for the Paris zone been alerted to an anomaly?

"Crew, as you were. Officer of the Watch, report."

"No change in status, Captain," a timid voice called out.

"Very well. Vitelli, come here," Faracon called. Vitelli, his confidence restored and his sense of elation from his confrontation with death still keen, strode fearlessly to the command chair and looked Faracon in the eyes.

"You're right," Faracon said. "I should have told you. Now, see if you can remember anything else that happened before you transported out. There was an order to fire . . ."

"Yeah, somebody gave the order to shoot us. Then you told me to get out. Then someone shouted real loud not to shoot, but there was a shot anyway. And then the explosion just as I . . ."

"Someone shouted at the troops not to fire?" Faracon asked, suddenly springing to his feet. He began pacing the bridge in the narrow space in front of the viewscreen. The turbulence in his mind formed an odd contrast to the placid image on the screen. It was night in the Tigris-Euphrates Valley. A thin cover of clouds drifted over the junction of the two rivers.

"Yeah, yeah, that's right. Somebody yelled out real loud

that they shouldn't shoot. But this Luftwaffe soldier, he shot anyway."

"What did the man who ordered them not to shoot look like?" Faracon asked quietly.

"It was real dark, boss," Vitelli pleaded, walking alongside Faracon. "There was just them flashlights to see by. Let me think—hey, you know what? He was dressed like you. Like a Gestapo guy. And he was running real hard, trying to tackle the guy who gave the order to fire."

"Are you sure he was Gestapo?"

"Yeah, yeah, boss, now that I think about it, I'm real sure."

"Helm!" Faracon barked, resuming his seat in the command chair. "Lay in a course for the moon, maximum sub-light speed. Assume synchronous orbit on the dark side, very low, as low as possible. Double range on all temporal shift scanners; I want to know if anything pops into this time period anywhere in the solar system."

"Aye, aye, sir," the helm duty officer responded. "Course plotted."

"Let's go," Faracon said, his voice low and serious.

A low, throbbing hum ran through the ship as the sub-light drive cut in, and the giant vehicle began to slowly vector away from the earth. "Under way," the helm officer replied. "Estimate lunar orbit will be established in twenty-nine minutes."

"Captain, temporal scanners are now operating at maximum range. No disturbances registering," the scanner operator called.

"Maintain continual scan at maximum range. Alert me the moment you pick up anything, anything at all. Vitelli, put the weapons crews on full alert, and if anything shows up when I'm not on the bridge, blast it to atoms."

"Uh, I don't get it, boss."

"That was no Gestapo officer who tried to prevent you from getting shot," Faracon explained, heading back to the dressing chamber. "Think about it. Göring and the SS are bitter enemies. He sent Luftwaffe troops to the Louvre out of fear that the SS and Gestapo were stealing art that he wanted. He wouldn't have a Gestapo officer with them," Faracon explained.

"Uh, okay, so this guy just showed up and . . ."

"Nothing in the universe happens by chance," Faracon said. "That was no Gestapo officer. That was a Temporal Warden, trying to prevent the gunshot that caused the explosion."

Place: Paris, France, Time Station
Time: 2:43:01 a.m., Paris time, May 10, 1943

Jean Vitterand collapsed in a heap on the Beamer platform, wisps of smoke and foul fumes rising from his seared uniform.

"Medic," he managed to call.

"Computer," C'hung C'hing shouted. "Alert medical crew. Emergency on Beamer platform." The Chinese rushed to Vitterand's side, peeled off his own tech coat, and used it to begin suffocating the slow fire. At the same time, he quickly examined Vitterand form hat top to boot toes.

The entire uniform was smoldering. C'hing noticed that the metal lightning bolt bars on Vitterand's collar, the insignia of the SS, had been semi-melted by some intense heat. They looked like tiny metal sculptures of deformed serpents. The tops of the leather boots had blistered and the sides were cracked open in several places.

Vitterand himself might be in trouble, C'hing decided. Beneath the cap portions of his hat his hair had fried, leaving only crisp, dry spidery threads that crumbled when touched. His entire face was scorched, and the flesh was already turning into a mass of blisters.

Vitterand began trembling.

"Cold," he muttered.

"He's going into shock," C'hing said.

Two medical technicians raced through the control room. They quickly placed Vitterand's now limp body on a floating cot, and the medical scanners began a thorough examination even as they raced the cot from the control room to the tiny sick bay.

"Alright, everyone back to stations," C'hing told the assembled crew.

The Beams operator knew events like this were disconcerting, even to experienced time travelers. To see Vitterand disappear in a flash of light in one instant, and in the very next reappear, charred to a crisp, would be demoralizing to even the best, including himself. Work was the best tonic, C'hing knew.

"Communications," he ordered, "report uptime and see if they can tell us anything that would give us a clue as to what happened. Equipment, take a look at that uniform after they get him out of it; we need to figure out what might have been the source of the heat that burned him."

"Roger that," Mulhoon replied, heading off down the narrow corridor toward the sick bay.

"Uptime com link opening," Vu Nguyen sang out.

"The rest of you," C'hing ordered, "back to work, back to work." C'hing paced around the crowded control room, shooing people toward their stations like a farmer's wife scolding chickens back to the henhouse. "The medical teams will take care of him. We have to figure out what went wrong and what needs to be done next."

C'hing paused between two console tables where Sandy

Deweese stood, shoulders drooped, staring at a meaningless display of energy output summaries.

"He will be fine, you know that," C'hing said.

"I know," the finely featured young blonde answered. "And if he isn't..."

"If he isn't, there is nothing we can do," C'hing said flatly. "You know as well as I that while time travelers can save ordinary humans from death, death is final for any human who has traveled in time."

"I never really understood that," Sandy said, her blue eyes moist.

"Well, you had better concentrate on understanding, rather than on things that you cannot change," C'hing said, punching in meaningless controls to change the graphs on the console. Perhaps if he pretended to be busy, Sandy would get to work and stop worrying. "It is a great wisdom to understand things you cannot change."

"No, I mean really. Why can't one of us just hop back in time and warn him?"

"If he dies, it would not matter," C'hing explained softly. "Suppose you did warn him, and he simply retrieved back to here. In a short time, he would die anyway—how, exactly, is unpredictable. A piece of the ceiling might fall on his head, or he might choke on a bit of dry bread, or just have a heart attack. No matter what else was changed, you could not change his death. That is just how time travel works."

Sandy shook her head, avoiding C'hing's piercing eyes. "Doesn't matter, anyway," she said, stifling the urge to cry. "He's going to be alright."

"And when he is better, he'll need new clothes. Better get on that," C'hing urged.

"Roger that, Beams," Sandy said. She paced bravely out of the control room, head held high.

C'hing muttered to himself as he returned to his own

principal work station. As second in command of Temporal Station Paris, he had seen several Temporal Wardens come and go through the years. But he'd never seen one break as many hearts in as few a number of days as this American. Half the females at the station were infatuated with him. Probably, C'hing thought, because he did nothing to encourage any of them. The man seemed to live like a monk.

"Sir, uptime com link is established," Nguyen reported.

C'hing nodded acknowledgment to Nguyen, then spoke softly into the computer's voice monitor.

"This is Beams Operator C'hung C'hing, temporarily in command of Temporal Station Paris," C'hing reported, pausing a moment to glance at the huge digital display clock above the arched entrance to the Beamer platform, "0248:46 hours, May 10, 1943. Temporal Warden Vitterand badly injured, apparently by burning, in temporal transport activated same date at 0243:01 hours."

"Roger," the anonymous voice of Temporal Warden Central responded.

C'hing ran his short fingers through his slightly oily black hair, then cradled his chin in his hands. "Request your observations on outcome of our Warden's mission," C'hing said.

"Update coming in now," Central replied.

C'hing waited, nervously squeezing his lips between his index fingers. "Sick bay," he called, when Central did not immediately begin with its report. "Status of Temporal Warden."

"Bad, sir," C'hing heard one of the med techs answer. "Third degree burns on face, second-degree burns over eighty percent of the body. He'll be laid up for at least two days while the nu-skin heals."

"He'll survive, then?" C'hing asked anxiously.

"Doc says affirmative that—but he'll have some significant pain over the next forty-eight hours. After that, he'll be ready for action."

"Thank you, sick bay," C'hing sighed. Again, he ran his hands through his hair. He was relieved that Vitterand would live, but still enormously anxious. The Time Station was still on a Priority Two alert, and he was in charge. Although trained to assume command, C'hing had never imagined he'd be called upon to do so when the entire future was at stake. How should he proceed? What orders should he give?

"We copied that, Paris." The voice of Central interrupted C'hing's nervous speculations. "Glad your Warden is going to make it."

"Thank you," C'hing replied. "Now, if you can give me any report on the anomaly wave that put us on alert in the first place . . ."

"Temporal Station Paris, you are secure from Priority Two alert. I say again, you may stand down from Priority Two alert."

C'hing flipped open his station-wide intercom mike. "This is Beams," he said. "Stand down from Priority Two alert."

Cheers rang out from the control room staff and quickly echoed down the several narrow corridors of the station. Nguyen grabbed C'hing's hand and pumped it up and down in elation. C'hing laughed and grinned, his relief so great that he did not yet realize his body was trembling.

"We copy that, too," Central called. "Sounds like things might have been a little tense there."

"I imagine they were a little tense at your end, too, Central," C'hing jested.

"Roger that. We celebrated just before you called."

"What, exactly, did Warden Vitterand do?" C'hing asked. As second in command, he still needed to know as much as possible about the situation.

"We're not certain," Central reported. "But at a minimum he saved Göring's life. The fat chief of the Luftwaffe will be able to keep 'em flying just like he ought to."

"I'm sure," C'hing said, waving his arms up and down to signal for silence in the control room, "I say, I'm sure our American Temporal Warden will be delighted to know that he saved Hermann Göring for the war crimes trials!" Cheers and howls of laughter rang out from the staff at C'hing's typically understated irony.

"But tell me," C'hing said suddenly, "why didn't his mission self-eliminate if the anomaly was removed?"

Good question, Nguyen thought to himself. Normally, if bad guy A goes back in time and changes something, and good guy B hops back in time and stops bad guy A before he changes things, good guy B's trip is paradoxically self-eliminated. Because, since bad guy A doesn't change time, there is no reason for good guy B to hop back in time to stop him. It was one of those little paradoxes that made Temporal Warden Corps duty so interesting. The best Wardens never remembered anything about their best missions because, from a purely historical point of view, they never happened. There was nothing for them to remember.

"Roger your query," Central answered. "The original anomaly was not entirely prevented, only its most devastating effect, which was Göring's death. Perpetrators were not captured, and some minor anomalous effects persist."

C'hing frowned. "Recommendations?" he asked.

"We recommend you get your Warden healed up and let him figure out what else needs to be done," Central responded. "We have three other Priority Twos going on now in other sectors."

The control room was suddenly silent again. If major anomaly waves were headed toward them from the past . . .

"Don't worry," Central said. "They're all uptime from you."

Again, relief passed through the control room. This time there was no cheering.

Place: *La Liberté*, in transit from Earth orbit to lunar orbit
Time: Exact hour and date unknown. Year 4903 B.C.

"A Temporal Warden? You think so?" Vitelli asked. The thin man screwed up his face, showing contempt for the very notion. "Nah, I don't think so. Now that I think about it, his clothes didn't even fit too well. Looked like the cleaner might have shrunk his uniform."

"Then that settles it," Faracon spit back. "He was a Warden. Haven't I taught you anything? You know the Temporal Wardens operate on a tight budget. They can't go around fabricating every item they need."

"Okay, okay," Vitelli said, starting to pace the bridge. "So if he was a Warden, why don't he just hop back a little earlier with a whole team of guys and arrest us when we show up?"

"Why not, indeed?" Faracon agreed.

"So he couldn't be a Warden," Vitelli concluded merrily. "Because if he was, he woulda done that, and we wouldn't have made the time hop back to here, see?"

"It means, you idiot, that he hasn't done that *yet*," Faracon explained, his patience nearing an end.

"So what? We got thousands of years between us . . ." Vitelli started to say, his voice trailing off as his brows furrowed in contemplation. "Oh. I get it. You mean, at any time, he could hop back to the Louvre, in 1943, arrest us, and we'd be in the clink, having never been here. Then we'd have never had this little chat. Jeez, that's neat."

And also the end of a multibillion-dollar, trans-temporal

criminal empire, Faracon thought with a chill. How could he
have been so stupid as to be involved personally at the Louvre?
For a moment he considered going back in time and telling
himself not to go, to send someone else on the heist with
Vitelli. Perhaps, he decided, he would do that later. But the
most immediate thing was to create a diversion, something
that would keep the Paris, 1943 Temporal Warden so busy
he wouldn't have time—paradoxically—to mess with the
Louvre job any more.

"We have to use the backup plan. Now!" Faracon said.
"Get going."

"I'm going alone?" Vitelli queried.

"Yes, you're going alone. I have to deliver some goods to
a king who's going to be very impressed." Faracon lumbered over to the central communications station, to his left
on the bridge. "Stand aside," he told the duty officer.

The man leaped to his feet and snapped to attention.

"Look away," Faracon barked.

The man turned his back to the console.

"Hmm," Faracon snorted. Then, his fat fingers flying on
the console touch pads, he sent an urgent message forward
in time to 1943 A.D.

In a small suburb of Paris, beneath the basement of an
impressive villa, a computer terminal flashed to life, with an
urgent message from the Wolf. The operator scanned the
screen, transmitted back an acknowledgment, and typed in a
set of preauthorized commands. The temporal damper field
around early May 1943 suddenly disappeared.

Aboard *La Liberté*, the bridge power monitors showed a
sudden upsurge in power storage. "Sir," the officer at that
console reported, "power transmission to uptime damper
field generator has ceased."

"Very good," Faracon said, smiling. "I want the Wardens
to be able to play around all they want to in that time

period." He glanced up at Vitelli, who had a worried look. "Time for you to make your little hop, just like we planned. You should enjoy being a snitch. And by the way, Jonesy knows to send you with a memory wipe, just in case anything goes wrong."

Place: Kingdom of Ukluk
Time: Late evening of the day of the king's visit to Enkidu-galal; exact time unknown. 4903 B.C.

Utnapishtim, King of Ukluk, discovered that it was very hard to concentrate on his counting. His throat and lips were bone-dry, and his tongue felt almost swollen. Utnapishtim had seen many strange things in his life. He had seen magicians pluck golden coins from the very air. He had seen priests who could turn sticks into serpents, and back into sticks again. He had even seen a high priest who could transmit his thoughts without speaking. That one had met with a sudden, fatal accident while inspecting the irrigation canals. But he had never seen a human being vanish into nothingness before his very eyes, not three paces away from him.

Had he counted three twelves or four? Utnapishtim could not remember. Was it important to the spell that he count? Was is important to the spell that he count accurately? Utnapishtim felt something he had not felt in a very, very long time. He felt fear.

The gods, he knew, could feel fear. When Enlil had slain his mother, the dragon of Chaos, she who swirled without form in the waters of that which was before the world, she had felt fear. Even Gilgamesh must have felt fear, Utnapishtim reasoned, when he encountered the death of his companion Enkidu. So now, he, Utnapishtim, felt fear. That did not mean he was not one of the gods, the incarnation of

Enlil, as the priests taught the people. It was just that, standing there amidst the strewn remains of a great banquet, alone, faced with something totally unprecedented and unknown, feeling fear, Utnapishtim did not feel like a god.

This fear was not a wholesome fear, he told himself. Wholesome fear was the fear one felt in battle, just before the moment of truth. It galvanized one to action, numbing the mind so that it did not race endlessly back and forth, but focused on the one thing, the one stroke of the sword, the killing stroke, that would mean that you would live, and the other man would die. But this fear, this fear was a sickness that set his mind reeling, wandering off in many directions, unfocused.

He thought about calling for his servants, or his guards. But what king could be seen stammering with fear, unable even to tell his dozens, in front of his servants? What king could prevail upon his guards, mere mortal men, to fight the power of a . . . god?

Was Enkidu-galal a god? Or was he a messenger of the gods? Utnapishtim had heard stories, very old stories, from the days just after creation, about men who walked among men but were not men. Beings who were neither men nor gods, but something in between. The priests disdained such stories. They made for bad politics and worse religion, for if there were beings in between men and the gods, of what value were priests? Or kings?

And yet this Enkidu-galal could not be a god himself. What god would need tin?

Utnapishtim's speculations were cut short by an event even more alarming and surprising than Enkidu-galal's disappearance. There was a soft *pop* in the air, and Enkidu-galal once more stood before Utnapishtim, in the very place from which he had vanished less than a minute before.

The astonished king's eyes bored into Enkidu-galal's.

"What manner of man or god are you?" he rasped. "No magician knows such a trick, and no priest knows such a spell, not even in the far land of the other river, Kush, from where our merchants bring back the most wondrous of tales."

Enkidu-galal stooped over, carefully lowering a heavy statue of Enlil from beneath his right arm to the floor. Then from beneath his left he lowered a similar sized statue of Ishtar.

The large man smiled at Utnapishtim. He clapped his hands loudly and called for a servant.

"Let there be brought to us the king's wax and seal," he ordered the serving boy, who hesitantly appeared.

"You do not answer," Utnapishtim stated.

This is too easy, Faracon/Enkidu-galal thought. "Is not the king a god?" he asked.

Utnapishtim's mind raced. Was this a test? Then he would pass it. "I am," he declared.

"And would you, then, not know another god when you met him?" Faracon asked, smirking. He paced around the king, chuckling as he stared at him, letting his gaze rise from feet to head and back again.

"Stop your pacing!" Utnapishtim ordered. Then, softening his voice, his gaze staying locked onto Faracon's face, he added, "Even the gods may be deceived."

"Well," Faracon snorted, leaning forward so that his face was mere inches from the king's, "I am no god. There," he said loudly, pointing to the statues, "there are your divine siblings! As I promised, from the very altar of Uruk!"

"We shall see," Utnapishtim said.

A slave scuttled in, his head bowed low, his hands held high. In his hands were a small stone container of red wax and a short golden rod with a large ball on one end. On the surface of the ball was the carved image of Utnapishtim, his name in cuneiform around the image.

"Slave," Faracon said. "You see the leather straps on each of these gods?" Faracon demanded. The slave stared for a moment at the two statues, his eyes widening with horror. Mutely, he nodded in the affirmative.

"Heat the wax," Faracon said. "The Great King shall set his seal on those straps, so that all men may know that these are the gods of Utnapishtim, King of Ukluk, and no longer the gods of the nameless mortal who pretends to be King of Uruk."

"Hold!" Utnapishtim commanded. The king stared intently at the statue of Enlil, examining it from every angle. At length satisfied, he turned to Enkidu-galal. "We would see the bottom," he said in a flat tone of command.

Faracon laughed aloud as he tiled the statue of Enlil, revealing the bottom of the piece, with the recessed opening where it would fit over a small upright stone rod on the altar of the King of Uruk.

"The other!" Utnapishtim commanded.

Faracon obliged, tipping up the statue of Ishtar.

"Heat the wax," the king commanded the slave.

Faracon laughed again, then approached close to Utnapishtim, lowering his voice to a whisper. "This is the message of Enlil himself," he croaked hoarsely to the king. " 'The gods of Uruk, the Enlil and Ishtar of Uruk, are yours. I, Enlil, will march before into battle against Uruk, for her king has displeased me. You may place your seal upon my leather strap, and upon that of Ishtar.' "

Utnapishtim nodded, trying to appear knowing, as though communications from the gods themselves were a serious but nonetheless commonplace occurrence for him.

"But," Faracon continued, "hear, too, the curse of Enlil. 'Once your seal is placed upon me, neither you nor any person shall touch the straps of leather on my person. The day that you do, I, Enlil, shall abandon you, and you shall be struck with fire from the heavens as though the sun itself fell to earth, and you shall surely die.'"

"It will be," Utnapishtim replied, holding the statue of Ishtar at an angle while the slave poured heated wax on the leather collar, "as Enlil has said." The Great King then stamped his seal in the hot wax and waited a moment as it cooled. Then, again with the help of the slave, he placed his seal on the leather strap of the second statue.

"There," Utnapishtim said. "We have placed our seal upon this Enlil and Ishtar. They shall march before us in battle," he said, his eyes beginning to gleam at the prospects of the next spring's campaign season.

"And what of your good friend, Enkidu-galal, who has brought you the gods of Uruk?" Faracon asked.

"You shall have your tin, in one year, as you required," Utnapishtim promised solemnly. "These gods are witnesses to the word of the Great King, their brother."

Faracon smiled.

"Until one year from this day," Utnapishtim declared, "you are banished from our kingdom."

Then Utnapishtim smiled. "We are grateful," he explained, "but not foolish."

5

A Diversion

Place: Paris, France
Time: 6 a.m., Paris time, May 9, 1943

This oughta be a piece of cake, Vitelli told himself as he gazed at the dreary early morning sights along the Avenue de l'Opéra. It was just a simple snitch job, and all he had to do was make sure the snitch, in this case himself, didn't get caught. He knew he'd done things like this before, although he couldn't quite remember exactly when, or where, or why. In fact, he couldn't remember hardly anything about himself, such as why he was here to snitch on "Max."

Despite the seeming simplicity of his task, Vitelli's strange memory lapses made him feel less than his usual cheerful self. Perhaps, he thought, it's this damned weather. The sky above was overcast with low, smoky gray clouds from which a steady, fine mist fell gently to both water and depress the city. For a moment Vitelli had wondered if someone had made a mistake. This was supposed to be Paris, the greatest city in the world, seat of culture, refinement, and romance. Here, in the monumental heart of the city, it seemed more like a drab German amusement park. There were more signs in German than in French. The street was filled with small groups of gawking German soldiers and a few early-rising, well-dressed, upper-class German tourists. The only thing French about the avenue was what could be seen of the architecture of the buildings, much of it hidden by signs and placards proclaiming a variety of new developments and regulations in both German and French.

Vitelli felt oddly out of place in this atmosphere of oppressive, Teutonic power. He didn't care much for the German style, he decided. He vaguely remembered hearing about the "Huns" of World War I, though how he'd heard about that he could not quite fetch into consciousness. From what he could see of occupied Paris as he strolled lazily along the avenue, they hadn't changed much in two decades. He particularly didn't like the way they acted as if they owned place. He stopped a moment to watch as two German soldiers gobbled up the sidewalk with their large steps, eyes challenging the French gendarme who slowly patrolled the street. They called out some mild insult to him; the policeman turned up his nose and looked away, too proud to suffer the insult without some show of rebellion, but too frightened to challenge the power of even the lowliest of the occupying force.

Vitelli himself gave the gendarme a nod as he passed. He felt strangely sorry for the fellow, even if he was a rotten copper. After all, they were the only two Frenchmen in the street.

Vitelli startled at this train of thought he was experiencing. What did he care about Frenchmen, especially a lousy French cop? He wasn't a Frenchman, he knew that. What was he? What was his name? Vitelli paused again in his meander down the street, this time pulling a packet of papers from the pocket of his loose-fitting, simple cloth workman's jacket. There was his picture, and there was his name. Jacques Darlon, the paper said. He was employed as a machinist at a small plant that manufactured bicycle parts, according to his work permit. Maybe he was French after all.

Again Vitelli startled. What was he thinking about? Time to focus on the matter at hand.

He forced his legs to pump faster and broke into a rapid stride down the avenue toward the Place de l'Opéra. The huge marble colonnades, arches, and friezes of the famous building loomed into view ahead through the mist, the dome atop vaguely defined through the gray haze. Pedestrian, bicycle, and auto traffic all increased as he approached the square. Even at this early hour in the morning, ordinary Parisians and their Aryan overlords were drawn to the Place de l'Opéra, not to hear music, but to transact business. They came and went not from the opulent opera house, from which at night the strains of Wagner, Wagner, and more Wagner eminated, but from a drab, soot-covered, concrete and brick building that dominated one intersection of the famous square across from the Opéra. A huge sign above the first floor of the building stretched all the way around a corner between two intersecting streets.

"*Platz Kommandantur*" it proclaimed in large, black, archaic Gothic script letters against a white background. A single Nazi flag extended out over the large doorway to the building. It was from this building that the German occupation authorities ruled France.

Vitelli saw his destination. To him, it looked like every police station he'd ever seen, and somehow he knew he'd seen several, even though he couldn't remember where or when. It was a big building, drab, oppressive, depressing, and crawling with scum. He decided to delay his mission just for a moment; a small cafe down the street was open, serving coffee, tea, and pastries. He'd fortify himself a bit before playing the role of a snitch. Besides, it was early; chances were the big boss he needed to contact wasn't even out of bed yet, much less arrived at work.

Vitelli, or Darlon, which was the only name he knew for himself, sauntered across the Place de l'Opéra and walked a few paces down the Boulevard des Italiens. The cafe was already doing a brisk business. Soldiers and Parisians filled the outdoor tables. Occasionally the soldiers would try to start conversations with the locals, who answered politely and terminated the interaction as quickly as possible. Some people, Vitelli thought, just don't know when they aren't wanted.

He made his way to a small empty table for two and plopped into a seat. He wanted coffee and a donut, but this place didn't seem to have donuts. He ordered *café américain* and a Danish pastry. As he waited for his order, Vitelli began to jiggle his foot and drum his fingers on the tabletop. He glanced about nervously. Somewhere, here, he thought, there must be a public telephone. He began to worry that perhaps he should just get his mission over with. All he had to do was place a single phone call, and let the Germans over at the Kommandantur place know where they could find a guy named "Max" this morning. Then he could . . . Vitelli couldn't quite remember, but he knew that once he'd made his call, he would be able to leave . . . Paris.

Funny, he realized, how he couldn't remember anything much about himself, but seemed to know a lot about Paris and the people in it. For example, the man at the table to his right sat alone, reading the morning newspaper and sipping hot tea. He wore a medium priced suit that once had been quite nice, but now had a distinct shine on the knees and sleeves. This man worked in a bank, Vitelli knew. He was probably a minor loan officer, a cut above a teller. The two younger men at the table behind him were obviously

employed in one of the many retail shops that lined the
street. He could tell from their dress, as well as the snippets
of muted conversation he could overhear. Those four
Germans, all privates, two tables distant—they were new to
Paris. Probably transferred here for garrison duty as a
reward for good service somewhere else—maybe the Eastern Front. They were enjoying themselves, laughing, joking,
gawking at the parade of passersby on foot and bicycle, but
they all had drawn, haggard faces, sure signs of hardship.

Then there was the woman at the table just in front of his,
toward the street. She was a girl, maybe eighteen, wearing
a long-sleeved sweater, calf-length plaid skirt, and pumps
with little straps up around the ankles. Single, Vitelli knew.
Possibly available. Vitelli stood, his coffee cup in hand,
anxiety gnawing at his stomach. He should get on with his
mission! Still, a pleasant little chat . . .

He squeezed his way between the crowded white metal
chairs to her table.

"Mademoiselle?" Vitelli doffed his beret and bowed his
head. "Might I join you for a moment?" Without awaiting an
answer, he pulled a chair back and slipped into the seat.
"Ah, what are you doing here?" Vitelli asked, noticing that
the girl was writing. "What is this?"

"Monsieur, do I know you?" she asked.

"Not yet," Vitelli admitted. "I am Jacques Darlon. A
machinist. I work in a little plant that makes bicycle parts.
Do you have a bicycle? Perhaps I made the spokes for your
wheels, or the chain."

She was brunette, with a petite nose, sparkling brown
eyes, and small thin lips accented with an application of a
pale pink lipstick. Her eyebrows raised slightly and her
brow furrowed as she suspiciously examined Vitelli's face.

"Monsieur, I do not know what you intend, but I do not
normally talk to strangers, and I have not the slightest

intention of becoming involved with a man of your age and occupation. Where is that waiter? Reynaud? Reynaud!" the girl called.

The waiter darted toward the table at the sound of his name. Patrons who knew him by name were more likely to leave decent tips. The Germans always tipped too little, if at all. The Parisians seldom had enough money to tip. But when a lovely French girl, who is a regular, calls you by name, Reynaud thought, a little service can produce several extra francs.

"Snooty, eh?" Vitelli challenged. "I like a little fire in a woman. It makes her more mature, more interesting, don't you think?" Vitelli's glance fell again on the girl's writing. She appeared to be filling out some kind of form, but it was in the shape and size of a postcard. "What is that?" Vitelli asked.

"You must live outside of Paris," the girl replied. "Reynaud, I would like another cup of tea."

"*Mais oui, mademoiselle.* Is everything else . . . alright?" Reynaud asked, gesturing with his head toward Vitelli.

The girl stared at the overeager man. Despite his age and coarseness, he appeared harmless enough. Besides, his ignorance of one of the most basic aspects of life in Paris intrigued her. "For now, thank you, Reynaud," she replied.

Reynaud nodded. He would keep an eye on this scum who was trying to prey upon the delightful young lady who would no doubt now leave him a very large tip. In the meantime, he went to fetch the coffee.

"You really don't know what this is?" the girl asked.

"May I?" Vitelli asked, reaching for the card. The girl nodded her assent and he picked it up, looking carefully at the front and back. "It's a postcard," he declared, puzzled. "But it's already printed up, with just some blanks on it."

Indeed, the card was a collection of phrases with blank

lines in between them. "(Blank) is in good health. (Blank) is tired. (Blank) is slightly, seriously, sick, wounded. (Blank) killed, prisoner. The (blank) family needs money, (blank) news. (Blank) is moving to (blank)." Near the bottom were three blank lines, then the printed close, "Fondest thoughts. Love and kisses," followed by a blank line for the signature.

"Of course, silly. You fill in the blanks with the names that apply, and scratch out any words or phrases you don't want, or just underline the ones that apply. Then you sign it and mail it," the girl explained. "Haven't you ever seen a simple postcard before?"

Oddly, Vitelli knew what a postcard was, but in his current condition of memory wipe couldn't remember having actually seen one before. Still, this method of communication defied logic. "Of course I have," he said. "But why not just use a blank card? Then you could write whatever you wanted."

The girl's face looked suddenly alarmed. "Shhh," she commanded, a finger raised in front of her lips. She leaned foward quickly. "Be quiet," she whispered. "What's the matter with you? Do you want to get us arrested?"

"What for?" Vitelli said expansively. "Jeez, I'm just talkin' about a simple postcard."

Reynaud, who had listened carefully to their conversation from the tea service, returned with mademoiselle's refill. "Is everything still alright?" he inquired.

"Alright?" Vitelli demanded. "Alright? What the hell is alright about some goddamn postcard that's already written for you?"

Reynaud smiled and made a sound that was a cross between a nervous laugh and a cough. "Monsieur is quite droll," he said, nimbly stepping away between the nearby tables as quickly as he could.

Vitelli threw his hands on the table, disgusted. He leaned

forward to the girl. "Look, just tell me what this is about," he suggested. "I'm, uh, kind of new around here."

"This is the only form of mail that is allowed between the different zones in France," she explained in low tones. "It's to make it easier for the Germans to censor our mail. They just check the form to see if there is anything that does not pertain strictly to family and personal business. It makes more difficult the use of any kind of code to write about things that . . . loyal citizens should not be writing about." The girl leaned back in her chair and raised her voice. "It is a good thing, too, for our own protection, what with Allied planes passing overhead all the time."

Reynaud ducked inside the cafe and walked quickly to the owner and manager, M. Raymond Drouet. M. Drouet did not like trouble, or even the hint of trouble, in his cafe. He would be grateful to Reynaud for reporting a problem before it became serious. That would be a good thing for Reynaud, because decent jobs, like everything else in Paris, were in very short supply.

"Monsieur Drouet? A moment?" Reynaud asked politely.

Drouet looked up from his work at the register.

"There is a gentleman at table forty-two. He seems to be bothering the young lady, although she is much too polite or softhearted or softheaded to complain. Also, Monsieur Drouet, I could not help but overhear some of his conversation. He pretended not to know about the *cartes postale*, and advocated the use of blank cards. I think some of our other guests overheard him as well, including some of our visitors from Deutschland."

Drouet raised a fat eyelid. "So. Thank you, Reynaud," he said quietly.

As Reynaud returned to his duties, Drouet picked up the telephone and quickly dialed a well-known number. His cafe depended on business from the Germans. Prices in Paris were so high now that only the wealthy could afford anything here except coffee and pastries, and even that was many times its prewar price. The Germans had money. It wouldn't do for them to think his cafe was a meeting place for malcontents, or worse, members of the resistance groups that had popped up like mushrooms.

Vitelli sensed from the girl's tense mood and her reply that he had violated a great taboo. So all mail was censored and the Germans had provided these postcards to make their job easier. That seemed like something he should have known—he knew a lot about Paris, why didn't he know that? Vitelli's anxiety grew. Perhaps he should make his phone call. This didn't seem to be going well at all.

"Would monsieur care for another pastry?" Reynaud suddenly appeared to ask.

"Huh?" Vitelli grunted, taken off guard. "Another pastry? At these prices? I don't think so, chum."

"Ah, monsieur may enjoy it with the compliments of the house. Our chef, he baked too many this morning," Reynaud said cheerily, placing a dish with a fresh cheese Danish on the table. "I will get monsieur more coffee."

"That's friendly," Vitelli commented.

The girl nodded, her eyes nervously scanning the street and the other customers. They lit on an open touring car that suddenly pulled up beside the sidewalk in front. Two men in expensive suits and fedora hats emerged. They squared their shoulders, shook the wrinkles from their jackets, and looked to the door of the cafe.

"I really must be going," the girl said, rising, gathering her purse, pen, and postcards.

"Hey, what's the hurry?" Vitelli asked. He stood, and then saw the two large, square-shouldered men in double-breasted suits and fedoras picking their way through the tables with all the grace of hippos prancing through a daisy field. They were heading straight for him. "Uh-oh, I get it," Vitelli said. "Cops."

Not even the memory wipe administered on board *La Liberté* could block out Vitelli's reaction to law enforcement officers, regardless of where or when he and they were located. The girl began to hurry away, nearly tripping over the tangle of white metal chair legs.

"Mademoiselle, monsieur," one of the large men called. "You will wait, please."

"Who's askin'?" Vitelli demanded, springing to his feet. "We wasn't doin' nothin' here."

"Then you have nothing to worry about," the larger of the two men said, grinning. He was the younger of the two, and Vitelli quickly measured him up. He stood about six foot one, a good 240 pounds, most of it muscle. Blond hair, blue eyes, thick hands that would make fists like meat hammers—not good, Vitelli decided. His companion was shorter, maybe five foot ten, about 180, slightly overweight but still in good shape. Thin wisps of dark brown hair fell over his forehead from beneath the fedora, and he sported a short, thin moustache. He'd be no problem. The men continued to close on Vitelli.

"I know I ain't got nothin' to worry about," Vitelli retorted. "I was just going to call you guys."

"Is that right?" the blond man said, grinning. He squeezed between two tables to a point about three feet away from Vitelli.

"That's right," Vitelli said, returning the smile. Then he grabbed the closed umbrella resting by the side of the chair occupied by the startled banker, who was beginning to rise, looking for an exit. Swinging the umbrella like a baseball bat, Vitelli stepped forward and struck Blondie, as he called

him in his mind, square across the side of the head as hard
he could. The man grunted, stunned. Then Vitelli drew the
umbrella back like a sword and drove the point straight at
Blondie's sternum.

Screams erupted from startled patrons as blood spurted
onto Blondie's chest through his clean white shirt. Tables
and chairs overturned as the local citizens began to scatter.
Blondie sucked in a gasping breath, grabbed the umbrella,
and plucked it from his chest. The point had broken his
sternum and bits of rib but failed to penetrate the heart.
Red-faced with rage, he reached inside his jacket.

"*Nein!*" his companion called, fighting his way forward
through the crowd. "We want him alive!"

Vitelli broke and ran, leaping over fallen tables, grabbing
passersby and tossing them behind himself to impede the
progress of the "cops." The girl was already beyond the
cafe, fleeing in terror down the Boulevard des Italiens.
Blondie roared in anger, dove into the crowd, parted it with
his powerful arms, and began the pursuit of Vitelli.

Vitelli cursed as he ran. All he had had to do was make a
simple phone call to the cops, and now all this—being
chased by the cops! How do ya figure, he wondered to
himself. If only he could remember a little more. He glanced
from side to side. He was racing past storefronts, the
windows loaded with expensive suits, dresses, jackets,
leather coats, purses, gloves—all the best. The war hadn't
changed some things, he thought sardonically. He turned his
head to look behind—and there was Blondie—right on
him!

The giant man lunged forward. Vitelli felt his vicelike
arms close around his body as he hurtled toward the
pavement. Then his head snapped back, and his face plowed
into the concrete.

Place: Villa of Carl Boemelburg in Neuilly, a suburb of Paris

Time: 8:05 a.m., Paris time, May 9, 1943

Vitelli drifted into consciouness. His nose throbbed with pain, and his mouth tasted of stale blood. His tongue probed at his swollen lips, only to discover two intriguing holes where he remembered there should be teeth.

He opened his eyes and quickly shut them again against the brilliant white light that shined directly into them.

A sharp blow to the back of his head snapped his head forward.

"Open your eyes, swine," a voice commanded in guttural German.

Vitelli groaned.

Another blow crashed into the back of his skull. "I said, open them!"

Vitelli opened his eyes, squinting. He tried to raise his hands to shield his eyes from the light, only to find they were tightly bound behind him to the back of the chair in which he sat.

The odor of tobacco smoke wafted in the air somewhere in front of him.

"Perhaps our guest would like a cigarette," a very different voice said. This German was cultured, urbane, smooth, Vitelli thought. "Would you care for a cigarette, Monsïeur Darlon? These are American, the very best Virginia tobacco blend," the voice said.

Vitelli/Darlon nodded. A smoke would be good.

A dark blob appeared in the brilliant light. Vitelli felt the end of a cigarette brush against his mouth. He drew the butt in between his swollen lips and took a deep drag. God, he

thought, that's good. He blew the smoke out his mouth and
nose at the same time. The pain in his nose made him cry
out.

"Oh, you are hurt, Monsieur Darlon?" the cultured
German asked. "I am so sorry. You see, the kind of people
I am given to work with know so little of gentle methods.
And, I am told, you did try to resist my men."

Vitelli twisted his neck and turned his head to one side,
trying to get a glimpse of the speaker. He saw the shadowy
form of a short, fat man sitting on the desktop where the
light was placed. He wore a uniform, a black uniform.

Gestapo, Vitelli realized. I'm being questioned by the
Gesatpo. Oh, my God. He quickly glanced down and saw
that he was nude. It was time, he decided, to be cooperative.

"I was frightened," Vitelli said. "I am sorry I resisted."

"Oh, Monsieur Darlon," the voice laughed. "I am very
certain that you are sorry! Yes, yes, I am certain that you are.
You have an amusing sense of humor, Monsieur Darlon."

"I have a message to deliver," Vitelli said. "Can I have
another drag?"

The cigarette was pressed again against his lips. He
inhaled deeply. The taste was so good, so familiar . . .
There was something he remembered . . . LSMFT?

"Perhaps you would be kind enough to tell me to whom
your message is to be delivered?" the voice urged.

"Sure, I'll play ball," Vitelli muttered. "My message is for
SS Sturmbannfuhrer Carl Boemelburg, Chief of Gestapo,
Paris."

"How wonderful! You are in luck, Monsieur Darlon!" the
voice exclaimed. "You are in the home of that very man!"

"Interesting place you got," Vitelli quipped.

The cold blue steel of a Luger barrel crashed into Vitelli's
right jaw. His head flopped to the side, and he screamed. He

felt hot blood begin to trickle down his cheek, and more blood spurted into his mouth from his right lower gum.

"Jeez, you broke my jaw! What's with you guys? I'm cooperating."

"You must forgive my associates, really," the suave voice replied. "They have a deep sense of devotion and respect for me. Any remark which might be taken as, well, let us say a jest at my expense deeply offends them."

Vitelli checked his desire to smart off again. He just wanted to deliver his message. Then, he somehow knew, this nightmare could end.

"May I deliver my message, please?" he forced himself to ask politely.

"Why, by all means, Monsieur Darlon, by all means!" the voice answered. "Why don't you tell your message to me, and I will be sure that Sturmbannfuhrer Boemelburg receives it."

"He's gotta get it right away. Time's important," Vitelli said, wincing as he spoke. His jaw was already swelling, pressing in against the right side of his tongue.

"Well, of course, I understand. If your message is so urgent, perhaps you should tell it to me right away. I can assure you the Sturmbannfuhrer will know almost immediately."

"Okay," Vitelli agreed. "Here's the message. Boemelburg is looking for some guy named Max. And he really wants to find Max before some guy named Klaus Barbie finds him and gets all the credit," Vitelli said.

Blondie, standing behind Vitelli, lifted his gun to strike the man again. But Boemelburg, the principal interrogator and head of the Paris Gestapo, abruptly signaled him not to strike. He wanted Vitelli to finish.

"Yes, yes," Boemelburg said. "I've got that. Please go on."

"Well, Boemelburg can find this Max at about ten o'clock

this morning. He's meeting some other people at a private apartment here in Paris," Vitelli explained.

"And the address?" Boemelburg quietly prompted.

"Number sixteen, rue du Four, Paris," Vitelli said.

"Excellent! Excellent!" Boemelburg exclaimed. "Now tell me, do you happen to know the exact identity of this 'Max'?"

"His real name's Jean Moulin," Vitelli said.

Boemelburg turned out the blinding light. "Take him below. We will question him more later. Prepare my car and two squads of men at once. We will take this fox Max in his lair!" Turning to Vitelli, Boemelburg added, "You have been very helpful. If I were you, I would pray that your information is correct. When I return, we will want to know all about you, and how you come to have such information. And in case you were wondering, your female companion was captured. She's being held at the Platz Kommandantur. If you do not furnish us with everything else we want to know, she will be thrown into a concentration camp."

"She doesn't know anything," Vitelli protested. "I was just trying to pick her up."

"We shall see."

Vitelli blinked as his eyes adjusted to the normal light, but he had little time to drink in his surroundings. His bindings were loosed, and he was quickly hustled out of the large, well-furnished room down a back staircase and into a cellar, where a row of cells stretched along a dank corridor. He was roughly tossed onto a cot in an empty cell, and the iron door clanged shut behind him.

Vitelli didn't care. He just wanted to be alone. As soon as he was certain that he was alone, he said the two words that popped into his memory as the keys to going home, back to where he belonged.

"Activate recall," he whispered.

Place: *La Liberté*, in transit from Earth orbit to lunar orbit
Time: Exact hour and date unknown. Year 4903 B.C.

Faracon rematerialized aboard *La Liberté*. A glance around caused him concern.

"Where's Vitelli?" he shouted to Jonesy.

The Beam operator shrugged. "Not recalled yet," he reported.

Faracon rushed through the decontamination and dressing procedures, then came straight to Jonesy's post.

"You made sure he had a memory wipe before you sent him uptime?" Faracon asked.

"Yes, sir. All he knew was the language, general culture of 1943, and his mission. He didn't even know who the hell he was, and he wouldn't have the slightest idea of how he got to Paris."

"Good," Faracon grunted. Now it was time, he thought, to take care of another disturbing little matter. He went to the bridge, checked on the ship's overall situation, and returned to the Beamer control room.

"How are we on power for personal trips?" he asked Jonesy.

Jonesy keyed in a query at his control terminal and watched as the colored graphs danced across one of his screens. "Enough for fourteen safe hops, thanks to the power we've saved by cutting off the damper field," he reported. "Twenty hops if we stretch it. After that, we'll be completely stranded in time until the anti-matter collector can be brought back on line."

Faracon nodded.

"There's also something the com officer thinks you should know about," Jonesy said casually. He wanted to ease into the subject without arousing Faracon's famous ire and paranoia.

"Why didn't the com officer tell me?" Faracon snapped. He plopped down in a swivel chair and wheeled it up next to Jonesy.

"Sometimes people are a little afraid of your temper," Jonesy said, his voice flat, expressionless.

"Bad news, then," Faracon concluded.

"Not the best," Jonesy agreed.

"Tell me, then we can both worry about my temper," Faracon said, smiling broadly.

"We had a routine report from the uptime stations," Jonesy began. "No use getting technical and specifying which uptime stations—the temporal mechanics of this are already getting so complicated I need the computer to help keep it all straight. Far uptime, okay?"

"Yes," Faracon agreed. Problems in temporal mechanics always involved mind-boggling paradoxes. The computers, using the known laws, could usually keep straight who was where, when, doing what, and which actions had canceled out others, and which actions would cancel out others after the passage of a little bit of time. Actually, the computers used a theoretically constructed metatime to sort out the paradoxes. The calculations didn't matter to Faracon; all that mattered were the results.

"It seems that this is what happened. You and Vitelli went into 1943 and snatched those statues from the Louvre. There was an explosion. That explosion killed Hermanm Göring, who happened, God knows why, to be at the Louvre that night," Jonesy said.

"Then that's why the Temporal Warden showed up!" Faracon exclaimed, jumping out of his seat with excitement. "Göring was killed? I can only imagine what kinds of anomalies arose from that!"

"Big ones," Jonesy said. "Apparently, it started a change wave that not only threatened the Temporal Warden Central, it started wiping out a lot of our post-twentieth-century investments. Reports were sent to our uptime stations and then relayed back to us."

"Then the Temporal Warden hopped in," Faracon continued, piecing it together for himself. "He didn't prevent us from getting the statues, but he did save Göring's life. Of course, Vitelli and I never even knew that Göring himself was at the Louvre that night."

"Correct," Jonesy said. "Now, if understand things correctly, you've sent Vitelli on a mission to divert the Warden from the Louvre on the night in question."

Faracon cursed. Actually, his real goal was to prevent the Warden from being reinforced at the Louvre that night and capturing Vitelli and himself, but the diversion might have the effect of causing the Warden to never come to the Louvre at all. The Warden might be off on some wild goose chase. In that case, Göring would die, the wave of change would start again, and either the future would be altered beyond all recognition, including the wiping out of Faracon's fortune, or Warden Central might overreact and Faracon would be captured in a massive effort. Neither alternative was acceptable.

Jonesy watched as the large man paced the Beamer control station, his brows furrowed, his hands clasped behind his back. Faracon might be a brutal murderer, a ruthless thief, or even a hopeless paranoid, Jonesy thought. But he was a genius at thinking through temporal mechanics problems. For all Jonesy knew, Faracon didn't even know the formulas. He was like some idiot savant, who managed to produce the right answers in some unknown way. Now he would need one incredible answer.

Faracon continued to pace. From time to time he would pause, lift his head at an angle, and stare into the thin air, shake it, and then pace some more. Jonesy sat silently, knowing from long experience that it was pointless and even dangerous to interrupt Faracon while he was in this mode of thought.

"The problem," Faracon said at length, "as always, isn't merely one of temporal mechanics. It's one of human behavior."

Jonesy nodded dumbly. He didn't have the slightest idea what Faracon was talking about.

"We will have to make a deal with the Wardens, sooner or later, at one time or another, " Faracon continued. "And in order to do that, we need something that they have to have and can't provide for themselves."

Again, Jonesy nodded and wisely remained mute.

"Maintain enough power to recall Vitelli. Plus enough for me to make two hops and two recalls. Plus enough for one other round-trip for one other person. That's seven individual hops, right?"

Jonesy agreed.

"I want all power put on a strict security hold. Maintain two power storage banks. One bank to power the hops I just described. The other bank to be used . . . as I direct, when I order it."

Jonesy's hands flew over his touch controls, creating two banks within the power storage modules. Even as Jonesy did that work, the recall alarm sounded, and Vitelli rematerialized in a heap on the Beamer platform.

Both men were startled for an instant by Vitelli's appearance. He was stark naked. His lips were swollen shut; his jaw was enlarged to the size of a softball; and another huge hematoma was visible on the back of his head. Dried blood covered the pulp where his nose should have been, and fresh blood dribbled from his lips down his chin and dripped onto his chest.

"Where the hell am I?" Vitelli demanded.

"Gestapo must have had at him," Faracon commented to Jonesy.

6

Confusing Times

Place: Paris, France. Temporal Warden's Station
Time: 1400 hours, Paris time, May 9, 1943

Temporal Warden Jean Vitterand scanned the routine daily reports from the morning's monitoring activities. There were the usual small-scale anomalies, the effects of minor change waves which began downtime, in another place and time. These were nothing to be concerned about for now. The Wardens in the appropriate places and times would be notified by Central as appropriate, and would take appropriate action. If there were any danger to the Paris Station in this time period, Central would alert him to take preventive action.

Other reports concerned the usual legal time travelers, visitors from the far future doing historical, biological, sociological, and anthropological research in the France of 1943. Vitterand noticed that most of the travelers were obeying the regulations and keeping to their appointed timetables. One small group, a university professor and two graduate students, were overstaying their leave in Lyon, where they were involved in a detailed study of the French resistance movement. Vitterand shook his head as if to clear that very subject out of it. The French resistance was one of the most complicated social, political, and military movements in history. It didn't involve that large a number of people, but it was so fragmented that only lifetime scholars could keep the players and the intrigues straight. It involved socialists, republicans, monarchists, communists, anticommunists, militarists, antimilitarists—almost every type of political group and orientation imaginable. All distrusted one another, and each had its own agenda to pursue in the course of resisting the German occupation of France. Well, Vitterand thought, soon he'd have to hop back in time a bit and shoo this group out of Lyon, before they wound up chucked in a concentration camp themselves.

But, aside from that minor problem, Vitterand was well satisfied. He had been here almost nine days now, and things seemed to be running smoothly. His Beams operator and second in command, C'hung C'hing, was, as Mason had promised, one of the best. His equipment man, Mulhoon, was a minor genius at engineering. Nguyen was proving to be competent at communications. The medical team kept themselves busy with study and drills—so far there had been no need for their services. And his costumer, Sandy Deweese, had proven inventive if nothing else.

As far as major missions, Vitterand had nothing to report, and that was the way the Temporal Wardens wanted it. Of course, that might mean one of two things: either there had been no threats to the timeline and he hadn't had to do anything, or there had been threats and missions, but they had been successfully accomplished. Successful missions eliminated themselves. A day or two or three after one, and you had no memory of it, because it had never happened, in a sense. Either way, Vitterand concluded he was doing a good and competent job in his first Warden assignment.

Vitterand leaned back in the large, twentieth-century

style, high-backed, leather executive chair and propped his feet up on the big oak desk. These were period luxuries that he had decided to allow himself—they made him feel more at home. The desk reminded him of his time at Harvard and Cornell, and the chair was not unlike the one his father had had in the Chicago office of their family firm. All that was lacking to make the office completely homey was the scent of high quality cigar smoke.

The large red blinker light in the ceiling of Vitterand's office suddenly began flashing, interrupting his reverie about his past life. "Temporal Warden Jean Vitterand," the computer called, "a temporal anomaly has been discerned. Please report for briefing prior to immediate corrective action."

Vitterand was on his feet before the computer finished speaking.

"Nguyen," he called over the station wide intercom. "What have you got?"

"Incoming anomaly report, confirmed at maximum uptime and by our own computers, sir," Nguyen's voice answered as Vitterand jogged down the short corridor to control room.

As he entered, Vitterand saw that Nguyen, Mulhoon, C'hing, and Deweese were already gathering near C'hing's workstation, the place where most informal but important conferences were held. One of Nguyen's assistants was already at the printer, creating a hard copy of the alert for Vitterand's use.

"Alright, everyone," Vitterand said, joining the group. "Let's see what we've got."

The assistant handed the printout to Vitterand, who began skimming it and reading relevant sections out loud.

"This station is on Priority Three alert, as of now," Vitterand announced as he glanced over the first page.

C'hing keyed in the alert status. Throughout the station, the computer began notifying appropriate personnel to take action stations.

Personally, C'hing was relieved to hear that it was a Priority Three alert. That meant an anomaly had been detected which would cause significant change in the future, but which would not threaten the existence of the Temporal Wardens in the far future. It was one of the many paradoxes of temporal mechanics that most changes in the Timeline eventually worked themselves out: at some point in the future, history would get back "on track" and far future events would remain unchanged. The interim periods, however, still had to be restored; otherwise history itself would become a meaningless jumble of events, a tale told by an idiot, as C'hing often commented to himself.

"What have you got, sir?" C'hing asked.

"Reading, reading," Vitterand replied slowly, his eyes sucking in the data. "Okay, here it is. At approximately ten a.m. this morning, about four hours ago, on this very day, May 9, 1943, the German Gestapo arrested one Jean Moulin, a member of the French resistance. As a matter of fact, he was a key member of the resistance," Vitterand explained. "He parachuted into France in 1942 and began a yearlong effort to unite the resistance factions into a unified fighting force. He was eventually successful in creating the CNR—that's the *Conseil National de la Résistance*—on May 27, 1943. The CNR was quickly almost destroyed by the Gestapo, thanks to turncoats in the resistance, but its historical importance is not diminished by that. What made it important was that the CNR recognized Charles de Gaulle and the Free French as the legitimate government overseeing all resistance efforts in France, a key fact that later kept France from going communist and coming into the Stalinist orbit after liberation."

"What do the uptime anomaly outcomes look like?" Sandy Deweese wanted to know.

"Not good. A communist France makes the formation of NATO shortly after World War II impossible. Soviet hegemony is established on the continent, with the result that the Cold War continues well into the twenty-first century, with a high-tech nuclear and post-nuclear holocaust unleashed in 2053 A.D. Things stay bad for a long time after that. Temporal Warden Corps is still formed on schedule, you'll be happy to know, but with massive personnel differences projected, given the major changes in the genetic stock available."

"So," C'hing said, "the Corps will still exist, but many of us might not."

"Those of you from uptime had better hope I can head this off," Vitterand said, not entirely in jest.

"Sir!" Nguyen interrupted. "We're getting a priority message from Central for your attention only."

"In my quarters, Nguyen."

Seconds later Vitterand was in his personal, spartan sleeping quarters. He verified that the com link was secure and soundproof from the rest of the station, then responded.

"Vitterand/Thomason, Paris Temporal Station, May 9, 1943, 1406 hours, responding to priority message, personal attention only."

"John," said the familiar, friendly voice of Bill Mason. "Good to hear you again. How are things?"

"Just got a Priority Three but I assume you know that."

"Yes, that's rather why I'm calling," Mason said casually.

"Afraid I can't handle it?" Vitterand asked. After all, it was his first major alert, and this was his first duty station as a Temporal Warden. He wanted to know whether or not he had Mason's confidence.

"Not at all," Mason responded quickly. "We have every

confidence in you, especially given your already sterling performance in the field."

"Sir?" Vitterand asked, puzzled. "I mean, I've only been here about eight and a half days, and so far nothing's happened."

"Yes, well, that's not exactly the case. It all depends on how you look at it. From our perspective, you've already . . . what's that American phrase? 'Saved our bacon,' I believe. Yes. You've already saved our bacon once in a big way."

Vitterand remained silent. Clearly, there was a complicated problem in temporal mechanics in the making.

"Well," Mason continued after a silent pause, "it's like this. Whatever you're going to do about this Moulin thing has to be done this afternoon and this evening. And, by the way, please don't allow yourself to be injured in the process."

"Wait a minute," Vitterand interjected. "This is only a Priority Three alert. The change wave won't ever reach you. And it begins after my recruitment. I should have, in a sense, all the time in the world."

"I'm afraid it's a bit more complex than that. You see, at a little after two a.m., May 10, your time, you're going to receive a Priority Two alert. You're going to hop back in time about three hours or so and prevent Hermann Göring from being blown up at the Louvre."

"I am?" Vitterand asked, momentarily stunned. "How do you know that?"

"Remember your temporal mechanics, son. Or better yet, just listen to me," Mason said, his voice conveying his unflappable manner. "We know that because you've already done it, from our perspective."

Vitterand thought for a moment, then got the basic idea. "I see. You aren't calling me in my present, here in 1943. There's a 'me' that's already existing ahead of myself in time, who has handled an alert that's coming at two a.m. tonight."

"That's it exactly."

"And you don't want this Priority Three alert to interfere with my handling of the more important Priority Two alert that's coming."

Vitterand could almost feel Mason's smile in his voice. "You did get high marks in your mechanics classes. I knew you'd grasp the picture."

"So," Vitterand said thoughtfully, "if I need to be hale and hearty later tonight, and have to be here, to do whatever it is that I'm going to do, or have done, depending on how you look at it . . ."

"Yes . . ."

"Why not just wait until after tonight to deal with this Moulin business? Let's deal with the higher priority first. Then I can always hop back, if need be, to deal with the lower priority Moulin change."

"I'm afraid it's not quite that simple," Mason said cheerfully. "After tonight, you're going to be laid up a bit in hospital."

"Nothing serious, I hope," Vitterand said, his stomach suddenly feeling like lead.

"Oh, no, nothing we can't fix up. You're not going to die."

"Glad to hear it," Vitterand said.

"But you will be out of action for several days, and by that time the change wave from the Moulin anomaly, while not exactly wiping us out here, will have become permanent," Mason explained patiently.

"Send in another Warden," Vitterand suggested.

"No personnel to spare. And no strike teams either, I'm afraid. Two other Priority Twos going on uptime from you right now."

"So I'm it," Vitterand said. "So, let's buy some time. I'll double back about three or four days. That way I'll have ample time to investigate and find a safe plan for dealing with the Moulin anomaly. In fact, I'll have two of me, if I need them."

Mason coughed, then cleared his throat. "Afraid not, old boy. Please set your personal chronometer implant for eleven hours, metatime. That's how long you've got to handle the Moulin thing, get back to your station, and be ready for the Priority Two tonight."

"Damn it, Bill!" Vitterand exploded. "What in the hell is going on? Why are we dealing in metatime? Why not give the Priority Two alert now? I can deal with it first and then deal with the Priority Three!"

"You've already handled the Priority Two, and done it nicely, remember? No, of course you don't remember. Never mind," Mason answered, fighting his own mind's wish to boggle and shut down at the complexities involved. "We don't want to change anything you've already done, from our perspective. And we've got to work this Moulin business in, and you've got eleven hours to get it done, and that's just the way it is."

Well, Vitterand thought, no one said saving the world was going to be easy. "Any helpful leads or tips on the Moulin anomaly?" he asked, not daring to hope for an affirmative response.

"It's all in the report," Mason replied. "No idea who tipped them off or how. You're a professional historian; you can appreciate how much of this cloak and dagger stuff remains secret forever. We do suspect that whoever it was did this for the purpose of diverting you from your mission later tonight, however. That really narrows the field down, doesn't it?"

"Sounds like the method of Faracon, a.k.a. the Wolf," Vitterand shot back.

"Quite. That's what we thought. And don't forget, he's got that bloody South American space-time ship with the French name . . ."

"I'll keep that in mind," Vitterand answered. "And by the way, I've got a little bit more than eleven hours metatime."

"Right. We don't want to cut it too close, do we? Better keep it to eleven hours, then. Well, good chatting with you. Good luck. Mason out."

Place: Place Blanche, Montmartre, Paris, France
Time: 0800:01 hours, May 8, 1943

Vitterand emerged from the small service alley behind the Moulin Rouge, closed and quiet in the morning's gray light, and stepped into the Place Blanche, or "White Square," the highest point in the city of Paris in the historic Montmartre section. He pulled his padded jacket closed against the spring wind that whipped across the hilltop. Even though broken and channeled now by the countless buildings of the area, the air currents were still powerful enough to send a chill straight to the bones on a cool morning. Walking casually, he pulled his beret tighter onto his head; he had no time to spend chasing a cap in the wind.

The square was crowded with pedestrian traffic. There were scores of working class men, probably unemployed, walking the street, enjoying the sight of the famous Moulin Rouge and fantasizing about pleasant evenings spent with the showgirls who worked there. Others trundled toward the rue Lepic, rations books and coupons stuffed in their pockets and clutched tightly in fists, proof against the petty thieves who would ruthlessly steal them from anyone foolish enough to leave such papers unprotected. Still others walked or bicycled to the jobs they were fortunate enough to have.

The person Vitterand was seeking was a working girl, but she did not have a regular job as such. In fact, it was probably too early in the morning for her to be stirring. Still, Vitterand had to go through a contact to reach her, and he wanted to get an early start.

He searched the square with his eyes, seeking an older woman with red hair. She would certainly be up at this time, Sandy had said, heading out to do her marketing. And she would certainly pass through the Place Blanche to head up the rue Lepic.

Still, he did not see his quarry. He paused for a moment to read the posters plastered on the sides of several buildings. They were announcements from the SS, listing the names of hostages, residents of the Montmartre district, who had been recently executed by the SS in retaliation for resistance attacks on German soldiers and officers. Many men and women would slow their pace just a bit while walking past these posters, their eyes scanning them for the name of a relative, loved one, or friend, but no one stopped to read them, and no one commented on them. There had been a time, earlier in Paris, when such signs would have been torn down or slashed to ribbons. Now, the grip of the Gestapo was tighter. Fear of the authorities was palpable among all the classes, and resistance to the Germans took more subtle and more savage forms.

Vitterand lit a cheap French cigarette and leaned against the dirty wall of a building. Loitering would not be tolerated for long by the authorities, but it would be in character for the role he was playing, and there were no gendarmes nor German military police in sight. Keeping his face turned down, as though desiring to preserve his anonymity in the midst of ecnomic failure, Vitterand puffed on the cigarette and kept a sharp eye on the traffic in the square. His patience at last bore fruit.

He saw Madelaine Dubose emerge from the rue Blanche into the square. The woman was physically distinct; she was tall, at five feet, ten inches, and her hair was still a mane of flaming red, piled high above her head and tossed in the wind despite the frail efforts of her cotton scarf to restrain it. As she came closer, Vitterand could see the signs of age and more in her fifty-two-year-old face. This morning, as most mornings, she had disdained vanity and appeared without the benefit of her evening's usual mask of heavy makeup. Now the skin sagged beneath her eyes into black, wrinkled bags, and deep worry lines could be seen indelibly etched into her forehead and along the line from the nose to the lips. She made no attempt at fashion; Vitterand noticed that she wore a plain brown cloth coat down to calf length, buttoned tight against the wind. Her feet, noticeable for the fiery red painted nails, were in open toe sandals. She wore no stockings, and he could only surmise that she must be wearing the plainest of dresses under the coat.

His trained eye also caught the fact that there were two men with her, although they did not accompany her openly. The first, a short man with a bronchial hack, clutched his jacket and bowed his head against the moving air, coughing and spitting as he walked across the square in front of her. From time to time he would pause, either to light a cigarette, or to take a drag, and gaze about seemingly without purpose, but always glancing back at the redhead, for whom he served as a bodyguard.

The second man, much younger, barely out of his teens, Vitterand judged, had to deliberately slow his pace as he followed her. He was newer to this work, Vitterand guessed, for he seldom let his eyes leave Madelaine as he tailed her across the square.

Vitterand ground out the cigarette on the cobblestones covered with a coat of white powder that was centuries old. He walked forward slowly toward Madelaine, on a path that would intercept her, his head slightly bowed. As the two approached, he removed his beret, bowed his head even lower, and called out, "Madame Dubose."

The woman slowed, gazing at him suspiciously with her hard, green eyes.

"Madame Dubose," Vitterand said again, "please forgive my intrusion. Might I have a word with you?"

The short man ahead of her was already walking back toward her, angling to come up behind Vitterand, his hand slipping quietly into the pocket of his jacket. The younger man hesitated, uncertain, awaiting a sign from his employer.

"Who are you?" Madame Dubose demanded, continuing to walk but at a slowed pace.

Vitterand fell in alongside her. "I am a friend of Cheri Darrieux, who suggested that I speak with you," Vitterand explained. He didn't mention that he knew Cheri Darrieux better as Sandy Deweese.

"Ah, well, in that case, by all means walk and talk with me a moment," Madame Dubose responded, her face revealing that her apprehension was not totally assuaged. "How is Cheri? I have not seen her for several days."

"She is well," Vitterand reported. "Although I believe you will see her . . . soon. There is some merchandise for which she is searching, and she hopes that you can help her find some in these times of terrible shortages."

"It is the time of *le système D*," Madame Dubose replied.

"*Oui*. One makes do," Vitterand agreed. Fortunately, his RNA implants on French slang of the period included the phrase "*le système D*," which stood for the verb *se débrouiller*, making do, or getting by under any circumstances.

"But surely Cheri did not send you to tell me about her

shortages?" The old redhead made the statement into a
pleasant but challenging question.

"*Non, madame*," Vitterand admitted. "I am looking for a
girl."

"You and the entire German army," Madame Dubose
said, throwing her head back in a sharp laugh and waving
away her bodyguards, who by now were hovering close on
both sides of her and Vitterand.

"*Non, madame*," Vitterand said again, keeping his voice
lowly and humble. "It is not as you may think. There is a
girl for whom I have an urgent message from her family,
and Cheri told me you might know where I could find her."

"Perhaps. Who is this girl?" Madame Dubose inquired.
She continued walking onto the rue Lepic, her keen eye out
for any decent fresh vegetables that might be had at the
open-air stands that lined the middle of the long block they
now strolled. "It is so hard to find good produce in May.
Sing out if you see any," she commented.

"Indeed I shall, madame. The girl's name is Helene
Mourier. Do you happen to know her?"

Madame Dubose stopped in front of an open cart on
which were displayed a pathetic collection of cabbages and
leeks. "Are these the best you have?" she demanded of the
weary-looking cart vendor, a short, thin little man with an
oily face and dirt under his fingernails. "Yes, I believe I do
know her," she remarked offhandedly to Vitterand.

"This is all that I have," the vendor replied. "You will find
none better on the rue Lepic today, or all week, for that
matter."

"No doubt, no doubt. How much for the cabbages?"

"Fifty francs, madame, for each. But only for you. For the
others it is one hundred francs."

"Fifty francs? I will not pay it."

The vendor shrugged. Vitterand knew that the man

couldn't care less whether he made a sale now or not. Before the end of the morning, starving Parisians, desperate for enough to eat, with no hope of obtaining food from the daylong ration lines, would eagerly clout one another over the head and steal fifty francs or even a hundred to buy a cabbage.

"I'll give you thirty," Dubose persisted.

"Fifty," the man said with a shrug.

"You of course have your license and permit, indicating the prices you may charge? And your pass is properly stamped from bringing your cart through the city gates?" Vitterand suddenly demanded.

The little man spit at Vitterand's feet. "What is it to you? Go call that gendarme over there if you doubt it," he challenged.

"That gendarme," Vitterand said, stepping up to stare directly into the man's eyes, "is on your payroll. He gets a cut from your profits, you little swine."

The man responded with an obscenity.

Vitterand grasped the man's throat and threw him against the wall, in a shadow, carefully keeping his own body in front of the man, so that passersby could see only with difficulty.

"How would you like trouble?" he asked. "Trouble with our German friends, perhaps?"

"Monsieur," Madame Dubose called, "this is not necessary. Please, we don't want a disturbance."

"Trouble, perhaps, with the FFI?" Vitterand whispered in the man's ear.

A look of terror blanched the greasy little man's face. He nodded, suddenly agreeable. "I have made a terrible mistake," he said. Vitterand released the man, who ran to Madame Dubose, gushing. "For madame, of course, the price is only th—" A glance from Vitterand showed displeasure. "Uh, twenty francs. Twenty francs for these beautiful cabbages."

"Excellent," agreed Madame Dubose. "I'll take them all."

The little vendor's mouth gaped as, with a wave of her hand, Madame Dubose summoned her two bodyguards. To the shorter man she handed her shopping basket, with instructions to count the cabbages and pay for them. From her bag she took a wad of one hundred-franc notes and gave them to the bodyguard. The taller youth was left to guard the money while she and her new friend continued their stroll down the rue Lepic.

"You are quite impressive for such a humble seeming man," Madame Dubose remarked.

"Madame is most generous."

"You had a message, I believe, for a friend of mine?"

"Yes, madame. Please tell Helene that her mother's garden is not doing well this year."

"That is a pity," Madame Dubose said, clucking her tongue.

"Yes, madame. Please tell Helene that her mother says, 'The tulips were spoiled, but the roses will be early this year.' "

"Really? I will certainly tell her that. How may she get a message back to her mother? Will you be seeing her?"

"As it turns out, I will. In fact, I was hoping to meet Helene this morning. At about ten, I will be visiting the grave of a relative in the cemetery on the rue des Abbesses. Perhaps she could join me for a brief chat," Vitterand suggested.

"If I see her, I will tell her," Madame Dubose answered. "And now, I really must get on with my shopping."

The two nodded to one another. Vitterand turned and climbed back up toward the Place Blanche, ducking into the alleyway that served the rear of the Moulin Rouge. Alone in the alley, he glanced about cautiously.

"Activate recall," he said.

Place: Cimetière de Montmartre, rue des Abbesses, Montmartre, Paris
Time: 1000 hours, May 8, 1943

Helene Mourier was a thin, pale girl of nineteen with raven black hair that tumbled down her back and shimmered even in the dismal light of a gray Paris morning. Seeing her, Vitterand could understand her success in her profession. Although thin, she had a full figure, and her face was almost angelic in its innocence. She had dark brown eyes, a small button nose that turned up ever so slightly, and small mouth framed by full red lips. She wore black on this occasion of mourning: a black sweater over a cheap black blouse, and a full black skirt that reached almost to her ankles. Only the black hose that slid into her plain, flat black shoes gave away the fact that she had access to money.

If Vitterand was to have any chance of contacting Jean Moulin, this girl was it. She was Madame Dubose's contact in the resistance, a member of the *Francs Tireurs et Partisans*, and the only resistance member of any stature with whom anyone at Temporal Station Paris had been in contact. Cheri, a.k.a. Sandy Deweese, had met her once through Madame Dubose, who was a valuable contact for obtaining clothing of almost any variety. Dubose had confided in Cheri the code that would indicate need for a contact with the underground, and the use of that code had brought a very cautious Helene Mourier to the Montmartre cemetery on this gray morning.

She strolled languidly among the graves, stopping from time to time to stare for long periods of time at a particular monument, or to gaze at the dome of the Basilique du Sacré-Coeur visible in the distance.

Vitterand shadowed her movements, gradually closing the distance between them, noting that Madame Dubose's two bodyguards also, as chance would have it, seemed to have business in the cemetery this morning. They remained alert but kept their distance.

Vitterand approached Helene as she stood by the grave of the famous painter Degas.

"Mademoiselle," he muttered.

"Monsieur," she replied, not looking at him.

"Your mother has told me, the tulips were spoiled, but the roses will be early this year," Vitterand began.

"What do you want?" she asked directly, still never looking at his face.

"A meeting," Vitterand replied.

"For what purpose?" Helene sighed.

"I must, quickly, get a message to a friend of yours," Vitterand said simply.

"Give me the message, and I will pass it along."

"I'm afraid there is no time for that. This is a matter of the greatest possible urgency. The fate of the entire movement rests on this one matter."

Helene turned and slowly began to stroll among the monuments, allowing the wind to toss her long black hair. "How often the fate of everything depends on the whim of some man," she mused aloud. "What friend of mine do you want to meet?"

"He is called . . ." Vitterand paused. Should he reveal that he knew the real name of the agent whom the Germans knew only by his code name, Max? Perhaps not. Probably this woman did not know Max herself, or know his real name.

"He is called Max," Vitterand said. "I must meet with him. Today."

The winds carried away the tinkling cymbals of Helene's laughter. "You are a fool, or you take me for one, in which case, you are still a fool," Helene said.

To Vitterand, her face was made all the more beautiful by her smile, even if it was a smile of youthful arrogance.

"Please, please, believe me. I must speak with Max," Vitterand begged.

"Yes," Helene teased. "Everyone wants to meet with Max. Perhaps your employers would also like to meet with this Max, whoever he is."

"I am not a German agent! I am with the resistance, but I am far from my home, and I must meet with Max today, or he will surely die tomorrow."

"If I knew what you were talking about," Helene said, her face grown stony and her dark eyes cold and lifeless, "which I do not, I would never trust you—a stranger out of the blue? A man whom no one knows? Do you think you can gain the trust of the underground by knocking a few francs off the price of some cabbages?"

"Helene, please . . ."

"I listen to men plead every night, and see them go out the next day to do murder," she declared. "Now go, before I have you arrested for trying to recruit me into the underground." She turned and walked away hastily. Vitterand started to follow, but her two "friends" suddenly moved to join her, and he thought better of it.

It had been a foolish attempt. Infiltrating the underground would take months. He would never reach Max this way. He ducked behind a large monument to a man who had been dead for more than two centuries. Out of the sight of Paris, he muttered, "Activate recall."

Place: *La Liberté*, in synchronous orbit above the Tigris-Euphrates Valley
Time: Exact hour and date unknown. Sometime shortly after arrival of *La Liberté* in 4903 B.C.

Jonesy was startled from his depressing calculations by the Beamer alarm. Someone was coming aboard, through time!

His fingers flew over the console, sounding the "Intruder Alert" alarm.

"Secure from intruder alert," a familiar voice called from the Beamer platform. "Computer override decontamination on my voice, retinal, and DNA scan ID," the looming figure continued. George Faracon placed one hand on a special sensor pad by the decontamination chamber, and his eye up to a retinal scanner.

"Identity confirmed," the computer agreed. "Decontamination requirement overridden by authority of Captain George Faracon."

Jonesy grabbed the laser pistol side arm from his belt holster, and Faracon emerged from the dressing room. He leveled it at the unknown intruder, who, he figured, must be pretty smart to fool the computer's ID system.

"I don't know who you are . . ." Jonesy threatened, "but you take one more step toward this control console and you're lasered toast."

"Stow it, Jonesy," Faracon said. "Get your captain in here. And shut off that damned intruder alarm. What kind of crew am I running here, anyway? There should be ten armed men in here by now, itching to cut me down."

The hatch to the bridge flew open. A company of armed security men, leveling photon rifles, flew into the control room.

"Slow, gentlemen, very slow. If I had time, I'd have you drill on that," the intruder said.

Captain Faracon stepped through the bridge hatchway, saw the confused looks on his men's faces, and glanced at the intruder. Instantly, by reflex, his hand went to the TCAF he routinely wore strapped to his belt.

"Don't panic—mine's on," the intruder Faracon announced.

"Clear the control room," Captain Faracon ordered from the bridge hatchway. "You, too, Jonesy. It looks like I'm about to give myself a good talking-to."

"That you are," the intruder agreed.

Captain Faracon entered the control room as the last of the troops left. "Go on, Jonesy, and seal that hatch behind you. No one in or out without my—our—orders."

"Aye, aye, sir," Jonesy stammered.

The two men waited until the hatch had sealed. Captain Faracon gestured to a seat; the intruder took one. Then the captain sat.

"I take it," Captain Faracon said, "that something has gone a bit amiss."

"Yes. You didn't have certain necessary data and consequently made a serious miscalculation," the intruding Faracon explained.

"What, exactly, have you come here to tell me?" Captain Faracon asked, irked at hearing that his current plan, still in the formation stage, was a failure.

"I can't remember where you are in your thinking," the intruder admitted.

"About what?"

"Göring, the statues of Enlil and Ishtar, the Louvre. Any of that ringing any bells for you?"

"Yes, indeed. The statues should be valuable, almost

irresistible bargaining chips with a local king if we're to get the tin we, er, I, need," Captain Faracon offered.

"They are. And we're getting it—haven't gotten it yet, but we're getting it. However, there have been a few complications with the Temporal Warden in Paris, 1943."

"Such as?" Captain Faracon asked.

"Never mind," the intruder replied. "I know you. If I give you too much information, you'll try to revise the plan and make it perfect. Don't. Trust me on this one. There are just two things you have to do, and be sure you do them both."

"And they are?"

"First, when you go visit Göring in his bedroom some night, before you awaken him, drug him up and bring him back to the ship. Then return him at once to his bed. Then wake him up and go ahead with your plan," the intruder said.

"But then he'll have traveled through time. If he should die by accident, there would be an irreparable anomaly," Captain Faracon thought aloud. "Oh," he said, his eyes growing wide, "we are in deep, aren't we? We need a temporal hostage to bargain with Warden Corps!"

"Don't think too far ahead or you'll screw this up, too," the intruder barked. "Now the second thing. When you pull the Louvre job, go ahead and use Vitelli, but don't go yourself. Pick someone else you trust, someone who will know which statues, and who'll get in and out quick. But don't go yourself."

"Why don't you come clean?" Captain Faracon demanded, standing and beginning to pace. "Tell me what the whole story is, and we can fix it from the start."

"No, we can't," the intruder Faracon thundered. "It's just too . . . complicated, damn it! Now do as you're told!" Seeing the suddenly hurt look on his own face, the intruder added, "Please, please, just do this. If you won't do it for yourself," he added, a broad grin spreading on his face, "do it for me!"

Captain Faracon grinned back and broke into a gale of laughter as the intruder activated his recall and popped forward in time.

7

If At First . . .

Place: Paris, France. Temporal Warden's Station
Time: 1425:38 hours, Paris time, May 9, 1943

Vitterand rested his head on his arms, which were folded atop the five-foot tall computer box beside C'hing's control console.

"The entire plan has to be scrapped," he told his assembled senior staff. "There's no way to penetrate the resistance from this end in the time allotted. I should have known that. For God's sake, I'm a professional historian and this is my period of expertise; I should have known that!"

"Regret will not, in this case, serve any purpose," C'hing offered. "We must find the course of right action."

"What C'hing is saying, in his Buddhist way, is that it's no good crying over spilt milk," Sandy Deweese offered. "Let's figure out the next step."

"Why not go for the obvious, using standard procedures?" Mulhoon asked. "You know, hop back to observe the arrest, maybe thwart it, or maybe figure out something else to do. Maybe we could spring the guy."

Vitterand raised his head, shaking it in the negative. "I don't want to have any loose ends left after this one.

Remember, we're going to have a Priority Two alert late tonight, and I'll be laid up afterward. By the time I recover, there's no telling what our new priorities might be. We could cut Moulin loose, or may be even interfere with his arrest, but that will leave the Gestapo on his tail. And whoever set this up is plenty smart. If Mason is right, and this is a diversion, then they'll go to any lengths to keep it up. If we interfere with the arrest, they'll just hop back in and set it up for later. We have to knock this out at the source."

"Then let's find the source," C'hing suggested.

"Right," Vitterand agreed. "And the place to start is Gestapo Headquarters."

Vitterand walked to a console near C'hing's and activated the historical records files. "According to the report, Moulin was arrested around ten a.m. this morning in an apartment at sixteen rue du Four. That must be a safe house for the resistance, because historically on May 27 of this year Moulin is supposed to officially create the CNR in a meeting of all the national resistance groups at that same apartment. Now, according to the historical files . . . Hmm. There are several Gestapo HQs in Paris, different HQs for different agencies. However, important prisoners from the resistance were taken to the personal villa of this man, SS Sturmbannfuhrer Carl Boemelburg, in the suburb of Neuilly."

"Let's start there," C'hing suggested. "By tonight this Boemelburg should have a full report on the Moulin arrest."

"Yes, and if our villain used a live snitch, there may be a report on that as well," Vitterand agreed. "It's our best bet."

"Of course, this means a forward hop," C'hing pointed out.

Vitterand paused. Forward hops were generally forbidden. A Warden could always time hop forward to Central, of course. But in the field, one was supposed to receive alerts, make any necessary time travel backward, and then recall to a time about one second after the time hop had been made. This was to prevent a Warden from hopping forward in time to a point on the timeline where he already existed. Without a TCAF activated, such a hop would lead to instant disaster.

But, in this case, Vitterand already knew that he existed on the Timeline in the future—more precisely, tonight, the evening of May 9/morning of May 10. So of course he would use a TCAF, and everything should be alright.

"We'll risk it," Vitterand said. "Mulhoon, I'll be needing a TCAF, if you don't mind."

"Here's a thought," Mulhoon offered. "I'll change the quantum vibration frequency on the TCAF. See, usually they're all set to one frequency, just a hair out of phase with normal reality. I can just as easily set it to a different frequency, a little higher or lower, so you're out of phase with normal reality, and out of phase with yourself wearing a TCAF, if you should happen to meet yourself in that condition."

Vitterand and C'hing looked at one another thoughtfully. Both nodded at once. "Right," they said in unison. "That ought to work."

When God blinks, C'hing thought to himself, the universe becomes a very, very complicated place.

"Alright then. Beams, I'll want to set down just outside this Boemelburg's villa in Neuilly," Vitterand ordered, again in full control. "Equipment, I'll need a Mercedes touring car, the kind these Gestapo types like to be chauffeured around in. Communications, see if uptime can send us down a couple of security types, preferably dressed as a sergeant and private in the Waffen-SS. We need them here now, and I mean now in metatime. Sandy, see what you can do about getting me a uniform. I need to be a Gestapo colonel, nothing lower. And I'll need some fake orders. Give me

plenipotentiary powers, straight from Himmler—no, check
that, straight from Hitler himself. That way if they check
with Gestapo HQ Berlin I can always appeal to the higher
authority and hope he's asleep! Let's move!"

The senior staff jumped to their tasks, their faces serious
but also enthusiastic, Vitterand noticed. That was good,
anyway. Now he'd have to go deal with his own demeanor.
He went to his personal quarters, sealed himself in, and
transmitted an order to C'hing to notifiy him when all was
in readiness.

Vitterand flopped down on his cot, hands folded behind
his head. He blew out a long breath, closed his eyes, and
allowed his feelings to begin to bubble up. He was carrying
quite an emotional load, and he needed to unwind.

"Self-indulgence!" he heard the voice of his father say in
his memory. "Already wasted an hour and a half trying to do
the impossible. Probably take another half an hour at least to
get ready, and now you want to indulge your feelings. That's
not how things get, Son," he could hear his father saying.

Father, Vitterand thought. Not a Parisian father with the
name Vitterand, but a real, living American with the name
William Thomason. Still alive, he mused. Alive right now.
Probably doing what? What time was it in Chicago right
now? About eight in the morning? His father would be just
settling down behind his desk at the Chicago office, phones
already ringing off the hook, three or four young executives
clustered around his desk like hunting dogs around a hunter,
awaiting the order to be set out on the chase. At home, the
Chicago house, his mother would be having a light, late
breakfast, and the phone would be jingling with calls for her
social secretary. Or would they? Were his father and mother
still alive, still well? With all his access to historical records,
he had never looked.

It was like the house and the office here in Paris,

Thomason realized. In eight, almost nine days here, he had never once wanted to go to the Paris house, or to what had been his father's office here in Paris. The temptation, he feared, might prove overwhelming. The sense of nostalgia, the chance to reclaim a lost life, to bring healing to parents who were no doubt grieving over his death still. That would be hard to turn down. Better not to start down that path at all.

His father would be furious with him, of course. William Thomason had opposed him joining the army. "Didn't get you all the way through Harvard with a Ph.D. in history to have you waste time in the military!" his father had fumed when he'd told him. The younger Thomason had argued that war was inevitable, that facism in Europe and militarism in Japan would have to be contained sooner or later, and probably sooner. That Roosevelt would never allow Hitler to dominate Europe and certainly would never let Britain slip under German hegemony. Better to enlist before the shells start flying and be in a position to make a real contribution, he'd told his father.

Hadn't convinced him, though, Thomason thought. He'd still been afraid. Afraid I'd get myself killed for nothing.

Did I? Look at my beloved Paris today. Under the heel of the Huns. People starving, and black marketeers charging and getting fortunes for a head of cabbage or a pound of butter or six small eggs. People divided—some so afraid of the Germans they'd do anything to please them, others so full of hatred they'd kill anyone to oppose them. Young girls like Helene, turned to prostitution to gather information on German troop movements, and turned into a professional killer by the FTP, the only expression available for her idealism, all that was best in her.

But victory will come, Thomason reminded himself. And besides, he remembered, now I serve higher purpose. "Son, history is a good field, an important field. The way a nation tells itself its own story, that's how it understands itself. That's how it formulates its values for today and plans for tomorrow. It's a noble profession, Son," his father had told him the day he received his doctorate. "Half the world is under the sway of dictators and generals, and all of them want to rewrite history to make themselves look good, or at least necessary," his father had said. "Don't let them get away with it. Keep history true. Keep it pure," he'd said.

If only he could know, Thomason thought. If only he could know. But I haven't kept it pure yet, he told himself. There are years of Soviet domination of France in the offing, and then a high-tech holocaust. Paris, my Paris, will be blown to atoms. And all the sacrifices of all the Helene Mouriers and Billy Masons in the world won't amount to a . . .

Billy Mason! A sudden insight exploded like fireworks in Thomason's mind.

"Warden Vitterand, we are prepared," C'hing's voice sounded over the computer controlled intercom.

Vitterand sat bolt upright, shook the surprise and astonishment from his mind, and got to his feet. For some reason, he couldn't wipe the grin from his face. Billy Mason. From Georgia, he'd said. God, what an actor. Now it was John Thomason, a.k.a. Jean Vitterand, a.k.a. a Gestapo colonel, who'd get to do the acting.

"Acknowledged," Vitterand responded to C'hing.

A chime announced the presence of a staff member at the door to his quarters. "Open," Vitterand ordered.

The hatch slid open and Sandy Deweese tossed a black and silver bundle of hangers and clothes onto his cot. "There's your uniform," she said. A great black leather overcoat flew on top of the pile. "Dress overcoat appropriate to your rank," she said. "And the other little items you'll

need." She named them one by one as the cot piled high
with a Gestapo uniform cap, Luger pistol in belt holster,
mid-calf high black leather jackboots, a leather folder
containing identity papers, transit visas, and orders, and a
riding crop.

"Is that really necessary?" Vitterand asked.

"Clothes make the brute," Sandy jested.

"Right," Vitterand agreed.

"By the way, I don't know what you said or did to my
friend, Madame Dubose, but she was certainly very curious
about you. She said Helene thought you were either a
madman or a German spy, and cautioned me to keep my
distance from you."

Vitterand made a mental note—he'd have to backtrack in
time and erase his meetings with Madame Dubose and
Helene. "Sorry. I'll take care of it," he told Sandy.

He quickly dressed, cursing the tailor who had made the
uniform, which was about one size too small for him. The
boots, too, were just too small. He could wear them, but
they pinched his feet and his toes rubbed against the front of
the boots. Oh, well, no use complaining. He flipped through
his identity papers. He was Col. Hans Jurgen, SS Gestapo,
on special assignment from Berlin to investigate resistance
activity. That meant he could also investigate the people
who were supposed to be investigating resistance activity.
He had plenipotentiary authority, and the orders were signed
by Heinrich Himmler himself. Vitterand reminded himself
to check with Sandy—why not have Hitler's signature on
the orders as he'd requested?

"Mirror," Vitterand called.

A side panel of the wall rotated, revealing a full length
mirror. Vitterand looked in the mirror at Col. Jurgen.
Despite the ill-fitting uniform, he was perfectly passable as
a high officer in the SS Gestapo. He snapped the riding crop

under his left arm, clicked his jackbooted heels, and raised
his right arm in the Nazi salute. "*Sieg, Heil!*" he practiced.
It seemed convincing, he decided.

Col. Jurgen left his quarters and stomped his way,
somewhat painfully to his feet, into the control room. As he
entered, two Waffen-SS men in *feldgrau* clicked their heels
and shot their right arms into the air. "Heil Hitler!" they
called in unison.

Jurgen returned the salute. "Good acting, men," he started
to say. Then, "Oh, sweet God in heaven, what the hell is
this?" exploded from his lips. Mulhoon looked the part, but
Nguyen? The incongruity of this frail looking, gentle
Vietnamese in the uniform of a Waffen-SS soldier was
almost unbearable.

Nguyen looked away, his face scrunched up with embar-
rassment.

"Central had no security personnel to spare," C'hing
called from his control console seat. "We have to make do
with what we have."

"No offense intended, C'hing, and none to you, Nguyen,
but . . ."

"Just not the Aryan type, is he," Sandy chimed in. "Told
you it wouldn't work, C'hing."

"Suggestions?" Jurgen demanded. Despite the laughter
Nguyen's appearance invoked, there wasn't time for frivol-
ity.

"Parisian chauffeur," Sandy said. "I've got the clothes
ready."

"Move, Nguyen. Quickly," Jurgen ordered.

"Yes, sir," Nguyen replied with enthusiasm, stripping off
the Nazi gear. "Thank you, sir."

"And, Sandy, what about these orders?" Vitterand asked.

"Hitler's signature seemed a bit too much. C'hing and I
agreed on that. It might raise more questions than it would

answer. Himmler is more believable. He was always having his people spy on one another," Sandy answered promptly.

Vitterand nodded. He was the historical expert; he should have thought of that. Was he really up to this mission?

"TCAF, set up like we suggested. I've got one on myself, and I made one up for Nguyen, too," Mulhoon said, handing the small black device to Jurgen.

"Good. Weapons?"

"Standard equipment for the period. You have the Luger pistol. Familiar with it?"

"Yes, yes. Anything heavier?"

"I'll be carrying a machine pistol, a kind of early automatic rifle, plus a standard combat bayonet. Plenty of rounds. Nguyen has a Luger—he'll have to carry that inside his uniform jacket," Mulhoon explained. "And the car, she's a beauty. Pulled her from stores. We picked her up under the previous Warden's tenure, back in 1940. She hasn't aged a day," Mulhoon said proudly.

Jurgen looked at the Beamer platform. On it sat a sleek, long, 1940 model Mercedes open touring car, limousine style, with a separate compartment in front for the driver. Jurgen whistled. Beautiful machine, he thought. Reminded him of a Hudson he'd once . . .

Jurgen shook that thought from his head. "Nguyen, let's go!" he called. "Beams, how about implants?"

"All done but yours," C'hing said, indicating the med tech who was entering the room.

Jurgen nodded and leaned his head forward, waiting for the familiar sting at the base of his skull. Although fluent in German already, he wanted the implant for its updates on slang. The French implant had already proven its value to him.

Nguyen appeared, redressed in a dark navy blue chauffeur's pants, jacket, and boots, complete with matching overcoat and cap.

"TCAF and Luger?" Jurgen asked him.

Nguyen flipped open the overcoat. The Luger was there, in a holster specially and quickly stitched into the lining of the coat. The TCAF, a tiny black box, appeared as no more than a mere bump on his belt.

"Activate TCAFs" Jurgen ordered, turning on his own.

The three men climbed onto the Beamer platform and into the car. "How, exactly, do you want to do this, C'hing?" Jurgen asked.

"When I give you the signal, just start driving forward, slowly," C'hing instructed. "You'll be on the road to the villa in Neuilly. Take the third turnoff to the right."

Nguyen nodded his understanding, hopped in the driver's cab, and started up the car.

Jurgen and Mulhoon sat facing one another in the open passenger seats, Jurgen facing forward.

The hum of the power conductors began to fill the Beamer control room. C'hing gave a "thumbs up" sign. Nguyen slipped the car gently into first and let her roll forward under the archway. The car disappeared in a brilliant flash of light.

Place: Neuilly, a suburb of Paris, France
Time: 2401 hours, Paris time, May 10, 1943

Nguyen turned on the headlights as the car passed through the Beamer arch. He kept the speed slow; he knew he would be blinded for a moment by the transition from the power flash to the pitch darkness of a Paris suburban lane at one minute past midnight.

Jurgen sat in the darkness, momentarily startled by his almost total blindness. He could feel the cool night air whipping in his face as the car picked up speed, and gradually his eyes adjusted to the night. The Mercedes' head beams pierced the light fog ahead, but there was nothing much to be seen along the road. To the side, stands of conifers raced by behind a short wall of mottled stones, hiding the gently rolling lawns, fields, and gardens of the exquisite homes that were typical of this section.

Jurgen ran his hands across the plush velure of the seat covers. The car was truly luxurious; the high ranking in the SS wanted for nothing. Jurgen thought of the defeated-looking Parisians he had seen in the Place Blanche, thought of their daily struggle for food, and thought of the work that the SS butchers were doing that very moment in Paris. His anger began to rise.

"Damned Nazi bastards," he muttered.

"No use getting emotional, sir," Mulhoon responded. "We've a job to do."

Jurgen thought about Mulhoon's remark, then decided the genuine anger he was feeling would stand him well in the role he needed to play shortly. "It's alright, Sergeant," he answered. "I want to be angry. How many happy Gestapo officials have you ever met?"

The car slowed to a crawl as Nguyen sought the turnoff through the fog. The area seemed quiet; they had met no traffic in their short trip.

"By the way, sir," Mulhoon interjected, "the car has the portable time drive installed, so if we need to hop directly from here, we can just get in and . . . go."

Jurgen nodded. The car negotiated a slow turn onto a white gravel lane and began to climb a low hill. The little rock walls continued to line both sides of the lane but quickly ran into a much higher wall of jumbled stones. In the center, guarding the lane, two Waffen-SS soldiers stood in front of a high, wrought-iron gate. One of the guards stepped into the car's lights, raising his hand in the signal to halt. Nguyen brought the car to a gentle stop, and the guard approached. He shined his large light into the chauffeur's cab, made a face of disgust at the sight of Nguyen, then worked his way back to the open passenger seats.

The light struck first Mulhoon, then Jurgen, full in the face.

"*Papieren, bitte*," the guard very properly asked.

Jurgen produced his Gestapo indentity papers and photo, but not his orders. The guard studied them intently in the beam from his flashlight.

"Herr Colonel, what brings you here?" he asked.

"I am here to see Sturmbannfuhrer Boemelburg on urgent business," Jurgen answered. "Open the gate at once."

"You are not expected, Herr Colonel, and the Sturmbann-fuhrer is asleep," the guard protested.

"The Sturmbannfuhrer is certainly asleep," Jurgen shot back. "I intend to rouse him from his lethargy. I have flown tonight from Berlin, and I will see him now. Open the gate and stand aside. That is a direct order."

The guard handed Jurgen's papers back to him, took a step back from the car, clicked his heels and saluted. "*Jawohl, Herr Oberst!*" Jurgen returned the salute.

"Open the gate," the guard called. "And ring up the Sturmbannfuhrer. He has guests . . . from Berlin."

Nguyen gunned the car forward as the gate began to swing open. Jurgen smiled at Mulhoon.

"You make an excellent Nazi, sir," the tall Irishman said with a straight face.

"It's a good thing you have a reputation for deadpan humor," Jurgen answered, "or I might take that personally."

Mulhoon smiled, then turned and looked forward to begin getting the lay of the land. The lane continued upward, winding a bit as it went, until it topped the low hill to reveal

an expansive, circular garden framed by the drive leading to
the front of the villa. The house itself was quite extensive,
and quite expensive, Mulhoon and Jurgen both realized. The
main structure had been built in the 1860's, during the
exuberant, neo-baroque period of the Second Empire. The
massive style of the heavy stone architecture reflected this.
Flat, gray, thick, solid stone walls, like those of a prison,
were set back from the colonnaded facade with its elaborate
cornices and friezes. A walkway ran the entire length of the
front of the rambling house, beneath the equally elaborately
decorated second-story balcony. Gas light posts, now gleaming with electric bulbs, illuminated both the gardens and the
front of the house. Little light came from the inside, save
from behind the large, window-filled front doors which
gave onto the entry hall itself. Armed guards patrolled the
grounds and walkways. Jurgen and Mulhoon saw two teams
of two strolling the hillside in a regular pattern. Two more
were posted by the main door.

Nguyen drove past a secondary lane that led to what
appeared to be a more recently built garage, and brought the
limo to a halt directly in front of the main entrance. He
hopped out the driver's side door, walked around the front
of the car, and opened the double doors for his passengers,
lowering the steps that popped out to the walkway. With his
back to the main entrance of the house, he bowed his head
slightly, like a good servant.

"Good luck, sir," he muttered.

Jurgen stepped out of the car, took two steps forward, and
played at impatience. "Come along, Sergeant. We haven't
got all night," he barked, slapping his riding crop across the
palm of his left glove.

"*Jawohl, Herr Oberst,*" Mulhoon shouted back.

"Victor," Jurgen called to Nguyen, inventing a name for
him on the spot, "you will wait here with the car."

Jurgen strode forward toward the entrance. The two guards snapped to attention and saluted. Jurgen returned the salute.

"I am Colonel Jurgen of the SS Gestapo, here to see Sturmbannfuhrer Boemelburg on urgent business," Jurgen snapped at the men.

"*Ja, Herr Oberst,*" one of the guards replied smartly. "You are expected. Please go inside. The servants will make you comfortable while the Sturmbannfuhrer prepares to receive you." The man opened one of the glass filled doors onto the entry vestibule. Jurgen stomped inside with Mulhoon close behind. He took off his leather coat, handed it to waiting, somewhat alarmed older maid inside, and began to pace down a hall, poking his nose into several rooms. Mulhoon followed suit, conspicuously slinging his machine pistol over one shoulder.

"Oh, sir, the Sturmbannfuhrer will see you in the drawing room," the maid said, emerging from the deep closet where she had hung Jurgen's and Mulhoon's coats. "Please, let me show you."

"You will show me the Sturmbannfuhrer's office, at once!" Jurgen demanded.

"Oh, sir, my instructions—"

"I will give the instructions here!" Jurgen screamed, red faced, at the frightened woman. "Let there be no mistake about that!" He stamped his foot loudly on the floor for emphasis, and in his mind cursed again at the tight fit of the boots. "His office! At once!"

"Oohh . . . this way, this way!" The woman flew down the hall, turning on lights as she went. The villa had a complex, expansive layout, with room after room filled with fine furniture and objets d'art. Storming down the hall, Jurgen drank in the fine oak woodwork, the hardwood flooring, the expensive but somewhat showy taste in the wallpapers and paintings that adorned the various rooms. He followed the scuttling maid through two turns in the hallway system until she came at last to a set of high, wood paneled double doors.

"This is the entrance to the master's office," the maid explained. "But I am not allowed to open this, ever. I don't even have a key."

"Sergeant," Jurgen snapped, seeing the heavy lock set in the right side door, "make us a key."

Mulhoon gave three hard kicks to the seam between the two doors. The wood cracked and splintered, and the doors flew open on the third kick.

"Lights!" Jurgen ordered the maid. She quickly reached inside and flipped a switch, illuminating the interior.

The light came from a small but exquisite overhead chandelier, a nineteenth-century, Jurgen noted, that had been adapted for electricity. The walls of the room were covered with a somewhat sappy floral print wallpaper, against which were hung paintings on German military themes. The backs of the two side walls contained ceiling height bookshelves, filled with leather bound volumes. Dominating the room from the rear wall, in front of a large window covered by layers of curtains, was the Sturmbannfuhrer's huge desk. The wood, Jurgen noted, was mahogany. The top of the desk gleamed, and the surface was bare save for the usual writing untensils, blotter, telephone, photographs of Boemelburg and his wife in two oval connected picture frames, and a small swastika flag on a short pole placed in the forward right-hand corner.

File cabinets were placed on both sides behind the desk, against the wall at the sides of the large window.

"What is the meaning of this insolence?!" an outraged voice shouted down the hall.

The terrified maid fled as Sturmbannfuhrer Boemelburg

stormed into the room, one boot still loose on his left foot, his hands fumbling with the buttons of his tunic. Boemelburg was short and plump, his balding head framed by a ring of graying dark brown hair. He had a large nose, close set eyes, and thick lips. His hands were thick, Jurgen noted, the product of soft living, while his face had the pale sheen of the professional sadist.

More footsteps thundered from the hall—SS goons, Jurgen saw, tromping along with their rifles in hand.

"I am Colonel Jurgen. Perhaps you would like to see my orders before we begin," Jurgen said curtly. "I am in no mood for delays, so read quickly, you sycophantic swine." Jurgen thrust his papers into Boemelburg's face. "Take them! Read!" he shouted. Jurgen shot a gesture to Mulhoon, who quickly grabbed a small chair from the side of the room and shoved it under Boemelburg's behind, buckling his knees. The man sat, his eyes scanning the documents.

"Whatever your orders, your conduct here is an outrage," Boemelburg shouted, standing up again.

"Dismiss your men!" Jurgen commanded. "Or do you doubt my authority to give you even that order?" Jurgen grabbed the phone from Boemelburg's desk. "Here!" he taunted. "Call Berlin. Perhaps you can explain to Himmler himself, personally, how you have bungled this Max business!"

Boemelburg's face went white at the word "Max." He licked his lips, then turned to his men, who had piled in through the doors. "Go. Dismissed. All is in order here."

One guard gave him a questioning glance, and looked askance at Mulhoon, who was covering him with his machine pistol.

"No, Karl, really, it is alright," Boemelburg reassured him. "The colonel and I have important matters to discuss in private. He is within his authority to act as he has done. Go."

• • •

"Your men show loyalty," Jurgen said, smiling. "That is usually the sign of a good commander. I am surprised, frankly." Jurgen paced over behind the desk and let himself sink into the large, full-backed swivel chair. He tossed his booted feet onto the desk, resting them from the terrible pinching of the too small boots.

"Now, you will tell me about Max," Jurgen said. "Sit down. Sergeant," he ordered Mulhoon, "go outside, close the door, and see that we are not disturbed."

Mulhoon nodded and left the room, pulling the doors as near to closed as he could. Boemelburg sank into the chair and fumbled with finally getting his left boot on.

"Talk, swine," Jurgen ordered.

"What do you want to know?" Boemelburg pleaded. "I captured him today, this morning, this Max, the one sent by de Gaulle himself to meet with the resistants. I thought Berlin would be pleased. What in God's name have I done? Of what am I accused?"

"Silence!" Jurgen screamed, crashing his riding crop down on the mahogany desk, and making, he noticed with pleasure, a nice scratch in it. "I will say this once, and once only, and you will understand it if you value your pathetic life. I will ask questions, and you will answer them. Do you understand?"

Boemelburg nodded.

"You arrested Max at approximately ten a.m. yesterday morning at an apartment at sixteen rue du Four. Is that correct?"

"*Ja*," Boemelburg confirmed.

Jurgen swung his feet off the desk, marking it with his heels as they scraped its surface. He stood and began pacing the room, seemingly at random, tapping the riding crop against the palm of his left hand, still gloved. "Was he alone when you took him?"

"No, there were three others with him. It is in my report."

Jurgen's pacing brought him up directly behind Boemelburg, who strained to turn in the chair and face him.

"Your report, yes. A copy is in these files, here?"

"Yes, of course," Boemelburg confirmed.

"Get it," Jurgen demanded.

Relieved to be allowed to stand up, Boemelburg raced to the file cabinet to the right of the desk, rummaged in a drawer, and at length produced the voluminous file. He handed it to Jurgen.

"Here. I believe it is all in order," he said coldly.

"Sit down," Jurgen snapped. "What was the basis of this arrest? I mean, how did you know when and where you could find this Max? Since there were three others with him, how did you determine his true identity?"

"It is all in the report," Boemelburg explained, annoyed and perplexed as he sank back into the uncomfortable, small chair. "We received a tip from an informant. He gave us Max's true name and told us where and when we could find him, right down to the address of the apartment on rue du Four. I conducted the interrogation myself," Boemelburg boasted.

"Wonderful. Did you happen to get a correct name for this informant?"

"His name is Jacques Darlon," Boemelburg answered promptly, but with a sinking feeling in the pit of his stomach.

"His real name?" Jurgen demanded.

"That was the name on his papers . . ." Boemelburg tried.

"His real name?" Jurgen repeated. "I don't like to repeat

questions, Sturmbannfuhrer. I really don't have time to play games with you."

"I'm not absolutely certain of his real name," Boemelburg admitted.

"You placed him in a cell here?" Jurgen asked. The question was a guess—an affirmative answer would be too good to be true.

"Yes," Boemelburg replied cautiously.

"Get him. Bring him to me at once," Jurgen snapped. "I will interrogate him myself immediately."

"I cannot, Colonel Jurgen," Boemelburg said slowly.

Jurgen whirled and stared at the man. His face was blanching again, and his hands were showing the slightest signs of trembling.

"Where is he?" Jurgen asked, speaking each word very slowly and in his lowest possible, tone of voice.

"He . . ." Boemelburg began. He choked on the words; his throat was suddenly so dry he could barely speak. "He escaped."

Jurgen drew back his riding crop and struck Boemelburg a hideous blow across the left side of his face, ripping the skin and leaving a slash from which blood streamed down the man's chin and splattered onto his pants. "When did he escape?" Jurgen asked, keeping his voice very, very low.

"We placed him in a cell downstairs as soon as he gave us the name and location of Max. I intended to interrogate him more once we had Max in custody. When we returned, with Max, he was gone. My guards were dumbfounded. The cell had not been disturbed, and was still locked. We cannot imagine how he managed it. The dogs could not even pick up his scent, which we had from his clothes. There was no trail anywhere."

Jurgen could well imagine how the man known as Darlon had escaped.

"What else did you learn about this Darlon before you lost him?" Jurgen demanded.

"Not much," Boemelburg said, his face buried in his hands. "He had work papers, but the plant listed on them had never heard of him. No one knows anything about him. He was acting strangely when we brought him in. He was bothering some girl in a restaurant, and didn't seem to know about occupation postcards. The owner of the cafe called it in. Two of my men went to question him, he resisted. They beat him. He claimed to have a message for me, so he was brought here. Then he promptly told me about Max. Then I left to make the arrest, and he escaped. That is all."

A sudden thought crossed Jurgen's mind. "What about the girl?"

"She knows absolutely nothing. But we still have her in custody. I plan on sending her to a concentration camp, as a penalty to Darlon for not cooperating with us more fully," Boemelburg explained.

"You are a fool," Jurgen said. "She knows nothing. Release her at once."

Jurgen took the file and walked to the door. "I will contact you from Berlin if it is necessary for us to pursue this matter further. You will discuss my visit with no one, do you understand?"

The broken Boemelburg nodded his assent.

"Sergeant, we're leaving," Jurgen announced.

The two men stomped through the house, got their coats, found the front door, and walked outside to where Nguyen was waiting in the car. He hopped out, like a good chauffeur, and held the doors for them. Then he raised the touring car's cloth convertible type top against the cool of the night air.

The car drove off slowly until it passed again through the main gate and turned onto the lane.

"Did you hear?" Jurgen asked Mulhoon.

"Yep. Sounds like he had a time traveler and didn't get anything out of him."

"Right. So let's go get him ourselves," Jurgen said. "Do you have anything from Boemelburg's on you?" he asked, carefully checking his own pockets.

"No," Mulhoon said. "You've got that file."

"Right," Jurgen said. "Flashlight?" Mulhoon handed him his torch. Jurgen flipped through the papers, finding the one bit of data he still needed. "Here it is. Arrest was made at 10:02 a.m. They left here about 9:30 a.m. Our time traveling M. Darlon must have left as soon as put him in a cell . . . Tell Nguyen to set us for this same place at 9:20 a.m. this morning, May 9," he ordered. Then he pitched the file out the open window.

Nguyen picked up the order from Mulhoon. He pulled the car carefully off to the side of the road. He opened the glove box, pressed a switch, and waited a second as the time travel drive control console swung up into place. Quickly, Nguyen entered the desired space-time coordinates. Then he turned the car around carefully and began driving slowly back toward Boemelburg's villa. Then he punched a tiny activation button hidden inside the gearshift knob.

Place: Neuilly, a suburb of Paris, France
Time: 0920 hours, Paris time, May 9, 1943

The black Mercedes touring car with Jurgen and Mulhoon in the passenger seats pulled through the main gate to the Boemelburg château and roared up the lane to the main drive. The cloth top of the car remained up against the gray drizzle of the morning.

Nguyen easily navigated the lane up the hill but had to stop as he approached the main drive around the gardens at the front of the house. A similar black limo and two trucks were pulling out of the lane from the garage area and lining up in front of the main entrance to the house.

"We're cutting it close," Jurgen commented to Mulhoon. He threw open the side door and stepped from the car into the drizzle, pulling the collar of his leather coat up against the rain. "Looks like they're getting ready to go to a little party at sixteen rue du Four."

"Should we hop back, sir, a bit earlier?"

"Negative. We'd have to recalibrate these TCAFs and it would take us even more time." With the speed of thought, Jurgen checked his own implanted personal chronometer. He had barely over eight hours left in metatime. He stomped off toward the main door of the house.

This time it was a butler who admitted them. Jurgen wasted no time.

"Fetch me a guard, and the Sturmbannfuhrer, *schnell!*" he told the startled servant. The tall, gaunt man nodded and walked gracefully away. "Some of these French are unflappable," Jurgen commented to Mulhoon.

"He seems more English than Gallic," Mulhoon noted.

It took only seconds for a guard, a mere private in the Waffen-SS, to come running into the foyer. The man nearly stumbled as he came to an abrupt halt and snapped to attention. "Heil Hitler!" he declared, giving the one armed salute.

"*Ja, ja, heil,*" Jurgen responded. "Now, take me to the cell blocks below. I want to see the prisoner Darlon immediately."

With a nod, the soldier trotted off through the door and down the walkway that led along the front of the house. In the garden along the walkway, a few tulips were already in full bloom. Their brilliant yellows, reds, and pinks contrasted starkly with the grayness of the day and almost prisonlike atmosphere of the archaic architecture.

The soldier turned at the side of the house and plunged down a set of stairs to a large cellar doorway. Two more guards were posted here.

Jurgen tromped down the stairs, waving his orders, Mulhoon behind him. "Open at once. I have come to take the prisoner Darlon to Berlin for immediate interrogation!" Jurgen ordered.

The guards glanced at one another. The older of the two, perhaps nineteen, gave a shrug in the direction of his junior companion and turned to unlock the door.

"The prisoner Darlon is in here—there!" he called, stepping through the door and pointing down the dank hallway. "They are just putting him in his cell."

"*Abhalten Sie!*" Jurgen shouted, running into the cell block hallway. "Don't let him out of your sight!"

Vitelli turned between the two gruff Germans who were hauling him to his cell. He saw a tall, thin Gestapo colonel running down the hallway, shouting at his guards. Jeez, he thought, won't they ever leave me alone for a second? All he wanted to do was be alone and say the two magic words that would take him . . . he couldn't remember. He knew they'd take him wherever he was supposed to be. But he also knew, knew in the very molecules of his mind, that he could not say those two words until he was alone and unobserved.

"I am taking charge of this prisoner, now," the colonel said.

Vitelli wondered if this was the same man he'd just been speaking to. The voice didn't sound the same at all.

"Take him, Sergeant," the colonel said.

The tall, husky, slightly pale Waffen-SS sergeant grabbed Vitelli around the arm.

"Hey, what gives?" Vitelli wanted to know. "What does it matter which of you throws me into a cell?"

"Be silent!" the colonel said, striking Vitelli across the face with his riding crop.

Vitelli screamed in agony from the blow, which impacted on his swelling jaw.

"God, don't you people . . ." Vitelli bit off his sentence. He didn't want another blow.

"Let's go. Quickly," the colonel said. He led the way down the dreary corridor, past the guards at the door and up a set of steps to the outside. Vitelli squinted his eyes against the gray-white light of the overcast sky.

"Just head straight for the car," he heard the colonel say.

Vitelli pondered as Mulhoon half pushed, half pulled and mostly dragged him along. This colonel was very different. He was strange. His pants weren't quite long enough, Vitelli realized. That was it. His uniform looked as though he was just about to pop right out of it, ripping it at the seams. Wasn't there something . . .? Vitelli couldn't remember.

"You there, halt at once!"

That voice, Vitelli realized, was the German who had questioned him.

Jurgen saw Boemelburg coming down the walkway with an armed squad in tow.

"What are you doing with my prisoner? Who are you? You are under arrest!" Boemelburg shouted.

Jurgen did not even slow his pace. He reached in his tunic pocket, produced his orders, and handed them to Boemelburg as he continued to walk right past him, through the squad of armed SS who couldn't decide whether to physically stop him or not.

"I am Hans Jurgen, from Berlin, with plenipotentiary powers from Himmler himself to investigate resistance activities, and to investigate you if I decide to," Jurgen said quickly. The red-faced Boemelburg fell into step beside him.

"This man Darlon is wanted, by me, for questioning, and

I am taking him. You, on the other hand, have something much more important to do, I am sure, than to interfere with me and my legitimate mission." Jurgen halted abruptly and turned on Boemelburg, leaning forward until his face was almost nose to nose with the other man's.

"You have read these orders?" he asked, snatching the papers back.

"Yes," Boemelburg said.

"Then go arrest Max, you dolt!" Jurgen exclaimed. "Sergeant, place the prisoner Darlon in our car. Sturmbann-fuhrer, as you were just leaving, my driver will let you and your vehicles go first."

Jurgen marched smartly over to his car, climbed in as Nguyen held the door, and told Nguyen to wait until the driveway cleared.

Boemelburg's car started down the drive, then stopped near Jurgen's. "Where are you taking that prisoner?" Boe-melburg wanted to know. "I have many more things to ask him myself."

"Berlin!" Jurgen replied.

Boemelburg cursed. His car drove off into the mist, followed by the two trucks carrying troops for the arrest of Max.

"Okay, Nguyen, let's go somewhere—anywhere—get us out in the woods somewhere," Jurgen ordered.

Nguyen gunned the Mercedes to life, and it was soon on an open highway, leading north and west of Paris. As soon as they were beyond the prying eyes of the city, Jurgen started in on Vitelli.

"What's your name?"

"Jacques Darlon," Vitelli said. "Look, I'll tell you any-thing you want to know. Just don't beat on me anymore."

"I won't," Jurgen promised.

The car sped over the gently rolling lands north of the

Seine, lands that had been a battlefield in World War I, Jurgen thought. In that war, at least, France had had her honor. In this one, there was little for France to celebrate.

Nguyen sped along until he found a country road that wound through the gentle hills. Finally, he spotted a copse of woods only a short distance from the road. He pulled the car over and awaited Jurgen's orders, although he knew that one of two things would have to be done, and done now.

Jurgen pumped Vitelli with question after question. None brought a meaningful response. The man acted, Jurgen decided, as though he were an amnesiac. After ten minutes of futile efforts in the back of the car, Jurgen looked at Mulhoon.

"Take it," he instructed the equipment specialist.

Mulhoon brought out his bayonet and flashlight. With the latter he clubbed Vitelli in the head so that he passed out. With the bayonet he began digging into the flesh at the base of Vitelli's skull. It took only a moment to locate the tiny but powerful implant that would allow the time traveler to recall to the Beamer site from which he had originally transported.

Mulhoon held the tiny piece up to his eye, shilhouetted against the sky, between his thumb and forefinger.

"Looks a bit old-fashioned," he commented.

"Umm," Jurgen half answered, deep in thought.

"You won't get anything out of him," Mulhoon told Jurgen. "He's been mem-wiped."

Jurgen's head shot up. "I know about mem-wipes," he said, irritated. "I just want to be sure that's the case, and that he's not just playacting."

"Oh, that's the case alright. See this recall chip?" Mulhoon said, wiping the bloody, tiny piece on his coat and then handing it to Jurgen. "That type's about one hundred or more years old. I mean, from Central's point of view. Not Warden period technology at all. Old stuff, from the period before the Wardens. It was used during the Time Wars, when they wanted to send back an agent who couldn't be traced."

Jurgen got out of the car. "Bring him," he told Mulhoon. The equipment man lifted the unconscious Vitelli in his arms and followed Jurgen across the open field. There were no buildings in sight here. The two men trudged silently toward the copse of woods across the muddy land, just now green with the first sprouts of grasses.

"Tell me again about that particular technology," Jurgen asked, his face stony, his eyes glued on the woods ahead. "How did it work?"

"Simple but time-consuming," Mulhoon said. "The chip contains a molecular computer that scans the entire brain, recording RNA patterns in crucial information storage areas—language, identity, personal memories, that sort of thing. It transmits these codes to a computer located outside the person's body, and the RNA programs are stored in binary, digitalized format."

"That must take quite a bit of time."

"It does," Mulhoon agreed. "But here's the nasty part. Then it destroys the RNA—breaks it up. You know that all data in the brain is ultimately stored in RNA. This is a selective, molecular level memory wipe. Leaves the guy a functional vegetable. All he has is his general knowledge of the culture he's going to, his programmed identity for that culture, and his mission. Once his mission is concluded, he can recall, but only when he's alone. That feature was to prevent him just poofing out into thin air and giving himself away as a time agent."

"So the only way he can get his memory back . . ." Jurgen said.

"Is to successfully recall. Which this guy can't, because we've taken out his chip."

Jurgen nodded.

"Unnnhh," Vitelli moaned, stirring slightly.

"Is the technique infallible?" Jurgen wanted to know. They had reached the edge of the woods. Jurgen continued walking. The copse was a stand of young oaks mixed with conifers. The floor of the woods was almost bare, only some grass sprouts and the muddy black soil. There was no underbrush to impede their progress.

"Not entirely. It almost always gets the identity, but the agent may remember bits and scraps, here and there. Nothing much that would be helpful, I'm afraid," Mulhoon said, laying Vitelli on his back on the ground.

Jurgen nodded. Mulhoon nodded back. Then he turned and began walking out of the woods.

Vitelli opened his eyes. He saw a canopy of leaf buds against a cold, gray sky. He squinted. The face of the Gestapo colonel in the badly fitting uniform loomed above him.

"Can you remember anything, anything at all, about your life before you came to Paris?" Jurgen asked.

"Not much," Vitelli admitted, too much in shock to even notice that Jurgen was aware of his memory problem. "I came to Paris just this morning. I accomplished my mission. I want to go back . . . where I'm supposed to go back to."

"Soon," Jurgen promised. "What else can you remember?"

"Nothing, really," Vitelli said, completely honest. "There was just one thing . . . You got a smoke?"

Jurgen shook his head.

"Too bad," Vitelli said, staring again into the sky. "Only thing was . . . LSMFT."

Jurgen smiled. "It's from the early and mid-twentieth century," he told Vitelli. "An advertising slogan. It means, 'Lucky Strike Means Fine Tobacco.'"

"Yeah," Vitelli said.

"Those things will kill you," Jurgen commented dryly. "Monsieur Darlon, you are a rogue time traveler, whose identity cannot be determined. Therefore you cannot be properly processed and returned to your Home Culture, your time and place of origin."

Vitelli looked dumbly into Jurgen's eyes.

"Therefore, with the authority given me by the Temporal Warden Corps, I, Jean Vitterand, Temporal Warden for Paris Station, 1943, in accordance with the laws governing unauthorized time travel and the creation of temporal anomalies, sentence you to death. Sentence will be carried out immediately. Is there anything you wish to say?"

Jurgen slipped his Luger from his holster and chambered a round.

"I don't know what you're talking about . . ." Vitelli protested.

"I know," Jurgen said. He leaned forward, aimed carefully, and put the first bullet squarely through Vitelli's forehead. With his boot he rolled the corpse over and put two more slugs in the back of the brain, making sure.

Standing back by the car, leaning on the window by Nguyen's seat, Mulhoon heard one shot, followed shortly by two more. Both men looked toward the woods. A moment later they saw Jurgen trudging out from the trees and slogging his way back across the field.

Nguyen's eyes met Mulhoon's. "He's going to make a good Warden," Nguyen said.

"At least he's not too soft," Mulhoon agreed.

Place: *La Liberté*, in transit from Earth orbit to lunar orbit
Time: Exact hour and date unknown. Year 4903 B.C.

Faracon rematerialized aboard *La Liberté*. A glance around caused him concern.

"Where's Vitelli?" he shouted to Jonesy.

The Beam operator shrugged. "Not recalled yet," he reported.

Faracon rushed through the decontamination and dressing procedures, then came straight to Jonesy's post.

"You made sure he had a memory wipe before you sent him uptime?" Faracon asked.

"Yes, sir. All he knew was the language, general culture of 1943, and his mission. He didn't even know who the hell he was, and he wouldn't have the slightest idea of how he got to Paris."

A whooping siren suddenly sounded, and yellow alert lights began to flash throughout the ship.

"What the hell is that?" Faracon demanded.

"Anomaly indicator," Jonesy said, suddenly near panic. "I've linked our computers throughout our stay here in 4903 B.C. so they're constantly checking with one another. We've just had an anomaly occur." Jonesy hurriedly scanned the readouts. At these temporal distances, he might have only seconds to even realize what the anomaly was, much less respond to it.

"Can you tell what it is?" Faracon shouted above the whoops of the alarms, leaning over Jonesy's shoulder, trying to read the console.

"Yes!" Jonesy said. "It's Vitelli. He should have recalled a few seconds ago. He didn't and, as far uptime as I can read, he never does!"

Faracon stood up straight, frowned, and then relaxed. "Secure from this alert, Jonesy. Turn off that damned alarm."

Jonesy killed the alarm system.

"That memory wipe you gave Vitelli," Faracon queried, "is there any way to fix it?"

"Not by anyone but us," Jonesy said. "All that remains of Vitelli's identity is the RNA codes in our computer file."

"Let's see that file," Faracon ordered.

Jonesy called up the file and displayed it on a terminal for Faracon to see. Endless strings of letters danced across the screen. "Those are RNA composition codes," Jonesy explained. "When those RNA strands are built in those sequences, replaced in Vitelli's brain, his memory will be restored."

"And this is the only conceivable way he could ever get his memory back?" Faracon asked.

"Absolutely," Jonesy confirmed.

Faracon reached down to the keyboard, punched up the file control, and hit the delete key. "Good-bye, Vitelli," he said.

Jonesy gasped.

"Doesn't matter," Faracon said. "That Temporal Warden got him. That guy is good, very good."

Now it was time, he thought, to take care of another disturbing little matter. He went to the bridge, checked on the ship's overall situation, and returned to the Beamer control room. . . .

8

The Gallic Factor

Place: Paris, France. Temporal Warden's Station
Time: 1426 hours, Paris time, May 9, 1943

The Mercedes materialized on the Beamer platform, and Jurgen jumped out, barking orders.

"C'hing, Sandy, Nguyen, Mulhoon, let's meet in five minutes," he bellowed. He was quickly back in his own quarters, changing into standard issue gear, and cursing.

The business with Darlon had been unpleasant, damned unpleasant. He didn't like killing, and he especially didn't like killing in cold blood. But it was necessary, necessary to keep history, as his father had called it, pure.

That was the same rationale the Nazis used, he realized sadly.

Still, he'd done what he'd done, and there was no use wasting time on regrets. He now had less than eight hours to solve the Moulin anomaly. For a moment, Vitterand considered simply hopping in and rescuing Moulin. That was the obvious thing to do. It was so obvious he'd rejected it earlier, seeking a more permanent solution. Any rescue would only cause a determined foe to make another attempt on Moulin, and another, and another. He had to find the culprit behind it all, the one who had sent Darlon into 1943 to betray Moulin.

But how?

The only way would be to assume that this Moulin anomaly was linked somehow to the anomaly that was yet to happen tonight. But Central wouldn't furnish him that data; they wanted him to act tonight just the way he had already acted. And after that, he'd be out of action for a while.

For an instant, Vitterand allowed himself to hope that the wounds wouldn't be too painful, or disfiguring. He wouldn't want to lose the obvious attentions of Sandy Deweese, which he intended to pursue... in another time.

Vitterand shut out that kind of thinking. The only thing left to do was to go back in time and warn Moulin. But he'd have to pick a time when the enemy, whoever he was, wouldn't expect it. He'd have to find Moulin and warn him at some random moment, so the enemy couldn't just intercept him trying to warn Moulin.

Even then, he'd eventually have to go back, after he healed up, and tie up the loose ends. But anything to confound the enemy at this point was better than letting the anomaly stand.

Vitterand joined his staff in the control room. C'hing was holding the floor.

"So, the question is really one of how to find Jean Moulin," C'hing was saying.

"Exactly the conclusion I've come to," Vitterand agreed. "Suggestions?"

"Who would know where he is?" Sandy asked.

"Some of the key heads of the resistance movement," Vitterand answered. "And of course General de Gaulle in London . . ." Vitterand broke off his sentence as the intellectual fireworks went off in his head.

"Get the London Station on a com link," Vitterand ordered. "I want to talk to the Warden there."

Nguyen flew to his communications console. It took several minutes, but Nguyen eventually reported, "Com link open to London Station, same date and correlated time. London Warden standing by."

"This is Jean Vitterand, Temporal Warden Station, Paris, France, at . . ." he glanced at the large digital chronometer in the archway over the Beamer platform, "1446 hours, Paris time, May 9, 1943."

"Brian here," came the response, "London Station and all that rot. No need to be so formal, old boy."

"Roger that, Brian." Vitterand had never met the London Time Warden for this period, and knew him from reports simply as "Brian."

"Well, what's on your end?" Brian asked. "I was called away from a meeting at the Admiralty for this."

"We have a complex emergency here," Vitterand began. "I can't explain all the details. But in a nutshell, I need to find out from General de Gaulle the exact location, today, of Jean Moulin, his personal representative—"

"Who's uniting the resistance factions in France," Brian interjected. "Yes, we're quite up on that here at the Home Office."

Vitterand recalled from his briefings and numerous reports that the London Temporal Warden held a "day job" as a high official in MI-5, British Intelligence.

"Well, I must locate this Moulin, and I have less than eight hours, metatime, to do it in. "

"Metatime?" Brian queried.

"Roger that. I say again, less than eight hours metatime."

"Must be a damned complicated mess you've got there in Paris," Brian said phlegmatically.

"Yes, and you'll forgive me if I find your British calm a

little difficult to tolerate at the moment," Vitterand snapped back.

"No need to be nasty while asking for a favor, old fellow. Of course, I'll see what we can do. What exactly is your intention when you locate this Moulin fellow? I do hope we don't have to kill him."

"Of course not. I'm trying to prevent his arrest earlier this morning."

"Quite," Brian responded. "Let me make a few inquiries and see what we can do."

Place: Paris, France. Temporal Warden's Station
Time: 1548 hours, Paris time, May 9, 1943

Vitterand had gone topside, out into the sunlight of the Paris afternoon. The clouds were gone now, and only the soot of the city lessened the blueness of the spring sky. The sun beamed down, warming the city above sixty degrees. Vitterand leaned against the wall of a building that had been long since abandoned but never torn down. A few bribes in the pockets of the proper Paris officials were enough to keep the building standing. Homeless derelicts sheltered on its first two floors, and the local gendarmes were happy to look the other way in exchange for a few francs and cabbages. The Germans didn't bother the place; no one of any importance to them ever had been, or ever would be, found there.

So Vitterand felt secure as he leaned against the side of the building, puffing on a foul Gaulois. Normally, he didn't smoke. But he had been waiting, cooped up in the station for almost an hour, and the tension was getting to him. He needed a break. His staff didn't mind. Though tense themselves, they didn't bear the primary responsibility for solving the anomaly.

Good God! Vitterand thought. Why didn't Brian hurry?
He certainly understood the situation. And it wouldn't do
any good for Brian to try some time travel tricks to get back
to him "earlier." Metatime was the ultimate time, the
absolutely real passage of time that couldn't be cheated in
any way.

Now Vitterand had less than seven hours of it left.

Sandy sauntered through the broken, leaning glass front
door of the derelict building. She caught Vitterand's eye,
gestured with a shake of her head, and went back inside.

Vitterand took another drag on the Gaulois and blew the
smoke out in a thick, blue-gray stream. Strong, he thought.
Strong, but good at a time like this.

He slipped inside the building and down the ratty hallway, stepping over the body of a sprawled drunk who
appeared to be sleeping it off at three in the afternoon. He
walked to the back of the hall, then through a second door
in a shabby, one-rooom apartment that contained no furniture save a mattress, sometimes used by the derelict who
made this his permanent residence. This man, of course, was
a security guard for the station, highly trained and a lethal
killer, if need be, in his own right. He gave Vitterand the
"thumbs-up" sign. The Warden opened a trapdoor cut in
the concrete slab floor and descended a short stairway. At
the base of the stairs, he entered what appeared to be a
simple lift, closed the grate, and pushed the lever.

Three seconds later he emerged into the subterranean
control room of his Time Station.

Nguyen was waiting for him anxiously.

"Brian's on the com link," he said. "Ready to go." C'hing
and the other senior staff were gathered, anxious looks on
their faces.

"Brian, this is Vitterand, Temporal Warden Station Paris,

1943, and all that rot," Vitterand said, trying to inject a light note into the deadly seriousness of this conversation.

"Roger that," Brian answered.

Vitterand sucked in a deep breath. "Do you have the information we need?" he asked.

"Well, in a way, " Brian said. "I don't suppose you could Beam on over here for a few metaminutes, could you, old boy?"

"I have to find Moulin," Vitterand said. "You understand the temporal mechanics of this. I have less than seven hours left now."

"Yes, well, I'm afraid it's not quite as simple as finding Moulin," Brian explained. "Oh, you can find him alright, of course. No problem about that at all. Find him right there in Paris, if you know where to look, don't you see."

Vitterand suppressed his impulse to scream the one word that mattered to him. "Where?" he asked, trying to sound casual to the imperturbable Englishman.

"Well, you see, the trick is, once you've found him, making him believe you. I suppose you've already tried the usual resistane channels and bumped into that brick wall, eh?" Brian droned on.

"Yes," Vitterand said, his tone dripping acid.

"Well, I have a fix for all that. I can get you a letter from General de Gaulle himself, instructing this Moulin to listen to whatever you have to say, at least about the danger from the Gestapo."

Vitterand was stunned. This Brian was nothing if not effective.

"Do you have that letter? Can you send it over here?" he anxiously demanded.

"Not quite, old boy. You have to come fetch it, you see. General de Gaulle will send such a letter, but he wants to meet you personally before he signs off. I'm afraid he thinks you're an American chap cooperating with MI-6 and all that. Anyway, meeting's all set up for one hour from now. Dress formal, and don't be late."

Vitterand looked quickly at C'hing, raising his eyebrows. The Chinese returned the same gesture, as if to say, "Crazy damned Englishmen." Vitterand swallowed hard, then responded, "Right. I'll be Beaming over as soon as I'm . . . properly dressed. Vitterand out."

Place: Classified Top Secret By Temoral Warden Corps Central HQ
Time: Classified Top Secret by Temporal Warden Corps Central HQ

The Rolls-Royce limo wormed its way through the afternoon traffic of London. Brian didn't like using the Rolls for this; it attracted attention, but Gallic pride must be served, and de Gaulle would not approve of an official visit that did not have the proper trappings of ceremony, even if it were a clandestine official visit.

"Do have a B and B, Vitterand. It will steady your nerves," Brian suggested, lifting a snifter himself from the bar in the limo.

"No, thank you," Vitterand replied. The time wastage involved in this trip was almost unbearable to him. He wanted this Moulin business done.

"Well, you'd best relax. Won't do to be a nervous Nellie in front of old Charlie boy. He's stiff as a board himself and has an ego bigger than Churchill's and Roosevelt's combined," Brian explained. "Almost as big as Monty's."

"Ego doesn't bother me. I just want to get that letter and get back. I'm running out of time. Metatime, that is," Vitterand reminded Brian. He was also tired of poorly fitting clothes. Now he was in full diplomatic tails with striped pants, black tie, spats, the whole works. None of it fit exactly right. It was another Sandy Deweese, instant-costume job.

"Doing the best we can," Brian said. "Do try to remember that I'm on your side in all this. I'm not a British official, but a Temporal Warden like yourself," he said, downing the contents of the snifter.

"I keep forgetting that. I'm so used to being this lower-class Parisian workingman, Vitterand, that it's sometimes hard for me to remember who the hell I really am, much less who anyone else might be," Vitterand acknowledged.

"Well, it does help to play the role at all times. That way one is less likely to slip up at an inopportune moment," Brian suggested. "I'm not British at all, but a sort of American myself."

"What sort?" Vitterand asked, suddenly interested.

"Nineteenth-century Sioux. Recruited from Wounded Knee," Brian shot back, his eyes suddenly hard and fiery.

"I'll be damned," Vitterand gasped. "You even look British, and your act had me completely fooled."

"Yes, well, a bit of genetic tinkering here and plastic surgery there and it all comes out right in the end, doesn't it?"

"Let's hope so," Vitterand said. "Let's go over my story again."

Brian looked out the limo window, peering ahead. "Quickly, then; we're almost there. You are an American, OSS type, on loan to MI-6 for operations with the underground resistance in France. One of your contacts is a Soviet mole who has penetrated certain sectors of the Paris Gestapo. You have information that the Gestapo know about certain meetings Moulin is planning, and that they will arrest him and his cohorts at such a meeting tomorrow morning. You need access to Moulin to warn him. As soon as your meeting with de Gaulle is concluded, you plan to fly back to France, aboard a military aircraft my office is providing, parachute in, find Moulin, and provide him the warning."

"What if he asks for details?" Vitterand wondered. "I don't know any of the key players yet, and they don't know me."

"Oh, I shouldn't worry about that. De Gaulle won't expect much from you; after all, you're an American."

The limo pulled to a stop in front of a nondescript building somewhere in the heart of London. Brian replaced the snifter on a tray and glanced out the window at the rooftops across the street. Although there had been very short notice, he had managed to post a few MI-5 security people in the vicinity. He hoped they were on their toes.

The driver opened the door, and the two Temporal Wardens stepped out into the street. They quickly climbed the short steps to the building's entrance, where a doorman greeted them by doffing his hat. They quickly removed their own and went inside. Down a short, red-carpeted hallway they came to a small lift. The operator held the grate while they entered, and then activated the device. Not a word was spoken; they were expected, and instructions had been given to bring them immediately into what Home Office insiders jokingly referred to as the Presence.

Another somber, red-carpeted, dark-paneled hallway greeted them as the lift creaked to a halt and the attendant pulled back the iron grate.

"All the way down the hall, please, gentlemen," the lift keeper said. "You are expected."

"Thank you," Brian said with a nod. Vitterand also nodded, taking a cue in manners from Brian. Better start doing that, if I'm to get through this interview, Vitterand thought.

The large, solid wooden door at the end of the hallway opened at their approach. But instead of the fluttering secretaries Vitterand had expected, they were greeted by two men in cheap, ill-fitting suits who looked like they had once played offensive for Notre Dame.

"Gentlemen," one of the men said in heavily Gallic-tinted English, "the general regrets the necessity imposed upon him by security; however, I have instructions to search your persons. There are many who would love to see the general dead."

Brian nodded his assent and extended his arms. Vitterand did the same. The pat down took several seconds; de Gaulle's men were thorough, Vitterand noted with some satisfaction. It was always good to see excellence, even in a menial task.

The pair were ushered through a second doorway, where a male secretary, also in formal attire, awaited them. The man bowed as they entered. "Gentlemen, I am Jean Debrouillet, personal secretary to General de Gaulle. Please be seated, while I inform the General of your presence. May I offer you something to drink?"

Brian demurred, and Vitterand followed suit. The two men sat in the slightly uncomfortable Louis XIV style chairs they had been offered. They were the kind of chairs, Vitterand noted, that made one sit upright, in a rather formal posture. Judging from the secretary's manner, and the furnishings of this room, the general was a very formal man indeed.

Debrouillet disappeared through two paneled doors which he opened and closed behind himself silently. Vitterand glanced about some more. A large portrait of de Gaulle hung behind Debrouillet's desk—the use of portraiture to promote leadership seemed to be a hallmark of mid-twentieth-

century rulers. Vitterand thought about the photo placards of
candidates at American political conventions, the huge
portraits of Stalin and Lenin that adorned every available
open space in the Soviet Union, and of course the overuse
of Hitler's image that had made his face the most well-
known and hated visage in all of Europe. To the right of the
portrait stood the tri-color of the French Republic, the
symbol of the legitimacy of de Gaulle's often challenged
leadership of Free France. Aside from a few exquisite small
tables and a plethora of uncomfortable chairs, the room was
empty of anything to attract one's interst or attention. It
was as though the visitor's mind was to be focused on one
thing, and one thing only: the personage who awaited them
beyond those double wooden doors.

The doors opened and Debrouillet reappeared.

"Gentlemen, General de Gaulle will see you now," he
said. "Please enter."

Brian and Vitterand stood and exchanged short nods with
Debrouillet. Vitterand gestured with his hand for Brian to
take the lead. The Sioux turned Englishman stepped through
the doors and into the presence of the greatest French leader
since Napoleon.

Tall electric lamps illuminated the long, darkly paneled
room, adding to the bits of drab sunlight that spilled in
through the tall windows spaced evenly along the left-hand
side of the chamber. The carpet was plush, red, and
expensive. Aside from the lamps and carpet, the room was
devoid of furnishings save a few paintings on the right hand
wall, two small Louis XIV chairs spaced evenly in front of
the general's desk, and the desk itself, which was large
enough, Vitterand thought, to serve as the deck of an aircraft
carrier.

De Gaulle himself sat stiffly behind that desk. He wore

his full military uniform, including the cap. Among the decorations prominently displayed on his chest was the Croix de Guerre. His famous face, dominated by the large, thin nose, rather bushy eyebrows, and thin lips, looked somewhat pale in the uneven lighting. At first, he did not even move, but stared directly ahead at his two visitors. Brian and Vitterand, for their part, stopped side by side at the far side of the room and bowed to the general.

My God, Vitterand thought, bending to the waist to show respect, the old bird looks like he's been stuffed by a taxidermist.

"Gentlemen," the general spoke at last, in French. "Won't you please be seated?"

Both men nodded, again a show of respect, and walked slowly down the length of the room to the two chairs which awaited them. Brian slipped into his comfortably; Vitterand felt awkward, especially as he feared his ill fitting trousers were starting to slip down his waist beneath the cummerbund. He ended up lowering himself into the chair slowly, supporting his weight with his hands on the armrests.

"I see, Monsieur Brian, that our American friend is a man of action. He is not comfortable in such formal clothes," de Gaulle said.

"I apologize, M. le General," Vitterand said in perfect French, "for my awkwardness in this setting. I assure you, it does not extend to the field, where I am much less awkward at battling our common foes."

"Ah, an American who speaks French, and speaks it well," de Gaulle replied, delight lightening up his heretofore granite face. "Where did you learn your French, Monsieur Thomason?"

Vitterand almost blanched at hearing his real name. Brian had forgotten to tell him that de Gaulle would know him as

Thomason—or had the jovial Sioux/Englishman done this deliberately, as a kind of joke?

"In Paris," Vitterand replied. "As a child. I had the privilege of spending much time in Paris in my younger years, and have spoken French as well as English from my earliest days. It is a beautiful language, and one well suited to both literature and diplomacy."

"I think you mean to flatter me, M. Thomason," DeGaulle suddenly flared.

"I flatter your country and language out of a genuine love for both, M. le General," Vitterand replied swiftly. "I do not see how that flatters you."

De Gaulle was instantly on his feet. "Do you then insult me to my face?" he hissed.

Brian rose, too, his visage pale with alarm. This wasn't going well at all, he thought. What in God's name did Vitterand think he was doing?

"Monsieur le General," Brian began, "I am sure that M. Thomason did not intend—"

"I'll speak for myself, thank you, Brian," Vitterand interrupted. He did not rise. Instead, he casually crossed his legs. "The general is well aware that correcting the misunderstanding of a friend is no insult, nor are common diplomatic courtesies to be considered flattery." Vitterand met de Gaulle's hard eyes head-on and neither averted his gaze nor blinked.

The tense silence persisted in the room for over ten seconds.

"*Mon Dieu!*" de Gaulle exclaimed at last, his granite face cracking into a broad smile. "I like this American! He has courage, M. Brian, courage and audacity! As Napoleon once said . . ."

"*L'audace, l'audace, toujours l'audace,*" Vitterand interjected.

"*Exactement!*" de Gaulle agreed, retaking his seat. Brian, smiling weakly, also sat down again.

"Now, to business," de Gaulle said. "I understand you have information concerning one of our Free French operatives in France."

"Yes," Brian smoothly answered, cutting off Vitterand. "Actually, we have information from inside the Gestapo which indicates that the planned location of Jean Moulin tomorrow morning is known to them. We can only assume that they will act on this information."

"We could broadcast a warning though the usual channels," de Gaulle said.

"And risk interception, code-breaking, or worse, misinterpretation of the coded message by our own side," Brian suggested. "His Majesty's Government is of the opinion that a personal mission to avoid this danger to M. Moulin is warranted."

"And how does your OSS feel about this?" de Gaulle asked Vitterand.

"My mission includes providing full support to the resistance by any necessary and feasible means. They will support my being seconded to MI-5 for such an undertaking," Vitterand said. "The problem is one of credibility. While I am very familiar with Paris, and with general aspects of life under the occupation, I am not well plugged in to the resistance network as yet. In short, I am not well known to your people."

De Gaulle nodded. "M. Brian's office has briefed me on this problem. That is why you seek a letter of . . . let us say, introduction, from me to M. Moulin."

"M. le General understands perfectly," Vitterand said, smiling.

"Do you have any knowledge of the work M. Moulin is

doing currently," de Gaulle asked, his eyebrows rising ever so slightly.

"In specific terms, no," Vitterand admitted. "In general terms, though, he is attempting to create a united resistance movement, bringing together disparate, even opposing forces under the single goal of resisting the occupation until such time as the Germans are defeated and a legitimate government is returned to the French people."

"This work is of the highest importance to us," de Gaulle persisted.

"Of course. A unified resistance would certainly recognize you as the legitimate head of the Free French government in exile, thereby undercutting your rival, General Giraud, who, I am ashamed to admit, currently enjoys some favor in the eyes of the American administration," Vitterand said, playing his highest card.

"You are quite knowledgeable," de Gaulle replied. "Why should I trust you? You are, after all, an American, and the Americans, as you so rightly point out, favor General Giraud."

"I am an American raised in France, who speaks the language of France from birth, and who has seen and felt firsthand the lives of the French people under the heel of Nazi tyranny," Vitterand said, rising to his feet. "And I am an American who knows, without the slightest doubt or hesitation, that Free France will be established under the leadership of only one man, and that man is you. This, General de Gaulle, is written in stone."

De Gaulle cast a glance at Brian. "A bit Gallis in temperament, wouldn't you say, M. Brian? This American friend of ours?"

Brian opened his mouth, but no words came forth.

"You shall have your letter," de Gaulle said, reaching for

a sheet of fine writing paper and taking up his pen. He quickly scrawled a few lines on the paper, then folded it and placed it himself in an envelope. From his desk drawer he took a seal and imprimatur, and personally made the document undeniably official. The front of the envelope he addressed in his own hand.

The general stood. He extended his right hand, the envelope in it. Vitterand walked forward and took the missive from him, placing it in his jacket pocket.

"Please deliver this to my dear friend, Jean Moulin, whom you will find tonight at the address in Paris written on that envelope. Go with God," de Gaulle said to the American. "As your adventure novelists love to say, 'The fate of France is in your hands.'"

Place: *La Liberte*, in orbit around the moon
Time: Exact hour and date unknown. Year **4903** B.C.

Faracon called into the beams control room from the bridge.

"Jonesy here, Captain, the tireless Beam operator reported.

"Jonesy, reactivate the temporal damper field," Faracon ordered.

"Aye, aye, sir," Jonesy responded. He sent the necessary commands to the ship's computer, which activated the power supply held in reserve for just this eventuality.

"Damper field in place, covering the first days of May 1943 up until Vitelli and Wilson hopped into the Louvre, give or take a few hours. At this range with the power tranfer, we can't be more accurate than that," Jonesy reported.

"Very good, Jonesy," Faracon replied. "Very good indeed."

Place: Classified Top Secret By Temporal Warden Corps Central HQ
Time: Classified Top Secret By Temporal Warden Corps Central HQ

"I thought that went rather well," Vitterand said as he relaxed in the back of the Rolls. The driver had been given instructions to "hurry" back to the abandoned travel agency that served as the entrance to London's Time Station. But hurrying, in London traffic, was nearly impossible. The great machine dodged and weaved its way among the double-decker buses, and smaller cars, bicycles, and pedestrians that cluttered the streets of the central city. Vitterand, for once, was enjoying the ride. Now he knew where he was going and what he had to do.

"You did give me quite a start at first," Brian admitted, "until I gathered that the old boy liked your brassy style. Now, of course, you know he's going to check out with OSS. Don't worry, I'll get on to one of our chaps in the States and have the proper files planted, or whatever is required. One less thing for you to worry about."

"Thank you," Vittereand said, genuinely grateful. "And thank you for all your help with de Gaulle. I wouldn't have stood a chance on this mission without your assistance."

"Think nothing of it. We Temporal Wardens have to stick together. God knows resources for our work are scarce enough. My man Arkady back at Central winces every time we use the Beamer," Brian shared.

"I report to Bill Mason," Vitterand confided. "And he's not too bad about resources, but it just seems they never have what we need when we need it."

"Perhaps you'll have to take a lesson from our Gallic friends in *le système D*," Brian quipped sardonically.

The limo pulled into a side street and came to a stop before a delapidated-looking building. A faded sign in the front advertised tours of France, and a crumbling sign above the door tried to proclaim the once proud name of the proprietor of the small travel agency. Brian hopped out. Vitterand followed. The two made their way inside, past a clerk at a shabby desk who barely glanced up at them, and moments later stood before the archway of the London Station's Beamer.

"All set?" Brian asked his Beams operator.

"Roger that, ready to go," the swarthy man reported.

"Thanks again, Brian," Vitterand said. He glanced again at the letter from de Gaulle, tucked it securely into the inside pocket of his jacket, lifted his cummerbund to make sure his TCAF was still securely attached and activated. Lastly he hitched up his trousers.

"Do have your girl do something about that," Brian said, laughing.

"Let's go then," Vitterand said. He stepped through the archway. Power surged through the dials on the control console. There was no flash of light.

Vitterand stood, his back to Brian, confused. Where was his Paris Station Beamer platform?

He turned around. Through the archway, he saw Brian standing, scratching his chin.

"Beams," Brian snapped. "What the hell is going on? He's still here, or now, whichever is most appropriate."

"He's both," the operator replied. "Come around and we'll try it again."

Vitterand hastily raced around the archway of the Beamer portal, stepped up, and glanced at the operator.

The man nodded. "Go!" he said.

Vitterand stepped through the portal and . . . nothing happened.

"What do you think it is?" Vitterand asked, racing over to the console to have a look for himself.

"Something is blocking our transmission," the operator stated. "There's no systems failure. Our computers run full diagnostics constantly, and there's no sign of any anomaly anywhere in the system. Power is at full force. There must be some sort of field . . ." the operator speculated.

"Get me a com link uptime to Central, now!" Brian barked.

His communications officer tried, once, twice, then three, four and five times. "Negative function, sir," he reported. "Com link uptime to Central cannot be established."

"There's one other thing I can try," Vitterand said. "Stand back from me a bit," he warned.

He closed his eyes, focused his mind carefully, and said, "Activate recall."

He opened his eyes. Brian looked at him with a pained expression. "Nothing's moving through the continuum just now, it appears," he said.

"Damper field—that must be it," Vitterand quickly concluded. "Someone has thrown a damper field over this time sector. It can't block out already established links— that's why your anomaly detectors aren't going crazy, telling you their uptime link is blocked. But it can prevent any new signal from being transmitted."

"How's that work exactly?" Brian asked.

"Temporal mechanics of it are damned complicated, and it requires a tremendous amount of power. The equivalent of several fusion reactors in series, at a minimum, using the most primitive technology that could do it," Vitterand explained. "I studied it in the optional mechanics course, but didn't quite grasp it all."

"Well, sir," the Beam operator suggested, "maybe Brian

here could find you a nice date for this evening. Looks like you're all dressed up with nowhere to go."

"Good God!" Vitterand exclaimed as the full impact of this development hit him. "Chronometer check, metatime remaining."

In his brain, the thought "five hours, twenty-three minutes" formed.

"I have five hours and twenty-three minutes to get this letter to Moulin," Vitterand told Brian, "or you may be experiencing some major personnel changes around here."

"Come on, then," Brian called. "Looks like we'll make good use of that story we gave de Gaulle. Go in there and change into something appropriate for meeting with Moulin. Costumes! Give the Paris Warden your assistance," Brian ordered.

Vitterand hustled off to a nearby room.

"Communications, get me a real time telephone line to the Home Office."

9

The Hard Way

Place: An aerodrome outside of London
Time: Classified Top Secret by Temporal Warden Corps
Central HQ

The modified Lancaster bomber, equipped with night radar, taxied down the runway faster than usual, Capt. Williams thought. And why not? This was a light load, indeed. One man with a bag of equipment and a parachute. And that one guy didn't seem to be too happy about the fact that he was going to be parachuting into France, near Paris, probably in the dark, judging from the position of the sun on the horizon.

"This is Captain Williams," the pilot said over the open mike, so everyone could hear him. "We have a routine mission here, but let's stay on our toes. We're going to take a little extra time to avoid that Jerry flak on the Guernsey Island. I don't think they'll bother to muster fighters for us, but let's be on the lookout, anyway. Flight time to target should be good despite our little detour; winds are favorable and we're traveling light."

Vitterand winced at the announcement. Still, it had taken all the strings Brian could pull, and maybe then some, to get this "instant" mission cooked up. In less time than it had taken Vitterand to change, Brian had arranged for a plane to fly him to France, pried some hardware out of the military for him to take with him, and alerted the Home Office's underground contacts in Paris to be on alert for him as he came parachuting down. At least, the radio signals were being sent out. Vitterand could only hope they were being heard, properly decoded, and acted upon.

Still, with all that speed, it had taken time: metatime. His chronometer implant was ticking away, telling him now that another precious hour had elapsed, and he had just over four hours left to make contact with Moulin. Then, he still had to figure out how to get back to the afternoon of May 9, without just waiting for it to roll around. That would make him metahours late for his activities on the night of May 9, and that was a Priority Two alert.

The hum of engines and gentle throbbing of the plane reminded Vitterand that he was tired. Still, there was no time for sleep. As his mind turned over and over the problem in temporal mechanics that was thwarting him, he examined the gear Brian had provided for him.

First, of course, was his parachute. Brian had assured him it was packed by a true professional. There would be no failure. There was a secondary chute attached to his tube of equipment. That, too, had been checked, rechecked, and double rechecked. Brian wouldn't let him drop in there naked.

Inside the tube were a number of handy items. First among them was a Thompson submachine gun with ten fifty-round, circular-shaped drums of ammo. Not good for long range work, the Thompson was unsurpassed for close-in fire-fights, the kind he was most likely to face if the Germans intercepted his drop, or if the resistance group that was to meet him encountered problems smuggling him into Paris. Vitterand knew that American soldiers would still be swearing by the Thompson as late as the 1970's, when it was a preferred weapon among combat veterans in Vietnam. He quickly checked the barrel and feeder mechanism on the weapon, and loaded a full drum. Then he placed the safety on and repacked it in the tube.

Equally important was an American standard issue Colt .45 automatic pistol. He made sure that there wasn't a round in the chamber; he didn't want the gun to accidentally fire on impact. There were five extra clips for the Colt.

The combat knife was of the type issued to the recently formed American commando companies. It had a long, razor sharp tempered steel blade, smooth near the tip but with rugged serrations near the hilt. It was perfect for silently slitting a throat, gutting an animal in the field, or for a hundred other uses. Vitterand allowed himself a moment to admire the knife, then slipped it into its sheath. He strapped the sheath and the Colt in its holster onto his belt.

Next were the radio, radio direction finder, booklet of maps of Paris and the outlying regions, and magnetic compass. The maps were unmarked; there was not point in risking giving away the locations of resistance cells. Brian had gone over them with Vitterand in the car on the way to the aerodrome. Vitterand knew where to go when he landed. In case the compass wasn't enough, he had the radio and direction finder. With the radio, he could contact any of a dozen frequencies Brian had hastily made him memorize— there was no time to prepare an RNA implant. These were top secret frequencies used in emergencies by the British to contact their own personnel operating inside France. With the frequencies Vitterand had also had to memorize code names. He ran over them in his mind again now, hoping that he wouldn't have to use them. With the direction finder he could triangulate on any radio source and pinpoint its coordinates. That would be a last resort if he became hopelessly lost in the tangle of country lanes and villages on the approaches to Paris.

Last but not least, partly in jest and partly out of caution, Brian had made sure the equipment pack contained an American survival flag, first aid kit, and three sets of C rations. Both men hoped Vitterand would never have to use any of these items.

Vitterand carefully repacked the equipment tube, fighting a mild nausea as the plane bounced and jolted in a tricky air current over the English Channel. Weather was always difficult over the Channel at this time of year, difficult and unpredictable. Vitterand tried to remember what the weather was like in the Paris region on the early evening of May 8 but could not. It was all just too complicated for his brain to make sense of . . .

That's it! The solution to the problem that had been nagging him ever since the discovery of the damper field exploded into his mind. The field had to be somewhere close to its effect! The power source could be anywhere, in any time; the technology to beam vast amounts of energy through the continuum had long been in existence. But the field generator itself, which absorbed that power and transmuted it into the temporal damper field, had to be in the present, and in close proximity to the area being affected. Otherwise, the power drain would be beyond the capacity of anything less than a star to supply.

Vitterand stowed his gear, reached up to the bar that ran horizontally along the length of the plane over the metal bench on which he sat, and pulled himself to his feet. His motion caught the attention of the navigator, crammed into his flight station.

"Hey, there, mate, I wouldn't be walkin' about right now if I was you," he said. "Bit o' turbulence, see? Knock you flat on your arse."

"I have to talk to the radio operator," Vitterand called above the drone of the engines. "Need to send a signal."

"Right then, just sit down," the navigator said. He keyed his own mike. "Walt, you there? Our cargo wants to send a signal."

"Need to get approval from the old man," Walt responded.

"What did he say?" Vitterand shouted.

"'E said 'e 'as to 'ave the old man's pass on it," the navigator shouted back.

Vitterand sat down. It was no use—the pilot would never want to call the Home Office emergency channel in any case. He'd wait until he was down.

Place: The cellar of a small house near the Bois de Malmaison, west of Paris
Time: 1848 hours, Paris time, May 9, 1943

Pierre Mourier turned the tuning knob on the whining radio receiver, trying to bring in the faint signal that was almost buried in static. Sometimes it was like that. Sometimes the signal came in very clearly. Other times he had to strain his old ears to make it out, until he thought his head would pop from the effort. And still other times he couldn't get it in at all.

Today was unusual. He had turned on the set at the appointed time—six o'clock in the afternoon, Paris time. The signal was fuzzy, very difficult to catch. It had whined and shrieked and howled. He could just hear a voice beneath static pop and crackle, but he could not make out what it was saying.

Probably the Germans were playing again at jamming the broadcasts. They did that from time to time. And when they didn't know which frequencies to jam, they would try to scan then send up jamming signals. Perhaps that was what they were doing. Pierre did not know.

What he did know was that something very important must be happening. London's broadcasts of code usually lasted five minutes, never more than ten. But tonight the voice went on and on. Here it was, going on seven in the evening, and they were still at it. That could only mean that the message was important. The Germans, Pierre reasoned, would certainly figure that out. And so that made it all the more important for him to keep at it, to keep trying to receive the signal, so that he would know if he were being called to action.

Pierre had been listening to the radio receiver, hidden in his cellar, every night for over a year. As a respected member of the FTP, he had on two occasions been called into action by the London broadcasts. In both cases, he had recovered downed Allied flyers. Then it was his job to smuggle them along to the next appropriate safe house in the underground line that ran all across France, from the Channel ports to the Mediterranean coast at Marseille. The first group he had managed to save; they had made it safely along the line to the Channel coast and were eventually picked up by the British on one dark night. The second group had not fared as well. The Germans were out quickly, looking for them, as they could be expected to do when someone dropped so close to Paris. His FTP squad had become involved in a firefight. Two members were killed, and flyers, both British airmen, were lost as well.

But that was all part of the struggle. Pierre knew the struggle would be very costly. It would probably someday cost him his life. Perhaps it would cost the life of his wife, and his son, and his daughter. For her, especially, the price had already been very high. She whored for the Germans and danced at the Moulin Rouge, seeming to all of Paris to be nothing but a collaborating piece of trash. Yet her activities paid huge dividends; the German soldiers, most of them younger boys or older married men with families, were sick and lonely in Paris. They wanted someone to talk to. And talk they did, in bed. Helene provided him with reports three times a week on troop movements, unit strengths, artillery positions, air squadron postings, supply situations, and gossip about the intrigues at half the German headquarters in the city.

That information Pierre used. Some of it he used to help plan the activities of his own FTP squad, which had blown railroad bridges at critical times, and assassinated no small number of German officers, even in the very streets of Paris. Most of the information he passed on through trusted channels to others who were in contact with other resistance groups. What he could not use, perhaps they could. Perhaps the British could, or even the Americans. It did not matter to Pierre. All that mattered to Pierre, after almost three years of rule by *les Boches*, was that the Germans be defeated, that France be set free, and that a true government of France be created. This would be, he believed, a government of worker Soviets, not the corrupt government of capitalistic parties, like the old republic had been.

Pierre jiggled the tuning dial yet again, his ear plastered to the speaker. Outside, keeping a close eye on the countryside around their small house and garden, Helene stood watch. It was her night of freedom from the tyranny of her calling. Pierre always enjoyed his one night a week to visit freely with his daughter. But he was willing to sacrifice it if he could further the cause of the resistance.

Suddenly, the whine and hiss ceased, and Pierre could hear the voice clearly, speaking slowly in French, but with a taint of British accent. Englishmen could never learn to speak French properly, Pierre knew. But it didn't matter. He could understand.

"For Otto, your aunt Matilda has a birthday surprise for your niece. Otto, your aunt Matilda has a birthday surprise for your niece," the voice said without expression.

Pierre laid his back on a bag of potatoes, resting as he listened.

"For Juliette, there are turnips growing in the old garden this year. Juliette, there are turnips growing in the old garden this year," the radio voice droned.

Pierre closed his eyes. He felt tired. Tired of fighting. Tired of the struggle just live from day to day. But he would never quit, he told himself. Never.

"Little Hans, your cousin will visit for the holiday," the voice said.

Pierre forced himself bolt upright, his eyes wide, his ears straining to be sure he heard correctly.

"Little Hans, your cousin will visit for the holiday," it repeated.

Pierre clicked the radio off. He reeled in the antenna wire that extended up above the cellar. He carefully took the radio and hid it beneath a pile of rotting compost underneath a wooden trapdoor in the cellar floor. Then he climbed the narrow wooden steps, opened the doors, and called to Helene.

Helene Mourier sat on the tiny porch of the small house in a plain wooden chair, peeling potatoes which her mother would boil into the evening meal. Throughout this casual task, she had kept a sharp eye on the fields beyond the house, on the roadways that linked them, and on the fringe of the Bois de Malmaison, a woods near the preserved house where the Empress Josephine had once lived. She watched for any unusual traffic, any sign of troop movements, and any sign of the dreaded black Mercedes, which were the favorite vehicles of the Gestapo.

She smiled as her father approached. He was older now, and seemed much older than she remembered from just a few years ago. His head was all but bald, with only a slight fringe of snow-white hair. He still had a full beard and moustache, although these, too, had turned white . . . when? She could not remember. He walked with a stoop now that he had not had when he was a younger man, and a much happier man, laughing with the daughter for whom he had such high hopes. She was smart, she was pretty, she had impressed her teachers. She could go, perhaps, to university and be a scholar.

Then the war had come, and his daughter had become . . . Helene could not bear to think of that word and her father at the same time.

Yet never once had he criticized, or complained, about her activities. In fact, he expressed pride in her abilities as an FTP fighter, for Helene could fire a weapon as accurately as a man, or fuse a bomb, and take it into places that a man could never penetrate.

"Helene," her father said softly.

"Yes, Papa," she answered, smiling at him sweetly. "Ah, look at you. Mama will scold you. There is potato dust all over your blouse and pants."

"Mama will have better things to think about tonight," her father said.

"What things are those?" Helene asked.

"Little Hans's cousin will visit for the holidays. We must all get ready for that."

Place: Near the Bois de Malmaison, west of Paris
Time: 1905 hours, Paris time, May 9, 1943

Captain Williams pushed the control of the modified Lancaster further forward, sending the careening plane even
lower as he wheeled her to the left and banked her back to
the right. Orange explosions that turned into dark black
puffs of cloud dotted the sky all around and above the
aircraft.

"Flak is pretty heavy, but it should let up as soon as it's
completely dark," Williams said to encourage his crew.

The sun had already sunk well beyond the horizon, but
the faint glow of dusk still illuminated the sky, making the
plane visible. Williams leveled her out at 3,000 feet and
continued evasive action.

Vitterand had been hanging on for life as the plane tilted
first one way, then another, always with the nose pointed
down. The violent lurches had thrown him around a bit, and
only the restraining straps had kept him from serious injury.

"We're close to target," the pilot's voice sounded over the
open intercom. "Let's get that cargo ready to go."

Williams had known from the outset that this was a
suicide run. Daylight bombing raids, although still practiced
with heavy fighter escort, were always deadly. Coming
close to Paris was also deadly. And tonight, he had to drop
a jumper right over Malmaison, less than twenty minutes
from the city.

Williams didn't know who had dreamed up this mission
on the spur of the moment, and he really didn't care. Some
damned bloody fool at the Home Office, he'd been told. At
this particular instant, he was surprised and grateful to still
be alive. And as visibility lessened second by second, he

saw that the flak bursts, though numerous, were less accurate.

Vitterand shuddered at the message from the pilot. Not only had he never jumped from a plane before, he'd never jumped into flak fire, and he'd never jumped with his stomach already practically clenched between his teeth. Still, there was no real choice.

Vitterand stood up, steadying himself. He made once last check inside his belt. The TCAF was active. At least he wouldn't end up as a cloud of antimatter particles, whatever else happened. He opened his gear tube and stashed inside it the pages of complex equations, complete with pencil streaks and smears, that he had tried to work out on the bumpy and dangerous ride. With luck, these might hold the solution to one of his biggest problems—if he lived long enough for that solution to matter. At least he'd be hard to see. He wore all black, commando style. Black pullover shirt, thick black pants, black boots. His hands were covered with blackout grease, and his face was smeared with it in lines. Although he didn't know it, the black makeup contrasting with the white around his eyes made him look ferocious.

He resealed the double checked equipment tube for the last time, and hooked its chute clip to the wire above. Then he hooked himself up.

"Navigator to pilot," the navigator reported. "Target ahead in fifteen seconds."

"Roger. Let's get the door open; I'll try to give him a little more jumping room," Williams replied. He nosed the aircraft upward, climbing as high as possible without putting too much yaw on the craft for the jump to take place.

Vitterand watched as the radio operator climbed out his post and stumbled across to the side hatch. He pulled back the handle, and the howling of the wind and loud, dull thuds of the exploding flak hit Vitterand's ears.

"Target in ten seconds," the navigator called.

The radioman maintained a tight handhold on a railing with one hand, while with the other he dragged the equipment tube up to the hatch.

"Good luck, mate," the smiling British youth offered to Vitterand.

Vitterand gave him a nod and a "thumbs-up" sign.

"Target in five, four, three, two . . ." the navigator counted down over the intercom.

Vitterand placed his body directly behind the equipment tube. He stared straight out into the darkling sky. He had already resolved not to look down before he jumped.

"One," the navigator called. The radioman shoved the equipment tube out the hatch and backed away as Vitterand took another step forward.

"Now," the navigator called. Vitterand felt the thump of the young radioman's hand on his back as he hurled himself into the black sky.

It was darkening quickly, Vitterand realized, somehow, while his brain adjusted to the wonder of weightless free fall. He strained his eyes to see the chute on the equipment tube; he could just make out the white silk in the dark below him.

Then his arms were jerked half out of their sockets.

His rate of fall suddenly decreased, and Vitterand was once again very much aware the greatest fact in all of life was not time, nor space time, nor the secrets of the great cosmos, but the simple fact of gravity.

He glanced upward, searching for the Lancaster. Already the plane had started into its steep, banking turn, turning west and north, circling away from the greatest city of

France and the ring of deadly flak. And it was higher and higher above him.

He glanced down again. He could still just see the chute of the equipment pack. He stared at it for what seemed like several seconds—the entire experience was happening in slow motion—and then he saw the earth, suddenly surging upward out of the darkness like the dirt covered paw of an angry god, intent upon swatting him like a fly. Just to his right was the woods—the navigator had been right on target, at least, and there was an open field below him.

Vitterand had just time to be thankful that he wouldn't have to try to steer the chute when he realized that the ground was about to hit him.

He fell and rolled the instant his feet felt sensation. He was still tumbling when he found himself thinking that it wasn't as bad as he'd thought, no more jarring than a leap from a second-story roof or a ten-foot wall.

He scrambled to his feet and reeled in the chute cords, damping the silk down, as it still wanted to flutter up in the gentle evening breeze. He folded the chute, stuffed part of it back into the pack, weighted the whole thing down with a rock in the field, and ran to his equipment tube. He had just got that chute stowed when he heard the click of a round being pumped into the chamber of an automatic pistol, and a strangely familiar female voice.

"There are many yellow tulips this year," the voice said.

Helene stood directly behind Vitterand, the Luger pointed squarely at the back of his head. In her mind, she began counting slowly to five. This man had that long to live if he didn't give the appropriate response.

"That is too bad for me," Vitterand said loudly. "My wife only likes the pink ones."

"Shhh!" Helene shushed at him. "Not so loud. Do you

want the Germans to hear you all the way from the gates of Paris?"

"No," Vitterand said in a hoarse stage whisper, throwing the strap of the equipment tube across one shoulder. "But I damned sure wanted you to hear me. I was told I'd be shot if I didn't give the correct response."

Vitterand turned around and looked into the face of Helene Mourier.

He stifled an impulse to cry out in surprise. She did not yet recognize him; the black on his face and the growing darkness of the night hid his features.

"Let's go! Quickly," she said. She cast a glance about in all directions as she broke into a low, crouching run toward the nearby woods. Vitterand followed. They had just reached the edge of what appeared to be a significant forest of old-growth trees when they heard the first motor in the distance.

"The Germans will be here soon," Helene said, her voice totally lacking in expression.

She plowed ahead into the underbrush, walking quickly and quietly; she knew the way by memory and could have walked it blindfolded. Vitterand followed, trying to watch his steps in the darkness, banging his equipment tube against trees and snagging his arms in thistle bushes as he went.

"*Mon Dieux*," the girl whispered. "Try to be quiet."

About a hundred yards into the woods, the pair emerged into a small clearing. There, Vitterand saw four rifles leveled at his chest as he stepped out from between two trees.

"It's safe," Helene reported. "He knew the code."

"Thank you for meeting me," Vitterand said in his best slightly provincial northern French.

"We were told you were an American," an old man with white whiskers said.

"Yes." Vitterand remembered his role. "I am. My name is . . ."

"No names. It is better that way," the old man interrupted. "Quickly, where do you need to get to? The Germans will be swarming all over Malmaison very soon."

"First, I need to make radio contact," Vitterand said. "And then I need to get into Paris as quickly as possible."

"You have a radio in there?" Helene asked, suddenly curious. She walked over to tap on the equipment tube. "God in heaven! It's you!" she exclaimed. In less than a second the Luger was leveled at his forehead. The four men in the small group also readied their weapons.

"You know this man?" Pierre asked.

"This is the madman I told you about. I met him yesterday in the Cimetiere de Montmartre. He wanted me to arrange a meeting for him —with Max."

"Hands on your head," the old man harshly ordered. The three younger men moved in behind Vitterand and quickly relieved him of his equipment tube, Colt, and knife. "I thought you were American, from London," the old man said. "Yet you were in the Cimetière de Montmartre just yesterday morning."

"Everything you say is true," Vitterand acknowledged. "How was I able to travel so quickly—well, let's just say I need some sleep," he said, smiling. "But I can prove the authenticity of my credentials," he offered.

"How?" the old man asked. "I will not ask a second time."

"Here, in my belt pouch, you will find a personal letter for Max from General de Gaulle himself, with whom I personally met earlier today," Vitterand declared. "Look for yourselves. If you do not believe me, use my radio. You can call London to verify it."

His belt pouch was being rifled even as he spoke. Vitterand kept smiling as the precious document was passed from hand to hand behind him.

"It is true," a male voice said. "This carries the official seal and imprimatur of government in exile. It is addressed to Max, and it has a specific location noted on the address."

"Then you were telling me the truth the other morning?" Helene asked, doubt still lingering in her tone of voice.

"Every word, mademoiselle," Vitterand replied.

The three men and Helene looked to Pierre. He puzzled for a moment. It was possible this man was a German agent, but not likely. He had seen himself as he dropped out of the airplane—as had half the Germans in the region. The letter had the official seal and imprimatur, according to Guillaume, who knew more about such things than anyone else in their group. Why would the British risk a plane for a German agent? And where would the Germans get that seal?

"He lives," Pierre declared. "Let's move out."

Vitterand took a quick visual inventory as the small group stowed its gear for transport. They had plenty of small arms firepower; two of the men had five-shot infantry rifles, Garands of American make, while the other three had German machine pistols. The girl carried her Luger and a Springfield. No doubt the American weapons were courtesy of the OSS. He also counted three satchel charges—great for explosions—and each man carried several grenades mounted on a combat belt. One of the younger men shouldered a large cloth sack; what it might contain, Vitterand could only guess.

"Here," one of the men offered, "I'll carry your gear. Quieter that way."

The group headed into the woods as the first voices reached them from the field.

"*Achtung! Hier!*" they heard a man cry. The Germans were patrolling the field and had found one of the parachutes.

"Dogs next," the man carrying Vitterand's gear whispered. In his mind, Vitterand quickly named the man Hitler Moustache, after the most prominent feature on his pale face.

As if in answer to his prophecy, Vitterand heard the howling of a dog pierce the dark night. The beast bayed and bayed, and soon several others took up the cry.

"Got your scent—and hers," Hitler Moustache said, quickening his pace through the trees and undergrowth.

Just ahead, Pierre held up a hand. The group halted for a moment. The old man looked at each of the men, then pointed to one with a Garand rifle, and pointed back the way they had come. Without a word the man began to double back, and the group pressed forward.

About thirty seconds later, Vitterand heard the flat crack of a rifle shot. There was a loud yelp, and then one less dog was howling.

The shot was answered by a rain of automatic weapons fire that crashed into the woods behind them. Pierre did not even pause, but instead quickened the pace even more, as another rifle shot answered, and another dog barked out its death agony.

The duet of rifle shots and automatic weapons spray continued as they reached the edge of the woods. Vitterand saw a small farm truck parked there, its bed full of straw and reeking of manure.

Pierre looked at Vitterand and made a quick, violent gesture with his thumb. Vitterand understood. Without hestitation he climbed into the back of the truck and began to cover himself with the vile straw. Other hands helped, more than he wanted. Then all was silence, save for the occasional gunshots, until the truck's motor kicked to life.

Vitterand lay in the stinking darkness and waited. In the silence, he checked his personal chronometer implant. "Three hours, fifteen minutes," came the answering thought.

10

One Problem Down

Place: A country lane near Malmaison, outside Paris
Time: 1921 hours, Paris time, May 9, 1943

Vitterand wanted to cry out from the stench, but he did not. Instead, he kept his peace and tried to mentally recheck his calculations as the truck bumped and jolted across the open. Then, with one large jolt, the sound of the tires changed, and the ride smoothed. Vitterand realized they had reached a road. The sounds of firing continued in the distance as the truck worked its way up through the gears.

Beneath his cover of straw and manure, Vitterand began to feel cautiously with his fingers. Eventually his hand found something round and stiff—the top of his equipment pack. Carefully, he checked the seal. He didn't want any of the corruption from the truck bed to seep in and possibly damage the electronics gear. The seal was still intact.

Relieved, he worked his hand down his side through the cold, clammy, clinging muck and touched the grip of his Colt, which Hitler Moustache had thoughtfully replaced as they began their trek through the woods. Moving very, very slowly, he drew the weapon and pulled it up under his chest. He wanted to be ready, just in case.

He did not have long to wait. He heard the truck gear down and felt in his body a slowing of the forward motion.

"Keep very still," a low voice said from above him. He felt pressure on his back; someone had rested their feet on the straw just above him.

The truck rolled to a stop.

"*Papieren,*" a German voice demanded.

"Yes, yes, of course," the old man answered in French. "Papers. I have my papers, here, somewhere."

"Oh, Papa, you haven't forgotten them again, have you?" Helene's voice said. "Look in that back pocket."

"Ah, yes, here, here they are. Papers, see?"

"What are you doing here at night?" the voice demanded.

Vitterand heard no answer to the question. In his mind's eye, he could see the old man shaking his head, making gestures to indicate he did not understand.

"Here, I speak a little German," Helene's voice sounded. "What is it that you want?" she asked, her tone sweetness and caring.

"What are you doing here? It is after dark."

"We live just down this road. But I work in the city. At the Moulin Rouge. I dance there," Helene said in broken German. "Perhaps you have seen me."

"Hey, this one's a dancer at the Moulin Rouge," the soldier shouted to his companions. Vitterand counted the voices of four men in all.

"Who are these others?" the soldier wanted to know.

"One of them is my brother. The other works on our farm. They are all taking me to work, to make sure I get there safely. Paris is so dangerous, you know."

More laughter arose from this remark.

"I must see the papers of these two men," the soldier demanded. Helene made a show of translating the demand into French. The three men riding on the sides of the back of the truck stood up. Vitterand nearly cried out as one of them stepped on his left hand. He heard their idle chatter as they produced their identity cards, and the joking of the soldiers as they checked them.

The Germans seemed satisfied, and Vitterand thought they were about to be allowed to pass, when he heard the distinctive squeaking of wheels made by only one type of vehicle.

"*Ach*, God, here comes the captain," one of the soldiers said.

"*Ja*, and he's got that damned Renault out," another replied. Another round of laughter broke out, but soon subsided.

Vitterand strained to hear. The captain was obviously approaching, and he was not happy.

"We have found nothing yet, and I will not go back in empty handed," he was saying. "Have you searched this truck? Who are these people?"

"Just a farm family, sir. Taking their daughter to work in the city, sir," a soldier reported.

"A likely story. Get them out here!" the captain demanded.

Vitterand's mind raced. A Renault—a French-made infantry support tank. Most of them were destroyed in the fighting in 1940, but a few undoubtedly survived. No doubt this one was a relic that some capain of a garrison outfit had managed to procure to satisfy his own bizarre sense of prestige. Sometimes, Vitteran knew, the Germans downassigned equipment to garrisons for the damndest reasons. Although the Americans were even better than the Germans at "extra procurement." He recalled the story of one

American infantry company with a highly ambitious supply officer that actually managed to have a platoon of Shermans assigned to it. Whatever the reason, the captain was running around in an old French tank!

"Line these people up" the captain ordered. "Let me check their papers. All of them." Vitterand felt the men disembark slowly from the back of the truck as Helene, distressed, translated.

A tank, Vitterand reasoned, might be useful. And a hell of a lot better cover than a truck full of manure.

If he remembered right, the tank would have a small main gun, probably capable of firing high explosive shells, and two machine guns. There would be a crew of four: commander, gunner, and driver and extra machine-gun man. Or did the Renault only need three to opereate it? He couldn't remember. But it didn't matter. All that mattered was how alert that machine gunner might be.

"Alright, their papers are in order. Now search the truck bed," the captain ordered.

"Captain," a soldier responded, "this truck is full of manure."

"Then poke it with your bayonet!" the infuriated officer shouted.

Vitterand judged the man's location by the sound of his voice. He chambered the first round into the Colt, drew his knees up beneath himself, and raised his body, the Colt at the ready.

He'd guessed right. His first shot took the captain square in the chest. The man sprawled backward onto the country lane, as Vitterand squeezed off a second round, right into the face of the young German next to the captain.

His new resistance comrades sprang into action, knocking down and disarming the remaining three soldiers.

Helene produced her Luger and quickly began firing into the men's heads.

Vitterand's hands flew through the straw pile, seeking. He found what he wanted: the handle of a German "potato masher" grenade. He leaped from the truck and ran the few steps toward the parked tank.

Already, the startled crew were starting to react.

"*Feuer, feuer!*" someone inside was screaming, no doubt at the machine gunner.

But the reaction time of the garrison troops was too slow. Vitterand scrambled up the side of the metal beast, twisted the handle of the grenade, and dropped it inside, slamming the hatch shut.

The machine gun sounded only half a second before the grenade exploded.

Vitterand climbed up the side again, threw open the hatch, stuck his arm over the opening, and fired inside until the Colt's clip was empty. Cautiously, he peered into the hatch. The Germans inside weren't moving.

"C'mon," he called to his startled companions. "Clean the bodies out of there. We'll take this along," he said. He was already standing over the dead captain, searching the body and snatching the man's identification.

"Are you mad?" the old man began to remonstrate him. "You nearly got us all killed!"

"But I didn't," Vitterand said, stripping the cap and uniform tunic from the dead officer. "And now we have a tank." Vitterand turned his attention toward Hitler Moustache, who heaved the last of the German bodies out of the tank. "See if the radio still works," he shouted in French.

"I don't know how to work it," the youth called back.

"I do," the old man said.

"Helene, you drive the truck," Vitterand ordered, slipping on the German tunic. "Everyone else, into the tank."

"Where are we going?" Helene asked, suddenly breathless with excitement as she realized what a brilliant action this strange madman was leading.

"Someplace where I can use my radio in peace for about five minutes," Vitterand said.

He clambered aboard the tank, buttoned the turret, and called down the old man. "How about that radio?"

"Still working. There must be a dozen calls coming in!"

"Hand it up, and get ready to broadcast," Vitterand ordered. "How about the rest of you, are you in positions?"

Grumbles and curses came back in French. The Pz II was a notoriously crowded vehicle, and this one was carrying extra baggage, because the men didn't know how to sit in the various positions properly.

"One of you ride with the girl," Vitterand decided.

Hitler Moustache eventually wound up in the truck with Helene, while Vitterand took the position as tank commander, his torso jutting out of the hatch. The old man, with a few instructions, served as radio operator and driver, and the youngest of the group Vitterand showed how to work the main gun and the machine gun. His youth was an asset, because he'd have to slide from the machine gunner's seat to the gunnery chair and back if they got into serious action.

Vitterand keyed the mike as he saw foot soldiers approaching, curious and cautious to see what the firing had been about.

"All units, this is Captain Brecht," Vitterand broadcast, giving his best impersonation of the officer's tone and accent. "All units, halt what you are doing and report."

He listened for a few moments to the cacophony of radio replies. "Listen to me!" he barked. "The parachutist has taken shelter in the woods by the mansion of Malmaison. All units converge on that position and prepare to attack. He is well armed, and supported by a band of resistance fighters. We have killed several here. Take positions, and await my orders to attack. We want them alive, if possible. Brecht out!"

The radio continued to crackle with reports, as, slowly, the units under Brecht's command moved to respond. Vitterand watched for a few minutes as the scattered infantry patrols began moving away from the tank to the north, toward the woods around the famous château that had once housed Napoleon himself, and where fat Hermann Göring had once sat on the imperial chair that still remained there. Eventually, he saw the head beams of trucks converging in the desired direction.

"Alright, old man," Vitterand said, "let's go." He motioned ahead to the truck and pointed south. Hitler Moustache gave a smile and a nod, and the truck headed down the country lane.

**Place: Main highway five miles east of Paris in the direction of Neuilly and Chatou
Time: 1945 hours, Paris time, May 9, 1943**

"Two hours and forty-five minutes," Vitterand's implanted chronometer told him.

The truck had just rattled to a halt outside a house off the main highway leading to the suburb of Neuilly. The tank rattled up behind it.

"How are we doing on fuel?" Vitterand asked.

"Well," the old man confirmed.

Vitterand jumped out of the tank, raced to the truck, and began digging out his equipment pack. The other man fished out the rest of their weapons and began looking for rags to clean them. Vitterand conferred briefly with Helene, and soon the entire group was safely ensconced in a dark barn behind the small, out-of-the-way house.

Vitterand quickly withdrew his sheets of calculations
from the equipment bag. It took him only moments to have
the radio up and working, and he shook his head to clear his
tired, foggy brain and remember the frequencies Brian had
given him to memorize.

His mind soon gave up the desired data, and he jotted the
frequencies down on his pages of calculations.

"What are we doing?" the old man wanted to know.

"I have to take a radio direction find. Then we may make
an attack on a German installation, or we may just go on
into Paris, so I can link up with Max," Vitterand replied,
never taking his eyes from his calculations.

The equations were meaningless to old Pierre, who
plopped down on a bale of hay to think. Hitler Moustache
and the younger man cleaned their weapons, and Helene
watched the strange American closely.

Vitterand made a final set of calculations. If these
approximations were correct, he might be able to locate the
damper field generator, if it were anywhere near Paris. He
had realized on the plane that the damper, in receiving and
transmuting energy from another source in time, would
create a powerful, localized electromagnetic disturbance.
Unlike the EMP from a nuclear explosion, however, this
pulse would be contained to a narrow band of the electromagnetic spectrum. Nevertheless, its effects would cause
some vibrations in the ions free floating in the atmosphere,
and thereby produce radio signals. He had calculated the
most likely frequencies to be produced, based on his best
guess as to the amount of power being used and the
minimum strenght required for the damper field. If his
assumptions were correct . . .

Vitterand quickly tuned the radio receiver to one high
frequency band after another. He listened briefly on each
chosen frequency and band, then switched again. His

equations had given him eighteen possible frequencies to check . . .

"Bingo!" he exclaimed in English. The Frenchmen startled, then laughed quietly. "Bingo," they said to one another.

To any ear except Vitterand's the radio was producing nothing but background hiss. To his ear, that hiss was sweeter than any symphony.

He switched on the radio direction finder (RDF) and quickly put in a call to one local receiver. He exchanged only a few code words, enough to confirm the bearing, and then placed his second call. Again, he kept the time on the air to only a few seconds. No use helping any listening Germans. He began his triangulation calculations. Although only a few minutes elapsed, the time seemed like hours to the exhausted and anxious Temporal Warden.

The final numbers emerged. He grabbed his map packet, tumbling through the plastic covered pages until he found the coordinates he sought.

"My God," he breathed in English. "They've got someone in the Gestapo."

The Frenchmen all heard the word "Gestapo," recognizable in any language.

Vitterand collapsed on the hay, resting his mind for a moment from its labors. Helene moved close to him, and took his head on her lap, stroking his manure-covered, smelly hair with her gloved hand.

Pierre stood, uneasy. "*Américain*," he said. "You have given us quite an evening. But now, before we are still all killed, what is it that you have in mind?"

"I want us to take that tank," he said, gesturing toward the vehicle still parked, now behind the house, "to the villa of Sturmbannfuhrer Carl Boemelburg and blow the hell out of that Gestapo headquarters," he said. "Then I've got to get into Paris."

The Frenchmen stared at one another. This was way beyond anything within their experience. The American was clearly insane.

"I believe we can do it," Helene said softly. "And why shouldn't we? What better chance will we have to kill Gestapo than with a tank?"

Pierre considered. For himself, he did not care, and to die fighting was best. Hitler Moustache would do it because he secretly loved Helene, Pierre knew, and would not want to look like a coward in front of her. And the younger man would do it because all young men who are not cowards are fools. As for Helene . . . Pierre considered some more, and sighed. She would go with this American, whether her papa said, "Yes," or "No."

"What is your plan of attack?" the old man asked.

Place: The villa of Carl Boemelburg in Neuilly, a suburb of Paris
Time: 2045 hours, Paris time, May 9, 1943

The tank stopped alongside the country lane. Vitterand watched as the truck pulled up in front of it and killed its lights. Vitterand clambored down from the commander's perch. From Hitler Moustache he took the three satchel charges. Slung over his shoulder was his fully loaded Thompson, and knife, Luger, and three grenades were hung on his belt. On his other shoulder was a length of rope, with a grappling hook tied to one end. This the FTP had also contributed.

The small group of resistants gathered around him.

"Now, you all know the plan?" he asked.

His question was greeted with silent nods.

"Give me ten minutes to get to the cells below. I'll spring the prisoners, then you come in firing. There are fifteen HE rounds in the tank, more than enough to level that place. I'll try to make it to one of the trucks in the garage. When you see me coming out, then you'll be on your own. Round up as many of the freed prisoners as you can. I'll take the truck on into Paris," Vitterand explained.

Pierre nodded. Hitler Moustache walked back to the truck, which he would drive in behind the tank. The other two men climbed inside the Renault. Helene waited for a moment in silence with Vitterand.

"You are crazy, *Américain*," she said.

"Yes, perhaps. But I can promise you one thing," he answered.

"Men always make promises. They almost never keep them," she teased.

"The world will be a better place because you were in it. Especially tonight," Vitterand said.

Helene looked deep into the mad American's eyes, then folded her arms around his neck.

Vitterand allowed himself one long, lingering kiss. At least, if he remembered this in days to come, he could say he had experienced the very best the nightlife of Paris could ever offer.

He pushed the girl gently away from himself. "Remember, you're on the machine gun," he said. "Fire in bursts, and keep it moving around to pin down as many as possible."

"Men always think they know best," she answered. "Who was it who saved you from the Germans tonight?"

Vitterand slipped away into the darkness, stepping cautiously over the small stone wall at the edge of the road, and into the trees beyond.

The ground sloped upward gently toward the higher stone wall. Vitterand studied the position for a moment. He saw

no lights, no place along the wall for anyone to stand with
a submachine gun.

He advanced quickly across the open slope to the foot of
the wall, unslinging the rope as he came. Then the grappling
hook flew up and over the top. He tugged on the rope, hard,
until the hook caught. He could hear the *clink* in the night
stillness; he wondered if anyone else did.

He waited a full minute for a response. None came. He
began his climb, scaling the wall easily. The large, jagged
stones provided easy footholds, and in only seconds he
peered over the top.

He was about one hundred yards from the main driveway
where it bent around the circular gardens at the front of the
house. Vitterand cursed softly. He'd hoped to come out
farther back, near the rear of the villa. Still, there was no
time to change the plan now. He retrieved his hook, reset it
at the top of the wall, and swiftly let himself down.

He began moving in a crouched run along the wall toward
the rear of the château.

The first patrol soldier appeared in the distance, walking
along the wall, leading a German shepherd. Vitterand dived
to the earth and rolled toward a shrub, digging into the soil
behind it. Damn the luck! A dog could spoil everything.

Vitterand watched as man and dog both came closer,
closer. Any second now, the dog would catch his scent . . .

"*Halten Sie*, Willy," the solider ordered. The dog heeled
and stopped. The soldier took a quick glance around, then
reached for his fly, turned to face the wall, and began to
relieve himself. The dog stood watch behind its master.

Vitterand slipped the knife from its sheath. He drew
his legs up under himself, ready to spring. He waited,
waited . . .

The dog turned its head.

Vitterand was on his feet and his knife was hurling

through the air in under a second. The blade caught the dog square in the throat. The animal went down with a whimper.

"What's that, Willy?" the soldier asked, shaking himself.

Vitterand's left foot stomped on the dog's throat. His right hand retrieved the knife. His left hand caught the soldier just below the chin and yanked his head up. The man gave out a stifled squawk as the blade sliced his neck clean through to the bone. A final stab, with the dog's muzzle held tightly in one hand, finished the animal.

Vitterand moved on quickly. He had reached the front of the villa and now was moving parallel to its side, along the wall, toward the rear. He slipped on farther back, until he could see down the back of the structure. Concrete steps at the back side led down to the cellar, where resistance prisoners were kept in a single double row of stinking, damp cells. Two guards were engaged in animated conversation beneath a floodlight that shone down from the roof onto the steps.

Vitterand wondered if he should simply wait, but decided against it. He flopped quietly to his belly and began crawling across the damp earth toward the cellar stairs. Was there any way, he wondered, to do them both with the knife?

The men were pacing in the narrow landing at the foot of the stairs, talking, smoking, not paying attention. Occasionally they glanced through the single window in the door to the cellar, but they saw nothing there to which they paid heed. Vitterand crawled farther off, circling around the rear of the building, until he was behind the structure. He stood, leaning his back flat against the back wall, and worked his way back toward the steps.

At the corner, he listened intently, not to see what the men were saying, but to judge their position. When it sounded as though both were turned with their backs in his direction, he stepped out and leaped into the crowded landing. His knife took one man in the back, slicing all the way through to the heart, before his feet hit the ground.

The other soldier spun around, trying to raise his shoulder slung rifle, but Vitterand caught him with a knee to the groin even as he drew the knife out of the man's companion. In another second, he was lowering both bodies quietly to the concrete below.

He quickly examined his kills and found the key ring he sought. Trial and error soon produced the correct key to open the cellar door.

He slipped inside, carefully closing the door but leaving it unlocked behind him.

A few moans could be heard in the hall, but no other sound, save low, muffled hum.

That was the sound Vitterand sought.

His gaze ran up and down the concrete corridor, lined with cells on both sides. The entrance he sought had to be here somewhere.

The drain. There was the faint outline of a square cut in the floor beside the drain in the very center of the corridor. Vitterand strode down the hall. The half starved and beaten prisoners paid him no attention. He still wore the tunic and cap of a German officer.

He knelt by the drain and studied it a moment. The grating was loose and tilted; it had been moved, recently.

A quick motion of his knife pried the grating up. He stuck his hand down the pipe and felt the sides. A tiny catch greeted his fingers. He pushed it.

With a creak, the square cut in the concrete began to rise, revealing a short stairway.

Vitterand heard footsteps running toward those stairs. He backed away, readying the Thompson. Now was no time for subtlety.

A crash erupted from above the cellar, and the vibration from the exploding HE shell rocked the walls and floor.

Vitterand rushed down the stairs, the Thompson blazing.

His rounds cut down two startled men in SS uniforms. Their bodies flew back over the curved metal housings of an enormous power receptor.

His eyes drank in the high tech consoles against the far wall, and he walked quickly to them. His hands flew over the controls, calling up the data on the damper generator's controls.

The commands appeared on the screen.

Vitterand typed in the one he wanted. With a whine, the damper field generator shut down.

Working quickly as the shelling continued above, he placed the satchel charges in strategic locations throughout the subterranean lair of the temporal criminals. Then he set the timers for five minutes.

It took him only two of those minutes to blow the locks off the cell doors above and herd the prisoners outside. In one more minute he had made it across the grounds to the garage, and in four minutes he was inside a small German truck, driving like mad for the main driveway and the villa gate.

The tank was still firing. He roared past it, through the smoldering rubble where the gate had been and on down to the lane which led on into the heart of Paris.

He heard the great explosion that literally tossed the villa into the air, as the satchel charges blew and released the stored power in the transmuters. The flash lit up the night sky almost like daylight, the way a sudden bolt of lightning does.

11

Two Down

**Place: A small apartment on the Left Bank in Paris
Time: 2150 hours, Paris time, May 9, 1943**

Vitterand parked the truck a block down the street from the
address on the envelope. He tossed off the German uniform
tunic and stowed his gear beneath the truck seat. Then he
slipped out the driver's side door onto the narrow sidewalk.

He walked quickly through the quiet, residential neigh-
borhood. It was only ten minutes until curfew. He didn't
want to be picked up by the Germans now, and he didn't
want prying eyes to notice the man who wore all black,
commando paint on his face, and manure smeared over his
clothes.

He quickly reached the apartment building, meeting only
one passerby on the street, who could not take time to stare
at the strange apparition that passed him. After all, it was
only ten minutes to curfew, and innocent Parisians had
ended up as hostages, dead, or in concentration camps for
violating curfew.

Vitterand climbed the narrow steps at the front of the
building, found the button for Number 3, and rang.

"It is very late," a voice called over the intercom.

"Yes, but it is never too late to enjoy the smell of a fresh rose," Vitterand answered.

A buzzer sounded, and Vitterand swung open the building door. He went straight to the lift to the left of the main hallway and took it to the second floor. As he got out, he saw the light from the cracked doorway of Apartment 3.

He walked boldly up to the door.

The door opened. He entered the tiny apartment, and the door closed quickly and softly behind him. He heard hands flying over locks, and from his right heard the click of the hammer of a pistol being pulled back. He moved his eyes slightly and saw the barrel of the pistol pointed directly at his head.

"I bear an urgent letter for Max," he said. "I am unarmed, and I apologize for the smell, but I rode part of the way to Paris in a manure truck."

"Where is this letter?" the man holding the gun demanded.

"Tucked beneath my shirt," Vitterand replied, taking care not to move.

Then everything went black.

Place: A small apartment on the Left Bank in Paris
Time: 2228 hours, Paris time, May 9, 1943

Vitterand awoke. His head pounded with pain. He opened his eyes and found himself staring at a cheaply papered ceiling.

"You'll want some ice for that," a gentle voice said in French.

Vitterand forced his eyes to focus. He saw a face, a face he knew from his historical studies. Who was it . . .

Jean Moulin.

"Max!" Vitterand exclaimed. He tried to sit up. The pain in his head hit him like a hammer, knocking him back down.

"Please, lie still," Moulin said. "There is no need for hurrying. I'm afraid we have to take rather extraordinary precautions, Mr. Thomason, in our line of work."

Through the fog of pain, full awareness dawned in Vitterand's mind. And a tiny thought struck him. "Two minutes remaining," it said.

"Max, I have an urgent message for you," Vitterand said. "Forgive my rudeness, and I won't be able to answer questions. You must leave Paris at once. The Gestapo are hot on your trail and will arrest you tomorrow if they can. The apartment at rue du Four is compromised for now. It will be safe again, later in the month. By the 27th."

"And you have come from London just to warn me. What you must have endured," Moulin said. "Let me get you something for your pain."

"No!" Vitterand shouted. "You must promise me, your solemn promise, that you will leave Paris immediately and heed the warning I have given you. You must promise to do this no matter what you see or hear in the next few minutes, no matter what else may happen. You must leave Paris!"

"One minute remaining," ran through Vitterand's mind.

"Do I have your promise?" he asked.

"You come to me with the authority of General de Gaulle himself," Moulin said. "You have my word of honor as a Free Frenchman."

"Thank God," Vitterand sighed. "Activate recall."

A startled Jean Moulin looked at the empty sofa where the stranger had lain not an instant before. Then he quickly packed up his papers, warned his comrades, and using the underground network, got himself out of Paris.

He would be arrested within a month, in the same

apartment, as a result of betrayal by fellow members of the underground. He would be tortured and killed by the Gestapo, exactly as history had always recorded, and always would. And his work would guarantee the integrity of a Free France well into the next century.

Place: Temporal Warden's Station, Paris, France
Time: 0257 hours, Paris time, May 10, 1943

Vitterand struggled back to consciousness. The pain burning from his face was unbelievable, but something had roused him back from the bliss of unconsciousness. He struggled to remember what it was.

His eyes opened on the sick bay of his Time Station. The med techs were fussing over him now. . . . Why?

Ah, yes, he'd been blown up at the Louvre. Saved fat Hermann Göring while he was doing it.

There'd been two of them, he remembered, but he could only see one . . .

Darlon. It had been Darlon.

The robbery and the Louvre and Moulin affair had been connected. The mastermind behind them both was whoever ran Darlon.

The statues—the statues that had been stolen—what were they?

"C'hing," Vitterand called weakly.

"He's awake," one of the med techs said, surprise in her voice.

"Not for long," another responded. "God, look at the pain thresholds on these neural readouts. We've got to put him back under."

"No!" Vitterand insisted. "That's a direct order. C'hing!"

C'hing entered the sick bay. "Sir?" he asked. "You really

need to rest, sir. I've already reported to uptime Central. All is well."

"No," Vitterand said, trying to shake his head to emphasize the word but finding that the pain was too great. "Find out what, exactly, was stolen at the Louvre. Before the anomaly reaches uptime and we lose this chance."

"Already have that," C'hing said. "After the debris was all sorted, some miscellaneous Mesopotamian jewelry was missing, and two statues, one of the god Enlil, the other of his consort, the goddess Ishtar. These were excavated from Uruk," C'hing reported.

"Approximate date?" Vitterand forced himself to ask.

"Of the excavation?" C'hing asked, puzzled.

Vitterand shook his head violently from side to side, exasperatedly signaling, "No."

"Ah, you mean the date the statues were made."

Vitterand nodded once. His mouth formed a grimace that he hoped looked like a smile.

C'hing moved to the side of Vitterand's medical bed. "Sometime before 4800 B.C. The early Sumerian period. Dating was uncertain," C'hing said. "Really, sir, I must insist that you rest. You are much too weak to go on. You need to heal."

"Later." Vitterand's brows furrowed. He moaned from pain as his face contorted with the effort of thought. It would be so much easier just to sleep. . . .

But the statues—why would anyone want them? The question stuck like a needle in Vitterand's consciousness. Of what possible use would they be to a time traveler? They had no particular value. They were just crude ancient gods. They had no value at all—unless you believed in those gods!

Vitterand suddenly raised himself up on one elbow, his

eyes wide, gleaming with excitement. "What margin of error?" he demanded of C'hing.

"Margin of error? You mean for the dating of the statues?" C'hing asked rhetorically. "Oh, not a great amount, less than a hundred years, I should think."

"Good, good," Vitterand whispered, his speech broken by a fit of violent coughing. "Activate uptime com link. Get a probe sent. Tell Mason he has to send a scanner probe, looking for orbital objects, beginning in 4700 B.C. and working backward," Vitterand said groggily. "About three centuries of scanning should do it. Over ancient Sumer. Report results to me. Don't let me go to sleep. We have to move in metatime on this."

C'hing gazed thoughtfully at his boss. If Vitterand were unable to perform his duties, C'hing was second in command. This request made almost no sense to him. Was Vitterand mentally aberrant? C'hing wondered. "What are the chances of delirium?" he asked the med techs. "What is his mental condition?"

Vitterand groaned. There wasn't time for this.

"Well," said the more senior of the two med techs, scanning Vitterand's neural readouts, "he's way past the pain thresholds. But these figures indicate he's still rational. However, he is also highly emotional, and that might be damaging his judgment."

Vitterand flopped back down on the bed. "Must . . . hurry!" he croaked. His eyes moistened with traces of tears.

C'hing had not known Vitterand long, but he thought he knew something about the man. He returned Vitterand's gaze for a silent moment. Then he ordered, "Keep him awake."

C'hing toddled back to his control console. He dreaded the conversation with Mason. Scanner probes were about the most expensive thing in the Temporal Warden's arsenal.

They were unmanned computer/sensor arrays, set to travel back in time, stop at designated instants, and sweep for a variety of anomalies. They were especially good at picking up energy outputs that didn't belong in a given time period. For example, a nuclear reactor in the pre-nuclear age would show up instantly. Properly programmed, a probe could sweep every year in several centuries in virtually a few hundred seconds. Probes reported their findings constantly uptime to Central. But use of probes was almost always denied. The power drain involved was considerable, and the computer time used for the constant tie-in, space-time guidance, and monitoring was enormous. Mason was going to scream. And C'hing had only his intuitive sense that Vitterand was onto something very, very important to back up his request.

Reluctantly, C'hing punched in an uptime com link to the main Time Warden headquarters. His prediction concerning Mason's reaction was proven true.

"He wants a what?" Mason shouted incredulously.

"A probe, scanning for orbital objects around the planet Earth, from 4700 B.C. back."

"For how long back?" Mason demanded.

"Three centuries," C'hing replied calmly.

"Three centuries! Do you know what the power drain involved will be? Do you know the computer space involved? Are you aware, has it ever crossed your or his consciousness, that there might, perhaps, be emergencies other than your own that require our resources?" Mason exploded.

"I believe he is in great earnest," C'hing said, keeping himself placid, not responding to Mason's emotional outburst. "I don't know his reasoning. He can barely talk, much less engage in difficult explanations of problems in temporal mechanics. But he insists. He is, as you know, sir, a stubborn man, a man of deep convictions."

There was silence on the uptime com link for several seconds.

"Yes, I know he is a man of deep convictions," Mason finally answered, his voice its usual flat calm. "Alright, he can have this probe. But tell him this had better pay off. Big."

**Place: Temporal Warden's Station, Paris, France
Time: 0336 hours, Paris time, May 10, 1943**

C'hing heaved a sigh of relief. Mason hadn't been too rough. There hadn't been any threats of heads rolling, or the equivalent, of people being "unrecruited." The Beams operator sank back for a moment in his seat. No use moving. Central would launch the probe immediately—any probe request that was granted had a top priority. And the instant the results came in to Central, Mason would contact him. Only he'd call downtime to an instant only a few seconds after the request was made. That was one of the advantages of communication across time.

"By all the gods!" Mason's voice bounced on the com link. C'hing couldn't remember ever having heard Mason's voice with this measure of excitement in it.

"C'hing here," he responded.

"By all the bloody gods in all the bloody hells, we've got it!" Mason exclaimed joyfully. "Your Warden was quite correct to make the request for a probe. Please inform him that we have located *La Liberté!* The space-time coordinates will be transmitted directly into your computer system."

"Ah, Warden Vitterand, he will be most pleased," C'hing answered. To himself, he thought, my Warden will not be Warden here for long. He'll be promoted with certainty for this. *La Liberté*, and her pirate commander, George Faracon, were the one thing and the one person that topped the Temporal Warden Corps' "most wanted" list.

"Tell him to be careful," Mason continued. "Faracon is no dummy. He probably spotted our probe, so if our action is off by even a few seconds, he'll be waiting. . . ."

"Certainly," C'hing replied. He understood perfectly. If the probe were detected, Faracon would be fully alerted, and with the time travel capability at his control, there was no telling what sort of ambush or worse he might prepare. "Ah, you mentioned, 'our action.' What action shall I tell Warden Vitterand you are planning?" C'hing asked Mason.

"Oh, it's all his show," Mason answered cooly. "We're pretty tied up here at the moment, don't even have a strike time available."

"Surely," C'hing suggested, "to capture Faracon and *La Liberté*, certain resources might be diverted—"

"Can't do it, C'hing," Mason interrupted. "We'd have two and possibly three temporal waves crashing over us if we diverted personnel just now. If we're going to catch Faracon, your Warden will just have to slog it out on his own for now."

"Perhaps we should wait until resources are available?" C'hing dared to suggest. "After all, we know where and when Faracon is now. So you can send a team whenever one becomes available."

"And if Faracon detected our probe, how long, in metatime, do you think he'll stay in 4903 B.C.? He'll hop back or forward or whenever and tell himself never to enter that time period, and that will be that. No, Vitterand has to move on this now. The clock's ticking, as it were," Mason explained.

"I will tell him," C'hing answered.

"Right. And tell him happy hunting! Mason out."

"We've got it!" C'hing exclaimed, bounding into the sick bay and peering into Vitterand's eyes. "How on earth did you know?"

Vitterand fought the pain as he pushed back with his arms to raise his burning body. Pain seared every inch of his face and hands. "*La Liberté?*" he asked.

"Yes, yes. Found it. She hopped in—oh, you know, the probe can't be exact, but she hopped in to 4903 B.C. sometime just after the turn of the year."

"Statues," Vitterand gasped. "Valuable—not in the future, but in the past. Power of the gods."

"Of course!" C'hing suddenly saw Vitterand's reasoning. "Faracon has scammed some ancient someone by promising them these gods!" C'hing exulted. "Brilliant. And more brilliant of you to figure it out."

"Yeah," Vitterand said, struggling to sit up. "Now, Beams, you remember when I hopped back in from my little meeting with Moulin?"

A med tech placed a warning hand on C'hing's shoulder. "He must rest," the tech said. "If he doesn't sleep soon—"

"Not just yet. Give me stimulants!"

The med tech glared at Vitterand incredulously. "Out of the question," he replied. "My job is to heal you."

"Do what I say, and I'll be so healed, none of this will have ever happened."

C'hing pondered the situation. "You're going back in time to when you arrived back here, at the Station, from the Moulin affair!" he suddenly exclaimed, his face beaming. "You're going to talk to yourself, and you're going to send yourself, then, back to deal with Faracon before the Louvre alert."

"Exactly," Vitterand said.

"Med tech," C'hing ordered, "give this man the largest

tolerable dosage of stimulants. He needs to be on his feet for about two minutes, tops."

Place: Temporal Warden's Station, Paris, France
Time: 1605 hours, Paris time, May 9, 1943

Vitterand materialized on the Beamer platform lying on his back, clasping the back of his head.

Sandy rushed up to him. Her nose wrinkled at the same time her eyes widened. "My God! You smell absolutely horrible. Where have you been?"

"In a manure truck, several explosions, and close combat," Vitterand replied. "And I was sapped in the back of the head, by a friend of a friend, you might say," he added.

C'hing toddled over and looked carefully at his boss's body, scanning from head to toe. "You need a med tech," he concluded. "And bath. Bath first, I think."

"Thanks," Vitterand said, rolling his eyes. "What a surprise that is to me." He stepped off the platform and gathered with his senior staff at C'hing's console.

"Please," C'hing pleaded. "Not to drip manure on the equipment."

Vitterand nodded his assent. "I need some sleep—and a bath. In fact, C'hing here is right. The bath will definitely come first. Make an uptime com link to confirm that the Moulin anomaly has been averted. Tell them I think I achieved a temporary solution, but it was bloody, and we'll have to redo it after the alert later tonight. Report to me right away. I won't be able to sleep and get ready for tonight until I know that this Moulin thing was successfully handled."

"Belay that order!" a voice barked. It was an all too familiar voice, Vitterand thought.

He whirled about, ignoring the pain the sudden movement caused in the back of his head, and looked at a man standing on the Beamer platform. The figure's face was obscured by swaths of wet bandages, and his clothing was a tattered ruin. But there was something about his stance, his voice, his carriage . . .

"Hey!" C'hing exclaimed. "That's you!"

"Yeah," Vitterand replied, his sense of dread betrayed by his tone of voice. He had always feared the day he'd end up talking to himself, like this, doubled in time. It could only mean that something had gone terribly wrong. He quickly glanced at his own belt.

"Don't worry, I'm wearing a TCAF," the Vitterand from uptime called out. "And I know what you're thinking, that something has gone very sour."

"Right," Vitterand agreed with himself.

"Does this kind of thing happen very often?" Sandy whispered to C'hing.

"Not when things are going as they should," the Beams technician whispered back. "There's been one big—what is your American word? Snafu—one big snafu, or he wouldn't be coming back to talk to himself," C'hing added.

"Not so," Vitterand shouted from the Beamer platform. "I've figured it all out, the Moulin business and the alert tonight. And if you do what I say, we can solve both anomalies at once."

"Tell me quick. I'm pretty tired," Vitterand said. "And since you're here, I can only conclude that the big night I'm expecting tonight is even bigger than I supposed."

"You're not as tired as you're going to be if you don't do as I suggest," Vitterand urged himself. "I'm trying to keep us from being toasted in an explosion, and having only partially solved our problems." He stepped down off the Beamer platform, staggered, and steadied himself.

Sandy saw that the man's hands were shaking, and that his eyes were glazed.

"You both need med techs," C'hing offered.

"Clear the room," both Vitterands ordered simultaneously.

C'hing shot a glance at Sandy, who shrugged. They and the other staff all moved to obey. The Vitterand who had come from uptime waited until the room was cleared. "Sound secure," he ordered the computer.

"Sound security confirmed," the computer reported.

The downtime Vitterand nodded. "So you really are me, from the future. The computer recognizes your voice."

"Yes," the trembling visitor from the future replied.

"Don't you want to sit down?" Vitterand downtime asked. He rolled out a console chair, pointed to it. "You—I mean we—look awful."

"Bad burns. Lots of pain," Vitterand uptime explained. He lowered himself slowly into the offered chair. "Now listen carefully. We don't have much time—this is all in metatime."

"Still?" Vitterand asked himself from the future. "I thought metatime missions were supposed to be rare."

The visiting Vitterand shook his head in disgust. Was he really talking to himself? Was he usually this slow on the uptake, or this much of a smart alec? He decided to save time, forge ahead with his story. "The culprit behind both anomlies, both the Moulin business and the thing coming up tonight, is George Faracon."

"Hmm. Mason and I had both guessed as much."

"Right. Here's what you need to do. Go back to *La Liberté*. She's in Earth orbit in early 4903 B.C. It's a synchronous orbit, above the Tigris-Euphrates Valley. The coordinates are on this readout," the future Vitterand explained, pulling a sheaf of papers from the small case he carried. "Beam on board and shoot that bastard Faracon in the head. All this should go away then," Vitterand from uptime said.

"What's the second anomaly—the one coming up tonight?" Vitterand downtime asked.

"Faracon gets Hermann Göring killed. Faracon goes to steal some statues from the Louvre, and while he's there, Göring gets it. The details don't matter—all that does matter is that Göring not get killed."

"Okay," said Vitterand downtime. "Can I clean up first, or does our metatime limit mean I can't take a shower?"

"Shower fast," Vitterand uptime gasped. "I think Faracon will be expecting you to come after him. He won't hold this temporal position very long. Activate recall."

Vitterand watched as his future self simply vanished into the air. He stared for a moment at the empty chair, then began to stagger himself, wearily, through the control room.

"C'hing," he called out over the intercom, "get me any plans we have in the computer banks on *La Liberté*. Set up a Beam Back to the coordinates you'll find on the printout by your console. And tell Equipment I want weapons, lots of them. I'll be ready to go in fifteen—no, make that ten minutes."

Place: *La Liberté*, in sychronous orbit above the Tigris-Euphrates Valley
Time: Early in 4903 B.C.

Jonesy hit the intruder alert alarm within a second of Vitterand's materialization on the Beamer platform of *La Liberté*.

In that second, Vitterand oriented himself. Directly in front of him, just as C'hing's fast briefing had indicated, was a clear partition. Beyond that partition was the temporal control room, where even now an operator was staring at him, obviously astonished, but not so astonished that his hands weren't flying toward a control. The partition, Vitterand knew, was necessary for biological containment. To his left he saw from the corner of his eye the sealed hatch that led to the biological decontamination chambers. Such safeguards were available at all Time Stations but were used only when one was traveling back in time, or coming back from a time, when infectious agents would be a problem. Their usefulness here, where obviously trips were being made to the surface, to ancient Sumer, were no surprise.

Vitterand, on the other hand, was a surprise to Jonesy. Still, the well-trained Beams operator didn't hesitate more than a second before hitting the alarm that caused a blaring Klaxon to sound throughout the vast ship. Whatever Vitterand was, he was three things that Jonesy didn't like. First, he was unexpected. Second, he was heavily armed. Jonesy saw that the man's weaponry was antique, but no less lethal for all that. He carried some type of ancient device for hurling lead slugs through the air at high speed. On his belt were a knife, rope, and much more conventional, far future, high-tech grenades. And Jonesy could see the straps around his shoulders that indicated he was wearing a breathing tank on his back. A tube snaked around to a mask mounted near the rear of his belt. This would protect him from gas attack.

Such armament, coupled with such surprise, could only mean that Jonesy's third conclusion was certain. The man was either a temporal assassin, sent by one of the numerous persons George Faracon had crossed all throughout history, or he was a Temporal Warden. In any case, Jonesy sounded the alarm.

It was his last action. Vitterand immediately lowered the Thompson and squeezed the trigger, sending a sudden burst of twenty .45 caliber lead slugs flying at incredible speeds into the partition before him. Built to withstand the penetration by bacteria or even viruses, it could not withstand the impact of the sheet of lead that shattered it. The bullets flew on through it. Jonesy's head was in the path of several. It exploded into a bloody mist, and bits of brains and bone were scattered on the walls and equipment of the control room as if they'd been sprayed from an atomizer.

Vitterand stepped through the partition, his feet crunching on bits of glass and plastic. He immediately went into a crouch and allowed his eyes to scan the room for televiewer cameras before coming to rest on the only door that led into this room with the exception of the entrance from the decontamination chamber—the door that connected it with the bridge of *La Liberté*. He found no televiewers. The South Americans had built cheap, and apparently Faracon had not seen a reason to rectify this particular lack. In that same sweep of the room, Vitterand's eyes drank in the multiple control consoles, and he saw Jonesy's headless corpse tip forward onto the control keyboard at what was obviously the main console.

Then he fastened his gaze on the bridge door. He wondered how long it would take before the first of Faracon's thugs responded to the alert. It was too bad the man at the console had had time to get off the alarm; Vitterand thought the man must have been very well trained indeed.

Then the door to the bridge hissed open, and Vitterand squeezed the trigger of the Thompson again. Another hail of lead poured forth. The first two of Faracon's thugs were caught squarely in the doorway and blown back onto the floor of the bridge beyond. Vitterand could see red blossoms appear on their white ship's uniforms before the door hissed shut again.

That, he thought, should buy him at least a few seconds. He stood, laid the Thompson atop the row of consoles before him, and vaulted them. He retrieved the weapon while at the same time kicking the chair on wheels, burdened with Jonesy's corpse, out of his way. Then he crouched in front of the console, with the Thompson still trained at the door.

Vitterand cursed mildly. The headless corpse had spurted blood all over the keyboards and control panels. Still crouched, he raced down the narrow walkway to where the chair had toppled over. With his knife he cut several rags from the clothes on Jonesy's corpse. He returned to the console and was sopping up the blood and wiping the keys when he heard the voice on the intercom.

On the bridge, George Faracon had scowled as the first of his security men were cut to ribbons in the doorway. "Duty officer," he barked. "Get that mess off of my bridge." Two more security men scampered to obey, grabbing the corpses of their bullet-riddled comrades and dragging them by the feet off the bridge.

Strange, Faracon thought. He'd expected an all-out assault. Why didn't whoever was in there simply burn down the bridge door—vaporize it—and come storming in? Of course Faracon had a good plan in mind should that happen—the intruder would have died instantly—but that was the way Faracon would have begun such a raid. This intruder, or intruder group, was more subtle. Of course, he had expected them. He had expected the Temporal Wardens.

His ship's sensors had spotted the probe even as it spotted them, but there had been no chance to destroy the time traveling device before it had vanished—and sent its report back to where and whenever the Temporal Wardens HQ was located. Still, he was a bit surprised. If he were leading a strike team, he'd have brought enough high-tech weaponry to have vaporized the security door between the bridge and the temporal control room in instants. And about one instant after that, he'd have vaporized the bridge. But that kind of weaponry would require a full strike team—could it be they hadn't sent a full strike team? Faracon pondered briefly, then ordered his computer to open an intercom channel to the control room.

Before he spoke, he reached into a recess in the side of the chair and brought out a small but powerful temporal transmitter—a device for sending messages through time. On this device was a large, spring-held switch, which he pulled back and held open with the fingers of one hand. Then he spoke.

"Intruder, this is George Faracon." Vitterand heard a voice call over the computer intercom. "Hold your fire. I'm coming in alone to talk to you. I'm holding a dead man's switch, and if you kill me, Göring dies," he announced. "You can respond by simply speaking—the intercom will pick up your voice."

Vitterand studied the console before him for a moment, then, still crouched, made his way over to Jonesy's bloody body. He took out his knife and cut some more rags from the corpse's clothes. Scurrying back to the console, he quickly wiped the keyboard, sopping up as much blood as he could with the rags, until enough of the keys were visible to orient his hands.

Fortunately, the technology, although primitive, was similar enough to what Vitterand knew that he was able to access the security programs. Simultaneously, a new alarm sounded on the bridge.

"Captain, the computer's security system is being accessed from the temporal control room," the duty officer reported to Faracon.

Faracon scowled, puzzled. What kind of raid was this? What kind of stupidity? "Computer," he snapped, "voice priority override. Cancel all access to security systems from temporal control room. And turn the intercom back on.

"YOU!" Vitterand heard a shout over the intercom. "I don't know what you think you're doing, but you can't accomplish a thing in there. You'd better agree to talk to me while you still can. My patience is growing thin."

Vitterand saw himself locked out of the security program, but not before he had secured the bridge door from his side—so that the door would not open without a command from him and from the bridge at the same time. He ignored the demanding voice—he knew from C'hing's study of the plans of *La Liberté* there was no other way into the control room except through the ventilators, and it would take them at least three, maybe five minutes to send a team in that way.

Vitterand's hands flew over the console. He called up the Beamer's log, studied it carefully, forcing himself to commit a string of dates and times to memory, and then deleted the entire file. Next he checked the power. And in an instant he saw Faracon's dilemma. The man couldn't hop the ship through time!

Vitterand paused. He could recall, inform Central, and wait for a strike team. On the other hand, if Faracon could find a source of power that he could tap into . . .

The risk was too great.

Now it was time to hear what the elusive criminal had to say.

"George Faracon," Vitterand called out. "If that is you—which I'm inclined to doubt—what is it you have to say?"

"First I'd like to know with whom I'm speaking," Faracon growled.

"This is Temporal Warden Vitterand, operating with the full authority of the Temporal Warden Corps. I would show you my identity card, but under the circumstances . . ."

"I quite understand," Faracon's voice calmly replied. "How do you propose we proceed? I'm a bit surprised, actually, that you came alone." Faracon wasn't sure the Warden was alone, but he hoped to bait him to revealing his strength.

"It only takes one man to deal with a rodent or an insect," Vitterand answered, purposely putting a sneer in his voice. He wanted to goad this man, assault his ego, make him reveal something.

"You're quite correct. However, if you were hoping to deal with me, at least in any violent way, I'm afraid there's something important you should know," the voice came back. From the tone, Vitterand judged that Faracon—if it were he—was unruffled.

"What's that?" he asked.

"I have to show you," Faracon responded. "Again I say, hold your fire, and let me come in. I'll be alone and unarmed. If not, you can gun me down in the doorway as you did my unfortunate associates a moment ago."

Vitterand scowled. Faracon had something—something that made him confident. What was it? And why did he want to parley? Surely he must know that even one man, properly armed, could destroy the entire ship simply by creating a hull breach, and recalling out before he himself was sucked into the vacuum of space. Vitterand decided to bite.

"Very well, we'll parley a bit. And since you want it face-to-face, so be it. Unlock the door from your side first, and restore my access to the ship's security system."

Faracon frowned. He didn't like the idea very much of letting this Warden back into his ship's security system. He manually switched off the intercom and verbally transferred override control of the security system to the duty officer. "As soon as I'm through that door, shut him back out of the system," Faracon ordered.

"Aye, aye, Captain," the duty officer replied, never taking his eyes from his station's monitor. Too many duty officers had died for the slightest breech for this man to behave as anything other than an automaton.

Faracon reopened the intercom. "I'll open the door from

this side. You'll have to do it from your side, I see. So I'll be waiting at the door. Whenever you're ready."

Vitterand leveled the Thompson atop the console, aimed it directly at the doorway, and with one hand released his lock on the door. The door hissed open. A single figure stood in the doorway, a large, bulky man with grizzled salt-and-pepper hair and a bit of a potbelly. He held a device in one hand, but otherwise seemed at first glance to be unarmed beneath his white ship's fatigues.

The door hissed shut behind him.

The big man stepped through the hatch with both hands held up and out in front of him. The device he held, Vitterand could now see, was a small, easily recognizable temporal transmitter. But there was an odd arrangement attached to it.

Vitterand stood, leveling his old-fashioned Thompson at the large figure's chest. "What's on your mind?" Vitterand demanded.

"First, let me compliment you on your excellent work," Faracon said. "It must have taken quite a bit to find me."

"It did," Vitterand agreed.

"Now, here's the situation," Faracon began, glancing about for a chair. He found one, strolled over, and lowered himself into the seat. "You don't mind if I sit down, do you?"

"Not at all. You don't mind if I keep this antique slug thrower leveled at your fat gut, do you?"

"Of course not," Faracon replied amiably. "You can see that this transmitter is rigged. This, you see," he said, extending the device so Vitterand could observe it clearly, "is a dead man's switch. Your friend and mine, Hermann Göring, will die if I let go of this switch. A message will be sent to all my agents, in all time periods, to kill Göring by any means possible. So if you shoot me, Göring dies. It's just a little insurance to make sure our meeting is a friendly one."

"Gee," Vitterand replied. "The death of a Nazi war criminal would be a tragic thing to have happen. I feel so threatened." Vitterand contorted his features into a snarl and rasped, "Why don't you cut the crap and come to the point."

"I will," Faracon said, smiling. "What's your hurry. You know perfectly well we both have all the time in the world. Why are you in such a particular hurry?"

"I'm not in a particular hurry to leave here," Vitterand replied. "It's just that I don't like the company."

"Ah," Faracon said, throwing his head back and opening his arms wide. "Insults, tough talk, all so typical of the self-righteous." Faracon slowly leaned forward in his chair and looked straight into Vitterand's eyes. "It's a shame you don't like my company. A man of your obvious abilities could prosper greatly if he were teamed up with me. Time has so much to offer, and one has only to reach out and take it."

"I'm getting bored. Do you want to tell me why I should care if you have Göring bumped off?"

"Tsk, tsk." Faracon shook his head in mock sadness. "I know, I know—you think that if I have Göring killed, you can always send someone back in time to prevent it from happening—just as you prevented it from happening—or will prevent it from happening—at the Louvre," Faracon taunted.

It was a slip. Vitterand pounced on it. "I see you've been talking to yourself," he said dryly.

"Oh, yes," Faracon acknowledged. "Just as you have."

"Okay. Guess what I learned from myself."

"No doubt that you should kill me—and that would eliminate all your problems," Faracon said quietly.

"Right. Now, are you George Faracon?" Vitterand demanded.

"I am," Faracon replied.

"Then, with the authority granted me by the Temporal Warden Corps, I hereby—"

"Not so fast. There's one key element in the equation you don't know yet," Faracon said, holding up his hands again, the dead man's switch prominently displayed.

"And what is that?" Vitterand demanded. "You have three seconds to give me a straight answer."

"You aren't yet aware . . ."

"One."

". . . that Hermann Göring . . ."

"Two."

". . . has traveled through time. If he dies at an historically inconvenient moment, nothing you or any other Temporal Warden or your whole stinking Corps put together can do will ever change that fact. You'll be stuck with an anomaly wave of some real importance, won't you?" Faracon leaned forward again, his eyes gleaming and the expression of a victorious predator on his face. "That must be why you've attached so much importance to this—his death nearly wiped out your precious uptime HQ, didn't it? Well, if it did before, it can do it again," Faracon said, and this time he was the one snarling. "I've got the entire Temporal Warden Corps in the palm of my hand. All I have to do is let go of this switch and 'poof,' no more Corps. And certainly—no more you." Faracon leaned back in his chair, grinning broadly. "Go ahead. I think you were about to say, 'three' and pull the trigger."

It was Vitterand's turn to scowl with frustration. "Two questions before I execute you," he finally responded. "The first, prove to me that Hermann Göring has traveled through time."

"Ah, my. I was afraid you might be hard to convince," Faracon said, extending his arm with his hand open and the palm up, a gesture of mock despair. "To tell you the truth, I don't know of any easy way to prove that to you that wouldn't be, let us say, inconvenient to me. If we time traveled to that moment together, you might want to do something untoward, like shooting that other me."

"That thought might occur to me," Vitterand said, smiling. "But it seems to me that proof of this point is essential to you."

"No," Faracon said, wagging a finger like a schoolmaster correcting a child's answer. "It's not essential to me. It's essential to you—to your decision. But you're a trained, and I might add, quite capable Temporal Warden. You're used to making critical decisions without full information. I fear that in this case you'll just have to trust me," Faracon taunted.

"That's what I thought," Vitterand said, trying to sound unconvinced. "That brings us to my second question, which you will please answer swiftly, before your security men come through the vent shafts and I'm obliged to kill the lot of them."

"I assure you, I have no such scheme in mind. I don't need it," Faracon interjected.

"My second question is this. If you have the power you claim to have, why haven't you already used it? Why not just have Göring killed—and the Wardens wiped out of history? Why are you even bothering to have this little chat with me?"

"Fair enough, fair enough. You are a worthy interlocutor." Faracon beamed. "Let us simply say that not all the consequences of Herr Göring's death are predictable, as you well know. Of course, we can get an idea of the gross scope of events, but the particulars—well, you see the problem."

"You might wipe yourself out," Vitterand snapped.

"It is a thought that has occurred to me," Faracon admitted. "Besides, I like the Temporal Wardens. The challenges of besting you keep me young, and the deals I make from time to time are quite handy."

"Deals?"

"You didn't really think you'd get rid of this threat"— Faracon again extended the transmitter—"without a price?"

"I should think your being allowed to live is fair price enough," Vitterand said. He fought to keep his face from betraying his dark emotions. He was bested, and he knew it. Still, something was tickling in his memory . . .

"Hardly," Faracon replied. "But I won't be exorbitant in my demands . . . this time. All I want for now is this: your promise that I will remain undisturbed in this period. In return Göring lives, and I further undertake to do nothing in this period that will significantly alter the future."

Vitterand was stumped. He was frustrated. There was something he could do, he knew, but he couldn't for the life of him put his finger on what it was, not with Faracon leering at him, gloating at him . . .

"It won't help you much, you know," Vitterand challenged. "I've seen your face now, George."

"You've seen the face I've chosen to show you. I'm a man of a thousand faces, as you've no doubt been trained to know. And any voice recordings you've made won't matter either, I assure you. Now, I grow weary of our little game. Give me your pledge, as I've demanded, and get off my ship." Faracon stood, as though to signal that this audience was ended.

"There has to be more in it for me," Vitterand challenged.

"We both win," Faracon snapped. "You prevent both Göring's death at the Louvre—you've already done that, in sense, or so I've told myself. You also prevent the Moulin anomaly. But I get your word that I will remain undisturbed in this time period. No strike teams. No interventions. No action taken against me," Faracon said.

"That's a bad deal," Vitterand replied. "You have a hostage for all time. We only get two anomalies cleaned up."

"You can hardly expect me to propose a deal that wouldn't be to my advantage," Faracon said, his face beaming. "Now, do you agree, or shall we both send all of history straight to hell?"

"I need to consult with Central on this," Vitterand said.

"Nonsense!" Faracon snapped. "You're a Temporal Warden, and we both know that a Temporal Warden has plenipotentiary powers to bind the entire Corps!"

"You've made deals before, then?"

"Of course. I've told you as much. How do you think I've stayed in business so long?"

Vitterand grimaced. In his gut, he knew that everything Faracon said was true. Even time travel couldn't change the age-old story—brutality brings riches, riches bring power, and the power to corrupt. And the most powerful criminals always remain in power for as long as they do because of the corruption they spread. This man not only held the Corps hostage; he had corrupted it from within. And he was about to get away, because Vitterand knew that he didn't dare shoot . . .

And then Vitterand remembered. He remembered the one niggling, nagging tiny detail that had been clawing at the base of his memory, struggling to find its way into consciousness.

"I agree," Vitterand said reluctantly, lowering both his head and his weapon. "I pledge that from this day forward, in this time period, the Temporal Warden Corps will take no action against you in the years 4903 and 4902 B.C."

"I knew you'd see it my way," Faracon gloated. "Now, get off my ship before I have you killed. My men are in the vent system, just in case, you understand."

Vitterand sighed. He let a red blush of shame rise up his face. He nodded resignedly. "Activate recall," he said, dejection dripping from his voice.

Place: Temporal Warden's Station, Paris, France
Time: 1611 hours, Paris time, May 9, 1943

"Equipment!" Vitterand shouted as soon as he materialized on the Beamer platform. "Get me a plasma rifle, now! Toss it up here!"

It took only fifteen seconds for Vitterand to have a plasma rifle in hand. He slung it over his shoulder, loaded a fresh drum clip into the Thompson, and called to C'hing.

"C'hing! Send me back again, only three days earlier, do you understand? Three days earlier! Do it now!"

"What's going on? I need to know!" C'hing demanded.

"Faracon went back and warned himself—he was ready, just as we suspected. But I saw his time travel logs—he didn't go back far enough! Three days earlier he's still unwarned, a sitting duck. Send me back, now!"

The startled C'hing set the controls as quickly as he could. Vitterand disappeared in a flash of light.

Place: *La Liberté*, in synchronous orbit above the Tigris-Euphrates Valley
Time: Three days prior to Vitterand's meeting with Faracon aboard *La Liberté*

Jonesy hit the intruder alert alarm within a second of Vitterand's materialization on the Beamer platform of *La Liberté*.

In that second, Vitterand oriented himself. Directly in front of him, just as C'hing's fast briefing had indicated, was a clear partition. Beyond that partition was the temporal control room, where even now an operator was staring at him, obviously astonished, but not so astonished that his hands weren't flying toward a control. The partition, Vitterand knew, was necessary for biological containment. To his left he saw from the corner of his eye the sealed hatch that led to the biological decontamination chambers. Such safeguards were available at all Time Stations but were used only when one was traveling back in time, or coming back from a time, when infectious agents would be a problem. Their usefulness here, where obviously trips were being made to the surface, to ancient Sumer, were no surprise.

Vitterand, on the other hand, was a surprise to Jonesy. Still, the well-trained Beams operator didn't hesitate more than a second before hitting the alarm that caused a blaring Klaxon to sound throughout the vast ship. Whatever Vitterand was, he was three things that Jonesy didn't like. First, he was unexpected. Second, he was heavily armed. Jonesy saw that the man's weaponry was antique, but no less lethal for all that. He carried some type of ancient device for hurling lead slugs through the air at high speed. On his belt were a knife, rope, and much more conventional, far future, high-tech grenades. And Jonesy could see the straps around his shoulders that indicated he was wearing a breathing tank on his back. A tube snaked around to a mask mounted near the rear of his belt. This would protect him from gas attack.

Such armament, coupled with such surprise, could only mean that Jonesy's third conclusion was certain. The man was either a temporal assassin, sent by one of the numerous persons George Faracon had crossed all throughout history, or he was a Temporal Warden. In any case, Jonesy sounded the alarm.

It was his last action. Vitterand immediately lowered the Thompson and squeezed the trigger, sending a sudden burst of twenty .45 caliber lead slugs flying at incredible speeds into the partition before him. Built to withstand the penetration by bacteria or even viruses, it could not withstand the impact of the sheet of lead that shattered it. The bullets flew on through it. Jonesy's head was in the path of several. It exploded into a bloody mist, and bits of brains and bone were scattered on the walls and equipment of the control room as if they'd been sprayed from an atomizer.

Vitterand stepped through the partition, his feet crunching on bits of glass and plastic. He immediately went into a crouch and allowed his eyes to scan the room for televiewer cameras before coming to rest on the only door that led into this room with the exception of the entrance from the decontamination chamber—the door that connected it with the bridge of *La Liberté*. He found no televiewers. The South Americans had built cheap, and apparently Faracon had not seen a reason to rectify this particular lack. In that same sweep of the room, Vitterand's eyes drank in the multiple control consoles, and he saw Jonesy's headless corpse tip forward onto the control keyboard at what was obviously the main console.

Then he fastened his gaze on the bridge door. Too bad that Beamer operator had been so well trained. But Vitterand had known that before he came. Just as he knew that now the door to the bridge would open with a hiss.

He sprayed the two thugs as they came hurtling through the door. Just as he remembered, their bodies were blown back onto the bridge, red blossoms blooming on their white tunics, and the bridge door suddenly shut again.

Vitterand laid the Thompson atop the control consoles, raised the plasma rifle, and began burning through the bridge door.

"Hold your fire," Faracon called over the computer intercom. "Let's discuss this."

"Come on in. We can discuss it all you want," Vitterand called back. He released the plasma rifle's trigger and dove over the consoles, coming up with the doorway covered. He watched as it slid open. Two thugs peeked inside. Faracon's voice called again.

"Will you hold your fire?"

"You can come in, and you only."

"Who are you?"

"A Temporal Warden," Vitterand shouted back. "I needed to get your attention, and thought this might do it."

"Ah, a Temporal Warden," Faracon said, practically beaming. He'd dealt with their kind before. This wouldn't be difficult. They could be bought, or bluffed. Faracon entered the control room, pistol in hand. He let the door slide shut behind him. "Okay, here we are, just the two of us. I trust you don't think you can outwit me?" Faracon said. "I'm sure that some future self of mine will figure this out in time."

"Precisely," said a second Faracon, who had just appeared on the Beamer platform, his TCAF activated. But then the Faracon from the future grew wide-eyed as he saw the shattered partition, and his earlier self standing, confident and unprotected, in the line of fire of Vitterand's plasma rifle.

"I doubt that," Vitterand said. He pressed the trigger on the plasma rifle, and downtime Faracon's body was vaporized in a stinking flash.

"No!" the Faracon from the future managed to scream, before his body, too, vanished into nothingness.

Epilogue

Place: Temporal Warden's Station, Paris, France
Time: 0200 hours, Paris time, May 10, 1943

The warrior stood atop the tall hill and looked out over the lush green of the valley extended far below. The small but important river reflected back the powerful light of the midday spring sun. The meadows far below were a quilt of riotous colors as the spring flowers erupted in them, dazzling him with their variety and beauty. In the fields he could see the peasants at work: men walking behind their cattle-pulled plows, children clearing rocks from the wet land, women pounding their wash on the rocks of river, or bringing light wood into the little gray stone huts with their thatched roofs, where tiny plumes of smoke curled skyward as the evening's stew was already being prepared.

The man reached up, patted the muzzle of his huge white war steed. It was a goodly horse, one that had served him well both in the sudden, short, violent shock of battle, and in the interminable days and months of riding and waiting between battles. Yet the horse was a strange beast, with a mind of its own, and no matter how loyal it might be to him, the warrior felt he would never truly know the animal. But he loved and trusted it nonetheless.

He glanced up at the midday sun, almost directly overhead. Like all true spring suns, it burned white-hot in the sky. Its rays were warm, but not as warm as they would be in summer, and its light was beautiful and white, but not the full, rich gold it would be in summer. Still, it was good to see the springtime sun, for the winter had been long and hard—at least, he thought it must have been so.

For the warrior found that just as he did not truly know his horse—because he could not recall its name—he also had no knowledge of the winter just past. His memory of such a time was clean, blank, like a slate a schoolboy might write upon—if there were schoolboys in this world. For was he not wearing a suit of armor? Aye, that he was. A beautiful suit of armor, white as snow—how it had been whitened, he could not say, for it was not paint, nor was it a white gold that covered the heavy plates, but white they were, for all that. Fluted, too, with the elegant design of the breastplate mirrored in the coat of arms on the great, white shield that was strapped beside his saddle. That design was of a river that flowed in a great circle about a strange and violent land—a land with huge trees and gargoyles' heads and flying things with mighty teeth and lizards' heads. And over this land surrounded by a river, hovering above them, were a set of broken lines, like dots and dashes. And he knew that these were a symbol from the Orient, the symbols of change, and of permanence.

The warrior wondered for a moment how he knew these things, but he could not remember.

The valley was far below him, and the hill atop which he stood was steep and sheer where it looked down over the river. Indeed, the way down would lead him back partway up the rear slope of the hill, and then along a winding road that slowly traveled back and forth, all the way down to the river, where it wound between this hill and another, and then led out into the valley. So his descent would be a long one. It would take most of the day.

"But there is not time," his horse suddenly said to him.

"What?" the warrior asked, turning, astonished, to gaze at the beast. "Did you speak? Could it be that you spoke?"

But the horse only neighed, and reared up on its hind legs suddenly, and then came crashing down to paw the earth with its mighty front hooves.

Clearly, something was much amiss.

Then the warrior, too, heard the sound that had stirred his steed. It was the sound of mighty horns blowing, the horns that summoned men to battle. And as he watched, he saw the tiny men in the fields below abandon their plows. They waved to their children, calling to them to mind the great beasts that pulled the plows, and to take them to safety. The men ran, each to his own little cottage or hut, and each emerged, in time, armed. Some carried sabers, some carried old straight swords. Many carried only their peasant's bills or hooks. But they came, and they began to gather in the center of the valley. And from afar, the horns sounded again, and again, and again. The blasts came from the east, and they were mighty warnings.

"Come then, good steed," the warrior exclaimed. As swiftly as his heavy armor would allow, the great white knight mounted his warhorse. He looked about him at his equipage—it was all there, neatly stowed: huge, great sword; the sharp pointed lance, already stained with the blood of evil foes; the shield with its strange, disturbing crest; and his great helm of gleaming white with red horsehair rising like a small shako from its crested top.

"Let's go," he called to the mount, gently clucking and tugging on the reins to turn the powerful steed toward the winding path. "Even though there is no time, I fear, for it will take the best of the day to go down this path to the valley, and by then a foe may have debauched from that draw far to the east. . . ."

But his steed would not heed him. Instead, it turned full around and trotted smartly across the top of the hill, directly away from the valley.

"What, what is this?" the warrior cried. "Have you forgotten who is the master here?" he demanded.

Then the horse turned again, this time with its mighty head pointed straight toward the sheer cliff, and forward it galloped. The warrior could feel the might of its powerful hind legs as they bit into the soft turf of the hill. He could feel the wind whipping his face as the horse galloped faster, and faster, toward the sheer cliff, and then . . .

And then he was aloft! For the great steed had sprouted wings—wings larger than an archangel's, and whiter than the face of Christ in the pictures on the walls of the great cathedrals of Byzantium.

Out over the valley the powerful horse carried the warrior, until he could look directly down upon the small muster of men who were falling to arms in the center of the valley. They looked up at him, and cheered, and tossed their caps into the air, shouting and screaming for joy that the great warrior had come to do battle for them, and ecstatic with the thought that he was invincible mounted on the back of the great white flying warhorse, the Pegasus-Jove of battle.

Then the warrior looked ahead, at the end of the valley, where the river again wound between two high hills; but these were not pleasant hills, no, but craggy, rocky, barren things, lifeless piles of hard gray rock that shot up from the earth with no thought but to block the horizon and hide the light of the sunrise on every morning, though they could not do so. But they could cast long shadows of a morning.

And it came from between the hills—rose between them, large, black, leathery, a thing as dead as those hills and yet alive. It rose with a great roar and wind from the flapping of its loathsome, ragged wings. It rose, suspended between those wings, with the body of a great bloated serpent, whose scales were all gray and black, and with the rear legs of a scrawny, moulted fowl dangling below its serpent's body, and with no forelimbs at all, and no head. No head—but a great skull, the skull of a leering man, and the fires of hell burning in the black, barren pits which should house fleshy eyes.

The warrior's heart was troubled as he saw this, for even at a great distance it was quite large and fearsome, and he was closing upon it atop his great steed at a speed that seemed, well, quite swift to him. Indeed, so swift that he could barely form a plan of battle.

The men in valley, he thought, no wonder they cheered, for as the thing rose in the sky, it spotted him from afar, and its serpent's body stiffened straight like a great arrow, with a last huge flap of its dreadful wings it launched itself through the air straight toward him. Yes, no wonder they cheered, for as it came for him it would leave them alone, and they were powerless against it.

The warrior's throat and mouth were dry, and his eyes stung both from the wind and from the tiny tears of fear that were springing into them. His gauntleted hands fumbled with his helm, until at last he managed to slide it over his head, and he quickly slammed the beaver down, for though he could not see as well that way—only a little, through a slit—it was better not to see so much. He wondered that his steed had no need of blinders, but it did not falter, nor slow; indeed it galloped across the air inexorably as doom itself

toward what now appeared to be—yes, were—the gaping
jaws of that skull head, and the darkness and blackness of
what lay beyond those jaws within in.

The warrior gathered up his shield and slid his left arm
through it. It locked into place on the arm. Then with his
right gauntlet-covered hand he reached down to his side and
pulled from its place of honor his great sword. And this he
raised on high, and with a great shout whirled it around and
around above his head, thinking that perhaps, if the creature
that was about to slay him appeared to him so fearsome,
perhaps he would appear fearsome to it.

And now the two, the fearsome beast of black, and the
great warrior of white, sped toward each other across the
white-gray sky of the spring afternoon. He, the warrior,
screaming his greatest war cry, and it, the loathsome, foul
beast, whose stench went before it to assault him, gaping its
great mouth, and shooting forth horrid vents of black
flame—fire as black as coal, fire that gave no light, but that
was searing hot.

And now the warrior braced himself and drew back the
heavy great sword, poised for a blow, as his steed, fearless,
charged through the black flames, its great white mane
burning black in the white of the sun, its eyes charred and
blinded, and his own armor searing his flesh. And the great
flying serpent beat the air beside him and his arm came
down, down, down with all his might and all his will across
the hideous joining of that monstrous skull to the black
body, and the great sword cut through!

Oh, the scream of the thing as that hideous skull
plummeted earthward, while the body, not yet certain of its
demise, still screeched through the air, the great wings still
beating, the body writhing, while great gouts of foul
blackness spewed forth from the severed neck to fall like a

hideous rain on the meadows and fields and men and beasts below.

The warrior, meanwhile, soared upward on his steed, as the great horse climbed higher in the sheer air, dipping its left wing far, far down, and raising its right higher and higher as it turned, turned, turned, until it, too, could see the filth-vomiting body of the black flying thing crash against the sheer cliff of the westernmost hill and tumble, bouncing, down and down off the rocks, ripped and torn by the branches of trees that thrust their crooked trunks out from the side of the hill, until at last it thudded into the wet earth by the side of the river, the last of its blackness running into the clear water.

And below, the hideous skull that shattered among the gathered, cheering men. And now their cheering turned to screams as the exploded remnants of that shattered skull flew like shrapnel among them, and the acid blood of the thing fell out of the sky upon them, and the blackness and the whiteness both ate into them, so that they perished in great numbers.

And the warrior heaved a great sigh of relief, relief that he had lived, that the valley was preserved, and a sigh of sadness, of deep sadness, for the death and destruction that saving the valley had brought to the people of the valley below. And he gently guided his now panting steed downward, gently downward, gliding in the light afternoon wind, downward into the laughing colors of the meadows, where there were now patches of smoking black mud where the foulness of the slain thing had fallen, downward into the fields where now the women and children slowly gathered to stare out upon the corpses of their husbands and fathers, downward into the midst of the destruction which would have been total had it not been for him, or might not have been at all had he, the warrior, not come.

And the great steed landed.

And the wailing of the women and the children assaulted the warrior.

"Do you not see?" a woman screamed. "Do you not see what you have done?"

"I see indeed," the warrior gasped, for he was unsteady now, atop his mount, and his body trembled, and his lungs gasped for air. "I see indeed, but think what would have been had I not bested this foul thing."

And the dead men rose up, and they said to him, "WE ARE THE ONES WHO WOULD HAVE BEEN. AND ARE WE NOT THE SAME AS YOU?"

"No! No!" the warrior cried. "You are not the same as I! For am I not a warrior, a knight pledged to the good, to protect from all evil, to keep the land pure?"

And an ugly hag with only a front tooth came forward from amongst the dead and held forth the warrior a mirror.

"Look and see, look and see what you are. You are the same as the dead whom you have slain," she claimed, cackling loudly.

And the warrior looked into the mirror. And he raised the beaver of his great helm, and looked, and looked, and looked. And he trembled, for inside his great helm there was no face—no—nor aught else. There was nothing at all.

And as the warrior trembled and wondered what this might mean, there came from the east the sound of mighty horns blowing, war horns crying to him.

And his steed reared up, so that he could barely keep his mount.

"There is no time!" the great horse whinnied, and it galloped off across the valley, its wings extending.

And the warrior clung to the steed, and asked it, again and again, "But who am I? But who am I?"

• • •

Temporal Warden Jean Vitterand awoke suddenly from a
sound sleep. He tried mightily to remember what it was that
had so frightened him, but already the fragments of the
dream were fading in his memory like wisps of smoke in the
air on a windy spring day.

He shook his head, as if to clear the last of the dream
images away, since they refused to come to consciousness.
Still, he had a strange feeling. He felt as if he should be
doing something.

"Computer," he called, "intercom."

"Intercom activated," the computer's voice replied.

"Vitterand to duty officer, report on status," Vitterand
ordered.

The familiar voice of C'hing responded. "I've got the
duty tonight, sir. Doing a double shift, so one of my
counterparts can get some badly needed sleep. Station status
is normal."

"What is our alert status?" Vitterand demanded.

"Why, there is no alert, sir. Our computers show no
anomalies meriting alert status, and there have been no
communiqués from uptime Central."

"Very well, C'hing. Vitterand out," the Warden responded. "Intercom off," he told the computer.

Funny thing about being a Temporal Warden, Vitterand
mused as he drifted back toward more peaceful slumbers.
All that training, and then nothing much ever happened.